POWDER TOWN

S.L.Bowe

CONTENTS

Title Page	
Chapter 1	1
Chapter 2	3
Chapter 3	8
Chapter 4	18
Chapter 5	22
Chapter 6	28
Chapter 7	33
Chapter 8	40
Chapter 9	43
Chapter 10	49
Chapter 11	52
Chapter 12	62
Chapter 13	70
Chapter 14	77
Chapter 15	84
Chapter 16	90
Chapter 17	95
Chapter 18	99
Chapter 19	110
Chapter 20	113

Chapter 21	121
Chapter 22	124
Chapter 23	134
Chapter 24	140
Chapter 25	148
Chapter 26	156
Chapter 27	168
Chapter 28	176
Chapter 29	183
Chapter 30	195
Chapter 31	201
Chapter 32	207
Chapter 33	217
Chapter 34	224
Chapter 35	235

CHAPTER 1

Slowly waking up to the sun beaming through my bedroom window, slowly my eyes open. I finally adjust to the light that is spilling in. With a slight murmur and a stretch out of my legs and arms, I roll over and place my hand on the opposite side of my bed. Once filled with my dearest husband, was now cold and bare. Hit again by the realization that I'm now here alone. I wrap my arms and curl myself up as my heart begins to break all over again.

Losing a few moments in my own thoughts, I gather myself together and finally the warmth of the shower controls my beating heart as it begins to slow down. A sudden feeling of peace runs through me as I stand under the falling warm water. The anxiety and panic attacks started when my husband passed away after a heart attack at work. This was nine months ago, but the feelings from hearing that news are still so sharp and vivid. Will these ever go away? I actually get dressed, apply some make up even though I know I won't leave the house. I make my way for the kitchen, for a desperate need of coffee. (Why does it always seem that the first cup in the morning the kettle takes the longest to boil.) I sit in my perfectly organised kitchen. Coffee taking effect when I glance towards the worktop and notice my mobile flashing. Shall I pick it up or ignore it like I seem to do these days. The wondering gets the better of me and I decide to have a look. Nine missed calls and countless text messages, a feeling of dread comes over me, why did I look? Slamming the phone back down on the worktop, I return to my drink, I sip away but can't take my eye of my phone. I count to ten to steady my nerves, unsure if I'm ready to face the world today.

'Bugger it, let's get it over with.' Snatching it up I begin to scroll, missed calls from my two beautiful daughters, they feel the need to check in more these days. Though they are both grown up and have their own families to look after. Having my two girls around more isn't actually a bad thing, bringing the grandchildren round is refreshing and gives me the nudge that I need on days like this. The rest of the messages are from my two best friends, who are desperately trying to pull me back into the world, but I'm not sure if I'm ready for that just yet.

CHAPTER 2

I read the messages from Rita and Doreen. A Feeling of guilt creeps in knowing that I've been a lazy friend these past few months. I know they've been worried about me, but I just can't seem to get into the mood to join them in our gossiping circle. They keep trying to pull me back in, but I just keep getting the feeling of something pulling me back. Although I'm so grateful that they haven't given up on me. I will get there I tell myself but not just yet. We've been friends for twenty-seven years, where we met on a hectic school run. I remember the morning like it was yesterday, my daughter Ellie starting her first day of school. I Started a new job a few months earlier and was still learning trying to do everything and not to make a mess in my new role before my soon to be maternity break. Thankfully work was understanding, but I couldn't shake the feeling that any other disruption I'd be gone. Putting myself into a mad panic, and not to give them an opportunity of them telling me I'm finished, I was determined to do everything perfect.

'Not long left I can do this.' I kept telling my exhausted self. Rushing as always as Ellie would refuse to get ready in a morning, (Do all kids do this?) Driving like a formula 1 driver, I just managed to get Ellie to school on time. Now to get to work, in my hectic fluster I began to reverse my car out of the car park. Next thing I knew there was a huge black handbag flying in my rear-view mirror and the loudest screech of…

'What the fuck are you doing?' I slammed on my breaks and sink my head into the steering wheel and began to cry. A working mom with a five-year-old, and the second on the way, the tiredness and hormones were off the chart. I felt so desperate, lonely and very emotional. I was feeling so overwhelmed especially hitting the last trimester of my pregnancy. These last few months really do hit you like a tonne of bricks, worrying how you will manage with two children, money, your relationship, let alone the stress I was feeling from this new job. I'd let it get a bit too much. The biggest thump on the window startled me back into reality. When I looked up, stood at my window I saw the most beautiful woman, angrily wafting her arms about, in that instance I sworn time stood still, she seen my eyes and I looked right into hers. She seen my tear-stained face and instantly calmed down. She was beautiful, tall and slim at least 5ft 10, a cleavage to die for, her sun kissed tan shined, her highlighted brown hair made her big green eyes stand out. I couldn't take my eyes off her she was stunning, which made me realise that I had started to let myself go, I look down at my clothes which were the ones I obviously grabbed first, my pale reflection and not so perfect hair, made me look like I just rolled out of bed, I was never like this, I always took pride in my appearance, but lately I've let it slip. From that moment I vowed to make more time for myself and my appearance. This was my first-time seeing Rita. Then suddenly Doreen joined our moment, standing slightly shorter and plump, Doreen was much plainer than Rita, still pretty, but you could tell Doreen was not fussed as much about her appearance, where it was clearly a priority for Rita. Embracing her natural beauty, I was instantly attracted to her warm caring nature. The feeling that she was truly concerned about myself as she opened the door, gave me the biggest hug that she automatically knew I needed. From that moment the two women welcomed me into their life and so it started a lifelong friendship. School runs, coffee trips and the occasional girl's night out became our thing. "A friendship born from almost running over Rita."

I snap back into reality with a smile, I decided to play the Voicemail left from Rita.

'Hey girl.'

I roll my eyes while listening, Rita always spoke and acted like she was a lot young than she is, considering we are all in our fifties, Doreen the oldest and most sensible at the age of fifty-nine, myself at fifty-seven and Rita still stunning as ever at fifty-six, who could easily pass for ten years younger. (Of course, with a little helping hand, which she is not ashamed to admit.)

'So, me and Doreen are here having our usual girl's night that you are missing again.' The little dig sends a squirm over my face.

'You know we care about you and respect that you need time, but we need to start getting you out of that house and your pyjamas!' (I look down at myself and smirk, as for once I've gotten dressed.)

'I am in clothes thank you.' I say to myself with a proud smile and then continue to listen.

'You can't keep living your life stuck in your home, so we are going to intervene!'

I Then hear Doreen gasp in the background. 'Oh Rita, please don't start this now.' This is when I've started to realise that alcohol must be playing a part in this conversation.

Rita cuts Doreen off instantly. 'You know she can't stay like this forever, if we don't it will never happen, we were just talking about this!'

'I know but maybe we shouldn't rush her too much just yet.' I sit and raise my eyebrows at this conversation that's happening, (as if I don't have a say in how I live my life, I am right here you know!) Rita continues with her rant, I can hear the tiny slur creeping in.

'Remember us talking about booking a trip to Greece? You agreed to come, well I've gone and booked it, we leave tomorrow, get them bags packed we will see you in the morning!' I gasp in shock, Rita always likes to drop things on us like this at the drop of a hat. Desperate to hear more I sit wondering if I should get excited or scared. I hug my coffee and continue to listen on. Doreen screeching and sounding like she's just spat her drink out at the same time makes me laugh, the shock must have hit her as much as me.

'You what? I can't go to Greece! What will Phil do?' Her screeches sound like a waft of panic, followed by a constant stutter.

Not realising that they are still recording a message, I listen on amused. Phil is her devoted husband, he works like a trooper, but really doesn't have any kind of idea how to look after himself, Doreen has looked after him for that long, that leaving him for a week, she probably thinks he won't be able to survive. Rita chirps back in on a frantic Doreen.

'I knew you both would try and find excuses not to go, that's why I didn't ask, its booked, we are going so get your bags sorted. Phil will be fine.'

'Oh look, we are still recording, well you got all that then Lynn, see you in the morning. Ciao.'

The message has finished, but I'm still holding the phone to my ear listening to the silence on the other end. I then place it down and look at the date and time. More shock hits me when I realise that we are going today! I jump from my seat and start a frantic pace around the kitchen. What should I do first? Do I go? Where's my dam passport?

'Shit!' I shriek to myself in a fluster unsure what I should do next. I feel my heart begins to race, I'm not sure if its panic or excitement. (Probably both.) My head is going into over drive, wondering what I should do, my palms are sweaty, so I wipe them on my clean trousers. I pour another cup hoping it's going to help me figure it out. I find myself pacing back and forth, I look down to see my coffee almost jumping out of my mug, I sit back down hoping it steadies my nerves. (I hate having things sprung on me like this, it puts my overly organised schedules to shit.) I'm speaking to myself like had have loads of plans, of course I don't, but my plans for sitting drinking coffee finishing my book will have to now be put on hold.

Suddenly the doorbell rings... I hear Rita, she's outside. I look over to the clock its only 7.30am. A surge of panic ripples through me. What am I going to do, I've only just found out, and why the heck is she here at this time in the morning.

CHAPTER 3

Another huge bang hits the door, I realise that I should be getting up to answer it, but for some reason my legs don't want to move. I hear Rita now shouting through my letter box.

'I know you're in there, Open the door!'

I sit waiting for a few seconds wondering what to do next. I peer my head round the corner and see in the glass side of the door Rita's frame waiting. It looks like she has now sat down on the steps, I can see her suitcase sitting beside her. (Looks like she's coming to drag me on holiday for sure.) I see my chance to try and sneak passed without being seen, I'm hoping I can give myself a little more time to think this through, part of me wants to go, but a little niggling voice is telling me I should stay in my comfort zone. I grab my phone and coffee and crouch down to begin a crawl along my clean shiny tiles. Finding out how tricky this is going to be holding a mug, I stop in the middle of the room, I turn my head slightly round to look at Rita, who's still sitting patiently. I move a little more, then come to my senses and realise how stupid I'm being.

'What am I doing?' I mutter away to myself as I try to lift my aching knees to stand. Fully upright I decide to go back and open the door, until I hear the screeching voice of Rita outside.

'I know you're in there, I can hear you clanking about!' Stupidly in a panic, I turn and bolt for my stairs. In my mind I know I shouldn't be doing this, but my body seems to think otherwise, and before I know it, I'm scrambling up the stairs in the most unladylike manor, my coffee swishing from side to side, my legs trying to clamber each step as fast as they can. Then I hear it! The flick of my letterbox, it makes me jump, I now stumble and fall forward into the stairs and my coffee flies out and starts dripping down each step.

'I can see you! Are you trying to run away from me? just open this door and let me in!' Rita's screeching echoes through my hallways. A ping of embarrassment comes over me and I can feel my face flushing red, I turn round to see Rita's two eyes looking through my letterbox! My cheeks now feel on fire, I don't know what comes over me, but instead of putting an end to this silly behaviour and opening the door, I turn back around and get ready for another bolt up the stairs.

'Don't you even dare!' She screams this time knowing exactly what I am going to do. I don't turn back instead I just run. I reach the top and press my back against the wall, clench my eyes closed, wondering why I'm doing this, but I just can't help myself. My heart is beating so fast it feels like it's going to pop out of my chest, my heavy panting sounds horrendous. (I Really need to start exercising again.) I hear someone else outside joining Rita. Hoping it's not my nosey neighbours, I peer my head round to see through the glass. Then I hear the warm tone of Doreen, i breathe a sigh of relief that it's not my neighbours, as the gossip would be all over the estate by lunch time. "That poor Lynn must be having a break down!" I can imagine it already. I try to listen to what Rita and Doreen are talking about as Rita's screeching has finally stopped.

'What are you doing? Why are you shouting through her letter box?' I can hear Doreen asking confused.

'She won't let me in! she knows that I'm here, I've just caught her scurrying up the stairs.'

'There will be a simple explanation, maybe just give her a little time instead of bombarding her like some maniac. Anyway, why haven't you just used the key lock, I know the combination.'

'Well why are we standing out here like lemons, get the key and let's get in.'

'Shit!' I totally forgot all about that spare key, now I'm going to have to explain my stupid self what I was doing, or I could deny it? Was only Rita that seen me. I pull myself together and straightened my now crumpled blouse and begin to head down stairs. I try to move a little faster than usual, so it looks like I'm rushing to answer the door. I see the two women thumbling with the lock, and two cases lined up next to each other. I manage to get to the door just before they manage to unlock it, I can hear them squabbling with each other. I open the door just as Rita pulls on the handle, her skinny little frame comes flying in. I act as if nothing unusual has happened.

'Morning, how are we all?' I say with a bright smile.

'How are we all? I'm better now to be finally let in!' Rita snaps as she walks herself in and tries to push her long hair out of her face, that's now sticking to her painted lips. Her eyes narrow at me as she waits for me to explain my behaviour. I try my best to look as if I don't know what she's going on about and hope my beaming red face has now calmed down.

'What?' I say arrogantly.

'Don't you be playing that one with me missy! I saw you scamper back up the stairs trying to avoid me.' I look back at her trying to look confused, but knowing fine well I've been caught red handed, my shame burns inside of me. Just as I'm about to open my mouth and reply, Doreen butts in and saves me from adding more to my shame.

'Good morning love, how are you? Are you ready to go?' Doreen asks as she moves the awkward conversation to the kitchen. I follow them into the kitchen, they are now making themselves at home, pulling out the chairs by the table ready to take a seat. I shift awkwardly from foot to foot, and look down, trying to buy myself some time, to figure out what I can say, to let them down gently. Rita picks up on this and raises her eyebrow. Doreen as pleasant as ever just looks at me with a smile and waits for me to answer.

'Erm... I've only just listened to the voicemail.' I look down at my hands, not being able to bare to look at them in the face as I explain my pathetic excuse. 'See, I was out for count last night and didn't check my phone. I haven't got anything packed, and nothing is sorted, I wouldn't want you to miss your flight, so I will just come next time.' I look at Doreen who is still smiling, I turn to Rita whose eyebrow is raised that high that I'm not actually sure it will go back down in the right position. The moment of silence is awkward. As we all just look at each other waiting to see who will speak first.

'Good job we came early then, we kind of gathered that you wouldn't be ready so that's why we are here now, let's get things started. Doreen you're on coffee and passport duty, you and I are going up stairs to get your case ready. Let's go!' Like a military operation they both set off on their tasks whizzing round. I'm just left standing their opened mouth unsure if I should join in, not that they are giving me much choice in the matter.

'Come on then.' Rita grabs me by the arm and begins to guide me back up the stairs. I let her drag me like I'm a defiant toddler not wanting to move. We then come across the spilled coffee stain. Rita looks down at it then looks back at me.

'So, you weren't trying to scamper up the stairs from me then?' She says while laughing.

My embarrassment reappearing its ugly head, and my cheeks flush once again. 'Err....'

'Don't worry about the stain I will sort it.' Doreen shouts from the kitchen saving me once again.

We both head up and begin raiding my wardrobe. Rita has begun flinging clothes out everywhere, she automatically started a pile of "yes and no." Watching the clothes fly everywhere, gets a bit over whelming, so I find myself trying to defend the no pile for some unknown reason other than to be awkward.

'Well I think this dress is a yes!' I pick up the dress and hold it against me, the plain black cotton maxi with long sleeves, "Is one of my comfy dresses" but I know deep down it's not an ideal holiday wear, but I still can't help myself by making more hassle than it's worth.

'No! We are going to Greece not Scotland!' Rita is now getting fed up of my awkwardness and stops my protests immediately. I look down at it and reluctantly agree, knowing I need to calm myself down from being like this. The only reason I am is because I was caught by Rita and pulled up on it, but instead of being like an adult and owning up to my silly behaviour, I'm acting like a child and rebelling out in any way I possibly can. My face squirms knowing how pathetic I'm being and that it needs to stop. So I finally put my big girl knickers on and apologise to Rita, thankfully she understands that I'm not just talking about the dress. She nods back and carries on helping me pick my clothes.

'Your right. Probably would be too hot.' I begin to scan over the no pile again as Rita catches me and then stops me from causing any more disruption.

'How about you go and sort underwear and swimwear and your toiletries, leave this to me.' She tries to cover her skinny arms over the piles as if to protect them. Not having any more fight left in me I reluctantly agree.

'Fine, but I don't want everything glam I want some comfortable things packed.'

'Don't you worry.' She smiles, knowing fine well there will be no comfortable clothing packed what so ever. Rita doesn't do comfortable clothes, she would be mortified if she got a glimpse of my big apple swingers, that's had so much use that the frayed edges are now clinging on to dear life trying to prevent a hole appearing, but I do love my comfy knickers! They are essential!

Within less than an hour we are heading back down stairs all packed and changed ready to leave. The once visible coffee stain is now completely gone.

'Wow Doreen, you wouldn't even know there was a stain there.' I shout through to the kitchen.

'I've had a lot of practice clearing up after men.' She says laughing. This is true as her husband probably barely lifts a finger in their house, not that he can't or won't, Doreen likes to be in control of that kind of thing, and if someone is going to do it for you, then why would he?

All of us back in the kitchen again, all cases packed and lined up waiting to go. We sit round the table wondering what else to do while waiting for the taxi to arrive. I decide to ring my two girls and tell them the news that I'm going on holiday. Rita heads towards the wine fridge and begins to scan for a bottle.

'Bit early for that isn't it?' I say while strolling passed with my phone to my ear. Hearing the pop of the cork tells me she doesn't care.

'We are going on holiday it's never too early.' She laughs while grabbing a nicely chilled rosé. 'One won't harm while we are waiting.' Rita winks while holding up the bottle to me.

I nod and give a smile back knowing there's not much point in trying to refuse.

'I'm just going to call the girls; I'll be back in a minute.' Rita nods while gently inspecting her chosen bottle.

Entering back into the kitchen after speaking to them. They both were delighted to hear that I was getting away and no doubt they already knew this was happening from Rita, as they weren't really surprised. I see three glasses already poured, Doreen looks disgusted at looking at alcohol this early in a morning, she's never been a big drinker.

'Cheers.' Rita says raising her glass. I follow suit and raise mine. We both look at Doreen who's clutching on to her coffee mug desperately avoiding the wine. Rita coughs to get the attention of Doreen.

'Oh okay, just the one.' She rolls her eyes and reluctantly raises her glass.

Half hour passes while we get lost in a well needed catch up. The excitement starts bubbling up inside me as I start to enjoy the thought of going on a girl's holiday. The taxi should be here any minute now as we all start gathering our things and do the last-minute checks. I drain the last bit of wine from my glass as Rita stands up and heads to the window.

'Where's this bloody taxi?' She's now starting to pace up and down getting more and more annoyed. She's never had any patience and being left waiting about is one of her pet hates.

'Oh Rita, just sit your little arse down, it will be here in a minute.' Doreen says annoyed at her inpatients. Rita has never liked being left hanging about, I've seen her cancel dates if they turn up late, even with a honest excuse, she still wouldn't give them a chance. If this taxi doesn't hurry up, I can only imagine she could easily cancel that. "Maybe that could be a good thing." I cheekily think to myself. "No that wouldn't work, she'd only demand someone else to take us, she probably already has a backup driver on standby no doubt.

'Don't tell me to sit down. I'm going to ring the company and find out where they are, this is unacceptable!' Rita snaps back and notice as slight fare to her nostrils, she's working her way up nicely to boiling point.

Doreen rolls her eyes and goes to answer her back. I jump up before she can, to hopefully defuse a little tiff between the two, because once they start bickering, they don't seem to stop, and I really can't be bothered having to listen to that before we even get anywhere, it would go on and on, then before you know it would be like a snowball effect, getting bigger and bigger until it crashes.

'I'm going to do a last bit of checking round before we go. Doreen there's some lime green ribbon in the drawer over there will you pop it on my case for me.' Hoping the lime green ribbon will help me identify my black case easier at the airport, as a black case will no doubt be a popular choice. I glance at Rita and Doreen's case and see the colourful and vibrant patterns and think to myself that I must buy a new one for the next time I go away, my tatter well used case has just about seen its day.

'Sure.' Doreen stands up to do this right away, as I quickly leave to check everything is off and locked one last time, even though I know they are it's a bad habit of mine. I've once seen myself trail up and down stairs at least twenty times to check my straighteners are off. Even though each time I checked I would try and convince myself that the light was defiantly off, only to reach the bottom of the stairs to doubt myself, but was it off... In the end up I had to unplug them and physically remove the straighteners from their usual place, for it to finally sink in that they were indeed switched off.

Joining the two again, I see Rita opening another bottle of wine a little too angrily. As she twists and pulls at the ever so delicate bottle.

'Thought the taxi was coming?' As soon as the words left my lips I knew I shouldn't have asked. I see Doreen's cheeks puff out trying to hold a laugh in, and Rita turns to look at me with scowl. Nothing is ever Rita's fault bare this in mind.

'They are, but Rita has gotten the time wrong, they will be another twenty minutes.' Doreen says before Rita can answer with a bemused look on her face.

'I definitely didn't get the time wrong.' She huffs. "Never mind, we shall have one more before we go.' Before anyone can say anything, she's pouring the drinks.

'I'm going to need it having a week with madam over there.' Doreen points in Rita's direction. I laugh and grab my glass knowing all too well what she is on about. The chilled fruity flavour fills my mouth, and I can't help but enjoy the sips a little too much even though it's still morning and normally it is only coffee that passes my lips at this time of day.

Rita scowls then laughs knowing that Doreen is right. That's one thing about Rita she can take the criticism and brush it off, plus she knows fine well she is highly strung, she always has been and more than likely always will be. The three of us are all very different in our own ways, which somehow makes our friendship even stronger: Rita the highly strung la de da, Doreen the quiet, reserved, won't let her hair down mothering type, myself, well I probably have a bit of each of their traits, the balance.

'You have a point.' She says raising her glass with a smile just as she is about to take a sip. There's a huge honk of the horn, it's so loud that it makes us all jump. Doreen almost spills her wine over herself but manages to lower her glass from her face just in time, so the spillage lands on my clean tiled floor instead.

'Bloody hell!' She shouts out in shock and runs to grab a cloth from the side.

'You are fucking kidding me, that's not been twenty minutes!' Rita storms over to the window and places her finger up to indicate one minute to the driver.

'We better drink up.' I say then down the rest of my wine. The sharp flavour hits the back of my throat and makes me cough.

'Heck!' Rita says surprised while watching me finish the almost full glass in one. 'Well bottoms up.' Rita giggles and does the same. 'We are going to be pissed before we even get there.' She pulls a face as the sharpness hits her too.

'Well, the taxi is just going to have to wait. I can't drink all that like that.' Doreen says while taking small sips at her drink, we watch on as it seems to take her ages. Seeing the more than half full glass of wine we realise there's going to be no rush in her, she certainly doesn't care.

'For goodness sake Doreen, drink the bloody thing.' There goes Rita's little patience again.

'I'm trying to.' Cries Doreen's feeling the pressure as we all watch her, waiting for her to finish, but she still slowly sips away as if we have all the time in the world.

'Well, I'm going to have to go to the loo while we are waiting.' Just as I'm wondering up, I hear the blast of the horn again. 'Bloody hell he's in a hurry isn't he!' I jump and shout back to them. Rita soon storms through, with the irritation of Doreen's slow sips and an impatient driver, she looks like she's about to erupt in a rage, I head up to the toilet before I can witness it.

'I'll sort him out.' She flings open the front door in a bubbling rage and begins to shout. 'Hey! Hang the fuck on, your early, so keep your hands off that horn, we will be out in a minute.' I glance passed her while stood on top of the stairs and see the sheepish taxi driver lower down in his seat and slowly nod. Satisfied with her outburst Rita closes the door and turns to me completely oblivious to her unnecessary reaction. I stare for a minute with my eyebrows raised, but I'm only met with a shrug from Rita. Typical, she would never think to apologise for her rude behaviour, although she's now noticed my reaction she quickly tries to divert to a different subject. "You carry on, I will sort everything down here, then we can leave.' I smile back and do just that.

CHAPTER 4

Finally making our way out to the taxi dragging our over filled cases along. The taxi driver jumps out to help us. Rita and Doreen are storming ahead. I watch them head further down the path as I suddenly stop walking, I feel my heart my heart do a flip then a surge of panic floods over me, my eyes begin to dart everywhere as I try to figure out what is troubling me. Then I get the feeling that I'm missing something. I start running an imaginary check list in my head, passport, I know I have that, money, got that I just need to change it over when I get to Greece, clothes, definitely packed, I dread to think what Rita has packed for me. The list in my head is endless, but knowing I've got the most important things I begin to wonder if I'm just overthinking. I go to grab my case again to make my way to the taxi when I see it. My shiny gold wedding band. I stop again and see the cases start to pile in the boot. I know I must go back I can't leave without it.

'Oh! Won't be a minute.' I shout to them not fully explaining myself as I leave my case and rush back inside. The door accidently slams behind me. I know I have full intentions of coming back out, but I've left the other two with doubts about that, with my quick bolt back inside and not much explaining. Leaves the pair shocked as I can still hear the confused pair mumbling to each other.

'What?' I hear Doreen shout.

'Oh no, not again!' Rita says angrily thinking I'm going to leave her on my doorstep again. 'Don't you even think about playing this game, I know the combination for the key holder this time!'

I hear Rita screeching and running after me, but I know I'm only going to be a minute, so I don't bother answering.

I head upstairs and there on the bedside table is Barry's wedding ring. I've taken it everywhere with me since losing my husband, I can't bare to take mine off just yet, I like to keep Barry's close to me, it makes me feel like I have a part of him here. I pick it up and give it a little kiss.

'I Almost forgotten you.' I clench my fist tight enough to feel the ring dig into my palm. I take a deep breath and head back down with Barry's ring now attached to my necklace. From the top of the stairs, I'm met by Rita's eyes peeping through my letter box once again. Her frantic wide stare almost makes me burst into laughter.

'What are you doing?' Her green eyes filled with panic wondering if I'm going to come back out. I almost get the urge to shout back "hello their Tom." I however think better of it.

'Calm down I'm coming, I just needed to grab something.' I shout from the top of the stairs; her frantic eyes watch my every move as I take each step down. I open the door and head back out. Rita stands looking over at me confused. I can't help but wonder if she's thought I had to run back for little number two.

"Are you okay?" She asks cautiously while she looks me up and down.

'I am now.' I smile and flaunt myself down the path, my mid length blonde hair swishing with every stride, my white linens and black silky vest top fitting just perfectly, my oversized sunglasses guarding my eyes from the beam of the sun. I feel great and it clearly shows, Doreen's mouth flies open when she sees me, unsure if she's surprised to see me back out the house so soon or surprised at my newly found confidence I've just gained. I notice the nosey neighbours across the road out on their steps, wondering what all the commotion is on the usually quiet estate. I don't even care that they are staring and gossiping. "I'd imagine they will be making a few good stories up." I slowly start to walk myself down to the taxi as if I'm walking on a runway. My confidence is beaming through me, Rita is loving seeing this and joins me, the two of us striding down with our long legs taking each step with ease, fully glammed up and looking amazingly immaculate, we both know we look good, as we carry on relishing in it and the gazes from the neighbours help, I could see some of the women nudging there opened mouth husbands who were clearly enjoying the view. The taxi man doesn't even know where to look so he places his head down. I felt great, the best I had in a long time.

'We know you both look great now come on we need to go.' Doreen shouts impatiently to us disrupting our imaginary cat walk, she is now seated into the far end of the taxi with the door wide open eagerly waiting. I pick up the pace, which is a mistake, because before I know it my little kitten heel sandal has got stuck in the gravel, but the momentum of my stride has kept me walking, with one foot bare, which makes me stumble, luckily Rita catches me before I fall and props me back up, stopping me from hitting the floor face first. I embarrassingly need to hop back for my stranded shoe.

'Oh shit!' I shout a little too loudly, while trying to fix my lopsided sunglasses from my stumble. I look up and see the nosey neighbours that have gathered begin to laugh. Even the jaw dropped husbands are howling, their wives loving that I have messed up my immaculate image. The embarrassment is eating away at me, and I just want the ground to swallow me up.

'What am I doing? I shouldn't be flaunting myself around like this, who do I think I am?' My face flames red as I mutter my shame to Rita.

'Ignore them.' Rita says while still clutching my arm until I get into the taxi. Where a sympathetic Doreen waits for me. Instead of Rita bending down to join us in here, she stands taller and faces the neighbours, and before I could stop her, she begins to shout at them.

'What the fuck you all looking at? You never seen anyone going on holiday before!' She holds her middle finger up and scowls at them until they turn away shaking their heads shocked at her outburst, then the nosey lot rightly so creep back into their homes. Then there's a shout from the middle-aged cocky man from further up the road.

'Go on Grandma, you tell them!' He shouts in excitement trying to egg her on further.

"Oh, no." I say dreading what is going to come next. Calling her grandma will not go down well, especially after she spends a fortune from trying not to age.

'You as well with your piss-stained kegs. Who are you calling grandma?' The poor man standing there in his shorts with a toned tanned body suddenly doesn't look so confident, and sheepishly steps back into his house without another word. The taxi drivers face has a look of horror, or he's maybe even scared, as he's still standing there beside the door waiting to close it once Rita has gotten in.

'What? You never seen a woman swear before?' She asks the shocked driver. The nervous man jitters then thinks carefully for a second before answering.

'Erm, not like that no, that was something new for me.' He laughs nervously and closes the door once Rita has stepped inside.

Finally, we set off for the airport.

CHAPTER 5

Arriving at the airport in plenty of time, the excitement is bubbling all over us. The taxi driver jumps out first, then runs over to our side to open the door for us. We start to clamber out. Rita goes first. The task is a little trickier than it seems, with our over-sized handbags, sunglasses and heels, we all seem to get tied in a knot together. The taxi driver debates lending a hand to help Rita out, but instead he just steps back to give a little more room, likely him remembering how fiery she can be.

'Bloody hell these seats are low to get out of.' Rita says in a fluster while trying to heave herself and her huge bag up. The soft leather seats sinking every time she tries to get out. Finally with one big heave up she manages to do it, but only with the loudest "Rip" following behind her. In utter shock Rita freezes for minute.

'That wasn't….' She begins to plead.

'My goodness Rita that was right in my face.' I jokingly say knowing fine well it was the leather of the seat making the sound and not her bottom. Doreen on the other hand is howling so much that she has lost all control of herself, her usual laugh and is now began to snort, she's loving the fact Rita is no doubt dying in shame, as the usual elegance rarely slips from her.

'It was the seat!' She pleads again, this time the taxi drivers grin is starting to creep over his face, as he desperately tries to hold his laugh in. He sees Rita looking at him and quickly changes his expression, he stops his smiling laugh and tries to look more professional with a stern look, but it's clear to see that he's dying to let it out.

'Oh yeah, that old chestnut "The seat"'. Doreen laughs enjoying every minute of Rita's awkwardness. Rita soon realises that trying to defend herself is pointless and instead puts a stop to the teasing with her fiery outbursts.

'Oh, piss off.' She fires back at Doreen. Now standing fully out of the taxi and next to the driver, he leans towards her trying to whisper in her ear, but we all manage to hear.

'It happens to the best of us.' He winks at her with a grin. This just makes Doreen lose it even more, as she's practically rolling on the back seats laughing. Rita doesn't acknowledge what he said, instead tries to keep her pride, and fixes herself up. We are just waiting for Doreen to pull herself together and get out. When Rita loses her patience at the snorting, laughing Doreen. She closes the door on her just as she is about to jump out. This makes Doreen laugh even more. Rita then turns to the driver to say.

'Can we just leave her?' He finally lets out his laugh an reopens the door for her. Rita tries to avoid Doreen's eye and stands waiting for our cases to be unloaded as far as possible away from her. Doreen composes herself then clearly re thinks about the moment and starts to laugh again. Rita grabs her case unimpressed and marches away to the entrance of the airport.

'Oh fuck off Doreen!' She shouts back at her and storms off.

'Enjoy ladies' The driver shouts with a slight giggle to his tone as we start to disappear among the rushing crowds. I lift my hand to wave bye and begin to follow Rita who's now dashing through the double glass doors.

'Let's get checked in and find the VIP lounge. I need a drink.' Rita says without slowing down.

'Oh, the VIP lounge isn't that fancy.' Doreen says enthusiastically with a hint of sarcasm.

'Yes, the VIP lounge, so best behaviour please.' Rita snaps trying to gain back her elegant composure. I roll my eyes knowing I've got a whole week of their bickering to listen to. Although they love each other they are the complete opposites, and it certainly shows.

As much of a chore it is carting our luggage about, we seem to do it with ease, finding our check in and squeezing through the crowds, Rita is still storming ahead still trying to hide her embarrassment or rage, even though the squeak was just caused by the friction of her hot body and the leather chair. Rita hates being made a fool of, this mainly started from finding her cheating ex-husband embraced with another woman, which you can't blame her for, no one wants that to happen to them. She vowed never to let another man do that to her and after all these years, she's stayed true to her word, probably a bit too much. We finally make it to the VIP lounge and our cases now gone with us all checked in. Finding a quiet corner, we sit down on the big comfy leather sofas with a Hendrick's Gin and tonic, served just right with a slice of cucumber. Each sip tasting better and better. (Or maybe that's just the alcohol kicking in.) Time seems to be flying by now, holiday mode has set in, Rita has finally calmed down, feeling relaxed our conversation is flowing greatly with plenty of laughs and reminiscence from over the years. Finishing the last of my drink, I notice how peaceful it is in here compared to the standard lounges I normally use. Thinking to myself I'd have to go VIP more often; I could get used to this more lavish life style. This is Rita's style all over, but I can now see why. There aren't many people in here so going to the loo or queueing at the bar for food and drinks takes no time at all unlike the usual hustle and bustle in the main lounges. I place my empty glass down and grab my handbag and stand up.

'Who wants another?' Rita immediately raises her empty glass to indicate another one, Doreen is still slowly sipping away debating if she should. I don't wait for her answer instead I make my way to the bar to order another round. Coming back to a table empty handed. Doreen looks confused.

'Where's the drinks?'

'It's table service, he's going to bring them over, and you don't need to pay.' I wink at Doreen. 'It's a free bar.'

'Ooh!' She says sarcastically with a posh tone. Rita rolls her eyes, knowing the teasing is aimed at her but doesn't take offence.

'Yeah, yeah I get it, but you both can't tell me that this isn't a better way to go on holiday.' Just then the drinks arrive, the young waiter places them down and smiles.

'Can I get you anything else?' He asks politely. I pick up my fresh glass and raise it slightly.

'Just keep them coming sweetheart, thank you.' He nods with a grin, probably not the first time of hearing that and walks back behind the bar. Rita has a smile all over her face clearly loving this moment. Doreen however looks a little horrified and looks at her now one and a half drinks sitting in front of her. She begins to stutter trying to get her words out in a fluster.

'Erm, shouldn't we take it easy, we don't want to miss the flight?' She says with a genuine cautious look on her face.

Rita laughs. 'Oh darling, don't worry about it, they will soon tell us when the flights ready. Just let your hair down for once. Look at Lynn over there, she is.' She nods over in my direction while I'm about to take another large gulp of gin. I do a cheesy smile back knowing I am surprisingly getting far too comfortable with this situation. Doreen looks over and shrugs her shoulders and allows herself to make the most of it.

'Oh, what the heck.' Then finishes the remaining glass that she was taking her time with. It's not often you see Doreen let herself go to enjoy herself but when she does, she gives it a good go.

A few more gins later, I start to feel the effects of it and loosen up with no panic or anxiety in sight, we carry on gossiping and laughing, getting louder and louder after each drink, we start getting the disapproving looks off the other guest, especially off the posh couple sitting not too far from us, tutting every time we have a burst of laughter. Rita has just noticed the woman tutting and starts to glare at her, the woman clearly annoyed with us ends up shouting.

'You should be ashamed of yourself carrying on like this at your age, this is a well-respected area, and look at you all drunk!'

"Oh no." I mutter to myself as I look over and see Rita's eyes have narrowed getting ready to burst into an argument. I start trying to calm her down but before I know it, someone else is shouting. I turn round to see a tipsy Doreen has stood up a little bit wobbly, waving her long finger to the woman.

'Oh fuck off and mind your own business!' She shouts back a little bit slurred from the alcohol. The woman is so shocked that she grabs hold of her chest and gasps.

'Well, I never...'

Her husband rushes to defend her and stands from his seat, his angry eyes are burning into Doreen. 'You're a disgrace, look at the state of you!' His wife sits there with a look of triumph, "Her hero coming to save her from the beasts." But it didn't stop there did it. Doreen puffs out her chest. (This means she's angry and ready for a battle.) I look over to Rita who's now looking on in amusement as for once it isn't her causing the trouble.

'You going to help me?' I say desperately knowing this is getting way out of control. Rita just rolls her eyes and smiles. The full Room has now gone silent, and everyone's eyes are fixed on us. I catch the young waiter from the corner of my eye, he's making his way over to us. I gulp knowing fine well what is coming. I turn to Doreen to try and calm her down but it's too late, she's off shouting again.

'You fuck off as well.' She now slurs to the husband as she tries to point her finger in his direction.

The shame is burning up right through my body, I'm pretty sure I must be glowing red! Rita is no help, instead she just stays sitting giggling finishing her drink. I grab Doreen and usher her back into her seat. I look over to the well to do couple and mouth the words "Sorry". The two look back and lift their noses in the air and turn away as if we are some peasants. As soon as we get sat back down in our seats the waiter finally reaches us.

'I'm sorry I'm going to have to ask you all to leave!' He shifts from foot to foot clearly uncomfortable confronting us.

'Why? Why not them?' Doreen asks as she points to the couple.

"Oh shit," Doreen is off again. I stand up and grab my things to get ready to leave hoping it defuses the situation.

'I'm sorry, she doesn't normally drink a lot, I'd say it's gone to her head. We are just leaving now anyhow.' I try to defend her rude actions and pull at Doreen to come with me to leave. The young waiter just nods but stays put until we all stand up to make sure we do leave. Rita finishes her drink, while Doreen stumbles up. We all start to walk out, I'm too embarrassed to look round, so I keep my eyes fixed on Rita who is leading the way out. She turns to the couple who are smirking watching us leave, holds up her middle finger and keeps it pointing at them until we are fully out the room.

"Oh dear God." I cringe 'get me on that plane.'

CHAPTER 6

Hearing the captains voice telling us we are about to land is a massive relief. It's been a long three and a half hours. Me and Rita had two more gins and then both got engrossed in our books. Doreen ended up falling asleep, with me being in the middle, her head was resting on my shoulder so had to listen to her snoring right down my ear for most of the journey. I hope by the time she wakes she is in a better state. She slowly stirs from hearing the captain's calls. I nudge her to make sure she wakes fully.

'What… where are we?' She jumps up still half asleep.

'We are here.' I softly say back.

'Really? Already?' Doreen becomes more alert and starts to look out the window. The tiny dots what are buildings are starting to take shape, the coast line looks so clean and fresh, the sea is bright blue and glistens from the sun beaming down on it. "This is going to be so good" I think to myself, lounging on the beach, reading a book, sipping a few drinks. The thought zones me out for a second. I jump back into reality when Rita starts chucking the bags down from the overhead compartment. I look over to Doreen who still looks a little tipsy from the drinks earlier.

'Come on, time to go.' I usher to Doreen to stand up. Doreen lunges herself out of her seat a little bit too harshly, jumping herself right up forgetting about the overhead compartment, her head bounces off it, with a huge bang.

'Shit!' She shouts then holds both her hands onto her head squeezing it tightly as if to stop the throbbing pounding pain.

'Watch your head!' Rita teases.

'Bloody hell that hurt.' Doreen cries out.

'I bet it did.' I replay it back over in my head and it makes me shudder. 'Are you sure you're, okay? It was a fair bang?' Doreen nods but still nurses her head. Once Doreen composes herself, we all start to leave the plane and head to the check in area.

After all the commotion getting off the plane and queueing for what seems like ages at the check in, we are finally huddled round waiting for our cases to come out. (This surely has got to be one of the worst parts of going on holiday.) It's getting really busy now, the bags haven't even started coming out and people have already started pushing and shoving trying to get to the front. With Doreen still recovering from her bang on the head and still slightly worse for wear, she has volunteered herself to stand back from the crowd and look after the luggage as each one comes out. Me and Rita hatches up a plan to be ready to jump into action when they start rolling along. Rita's going to grab the bags off the conveyer, pass them to me and I will move them over to Doreen. "If only it's going to be as simple as that."

The loud sound of the belts starting to move, sends all the passengers into a frantic frenzy, everyone starts to push even more desperately trying to get to the front. It really doesn't matter who you are, if you are in someone's way you are definitely going to get flung about. I get myself in to position and try to hold my ground against the rushing tide of people, I turn to Rita to check to see if she is ready.

'Are you ready?' She asks beating me to the question. I nod back. Rita turns back around to head for the conveyer belt, her eyes wide and alert, her skinny tall body towers over people, then off she goes, she manages to wiggle herself to the front and is now ready to start grabbing the bags. I look round to check on Doreen whose standing waiting patiently. I catch a family on the other side of me who have now erupted into an argument over her husband bringing over the wrong bag. Everyone seems to have the same bag, and you can always guarantee you grab someone else's by mistake. (Luckily my black case has a lime green ribbon attached, a wise move, I think to myself with a smirk.) Rita brings over the first bag, fighting with her elbows to squeeze past the rushing crowd.

'That's Doreen's.' She says as she desperately tries to reach it out to me. I then see a lime green ribbon on a case pop out.

'Quick there's mine coming out now.' I say to her pointing in a rush in case she misses it. Rita squeezes herself back through any gaps she can get in and manages to pull the case off, once again she come clambering through the crowd.

'This is hellish, people are like wild animals in here. Your ticket and ribbon have come off when I was trying to pull it off the belt. I look down and see the remaining part of the ticket still had our hotel name on it. Rita then dives back into the crowd to wait for hers. I wheel the two cases over to Doreen; people have now started to crowd around her and some are trying to rush out of the door. It really is hectic in here, people are running everywhere and bumping into everyone. Which makes me remember why I hate airports!

'There's mine and yours, I'm just going to go back and help Rita find hers.' Doreen nods and closely keeps the two cases next to her. After what seems like forever pulling cases off and placing them back, we find it.

'Well that was something.' Rita says huffing and puffing while dragging her overfilled case away from the crowd.

'I know it's carnage in here!' I say just as flustered as much as Rita, my once clean crisp clothes now feel damp with the heat and sweat. The pair of us drained from it all, start to head back over to Doreen, who has now vanished in the hectic crowd that's all trying to head out of the door at the same time. We quickly scan round trying to find her, but the bobbing heads and rushing bodies make it hard to see.

'There she is.' I point over to see a flustered Doreen trying to gather our knocked over cases. There seems to be cases spilled over everywhere, everyone scrambles desperately trying to retrieve their own. We manage to get there quickly to help her gather up the remaining case that's still toppled over. The heard of people are now spilling out of the doors rushing to catch their transfers, the area is now starting to calm as we finally catch out breath.

'This is just ridiculous.' Doreen shouts, her face beaming red in a flustered craze. 'People have come rushing over knocked everything everywhere and I even got pushed and nearly fell over!'

'It's crazy in here isn't it, it was the same at the conveyer belt, it's likely with the delay of the flight people are trying to catch their transfers, which by the way, we need to hurry to get, have we got everything?'

'Yeah, it looks like it, although my ticket has now completely torn off, remind me to get one for the way back.'

'We will sort that after let's just get out of here, our taxi should be waiting.' Rita rushes us out, having had enough of all the pushing we follow, trying to scramble through the overly crammed door.

Thankfully the taxi is outside waiting for us. Luckily, we decided against the transfer bus. "As that's certainly not Rita's style of travelling anyhow." Having seen that bus has already set off in the distance, I watch the fury of people being left behind shouting and scrambling for the available taxis. We begin to run over hoping he doesn't decide to leave before we get there or take on new desperate passengers. I cling on to my floppy oversized hat while dragging my big bulky case behind. He notices us heading to him and rushes over to help, he grabs our cases and places them in the back quickly, slightly annoyed that he should probably be already on another run by now. Our apologies don't seem to soften the scowl on his face as he wastes no more time waiting about as the taxis begins to zoom off to our destination.

The three of us take a deep sigh of relief at having not being left behind, although you do feel sorry for the people that have had to be left waiting on the curb with the cases, your just kind of glad that it isn't you.

'That was absolutely horrendous.' Doreen mutters still reeling from the chaos in the airport, or perhaps she's still slightly tipsy and that is why she seems to be repeating herself.

'You what? All you had to do was stand with the cases, try fighting over everyone to drag them off the conveyer belt. Now that was horrendous.' Rita shakes her head at Doreen.

I giggle to myself as the two-start chuntering away at each other. I lay back in the seat and close my eyes for a second taking in the calmness of the car motoring us along. I almost drift off into a sleep when I feel the jolt of the car wake me up. The journey hasn't taken long. No sooner from me closing my eyes to opening them, we were here pulled up outside. I gaze out the window and can't help but gasp. The hotel looks beautiful, the marble grand entrance, easily lures you in. Palm trees decorate the path leading up and sat on either side stood two elegant water fountains, that completely fall in sync with each other. I know before I even enter that I would never be able to afford this place.

CHAPTER 7

It is late afternoon when we arrive outside the hotel. Although the heat of the sun has started to die down, the heat still smacks me in the face as soon as I step out of the taxi. I stand there in awe, taking in the amazing view, if you look in the opposite direction of the hotel, you look down on to the brightest blue coastline which is not too far, but far enough that I'd probably need a taxi to get there. A shudder comes over me when I try to imagine myself trekking back up the big hill feeling the imaginary sharp burning pain that my knees would feel. I turn myself back around and take more of the view of the hotel. It really is beautiful, standing tall with big, stretched windows covering the entire building, surrounded by trees and flower displays, the black and gold décor finishes it off perfectly. The décor makes the place look expensive and posh. "This is Rita's style to a tee." The lavish elegant finish with not one thing out of place, apart from my sweaty self. I can't help but wonder how much it would cost to stay in a place like this. Not that it would make much difference to Rita. She has the money.

'This looks expensive.' I say hoping to get some clue to the price, I know she would never tell, she has money of course but she certainly wouldn't glory in it to other people. Rita who's now standing smiling to herself taking in the view knowing her choice has blown me and Doreen away. She wanted to treat us and she's certainly done that indeed.

'And posh.' Doreen sharply butts in trying to keep herself grounded and not get lost in all the wealth that must be here. She's very minimalistic and is not one for show boating. She can't stand when the rich and wealthy use their fortunate lives to show off against the not so fortunate. Although I wouldn't say she is poor, neither of us are, but we certainly aren't as wealthy as Rita.

'It is, isn't it beautiful.' She says to us, having already been here before herself, she adamantly kept this a secret to where exactly we were going. If we googled the pictures, which we would have no doubt done, it definitely would not have given us this same affect and that's exactly what Rita wanted us to have, and my goodness it's certainly worth it, this place is utterly breath taking. We all agree while standing taking in the view waiting for the cases to be unloaded.

Rita wasn't always well off with money, but after discovering her now ex-husband was having a long affair. "Not that this was only the one, as he couldn't keep it in his pants." This dirty affair he couldn't slither out of this time though. Caught red handed when she rang his assistant after their son Jackson got rushed to hospital from falling down the stairs at school and splitting his head open. Hours of trying to get hold of him and fobbed off from his assistant, an already suspicious Rita took drastic action, and called me to join her and Doreen to go to the hospital to wait with her son, who was now ok and waiting to be discharged. A raging Rita marched to his office, where the investment banker should be. Rita and I, march right up to his shocked assistant that was trying to stop us from entering his office but failed miserably. She busts the doors open to see him embraced with another woman, (His co-worker. That he often went on business trips with.) Rita spots the remainder of the lunch date across his desk and the two glasses of wine, grabbing one glass and throwing it right at a shocked Jim, who just manages to duck in time, as it smashes on the wall behind him. Ever so calmy Rita speaks, 'I've been calling you! Our son is in hospital, so how about you sort yourself out and join me there like the loving husband and father you pretend to be!' Rita turns around and we march back out leaving everyone shell shocked, and a desperate Jim stumbling with his pants round his ankles trying to explain his pathetic self. His assistant, embarrassingly says:

'If there's anything I can...'

Rita cuts her off instantly, 'You can get me a dam good lawyer, that's what you can do!' The assistant nods her head, truly embarrassed and ashamed, but did just that. Her ex-husband didn't put up much of a fight and generously paid her a hefty sum in the divorce which she wisely invested, not for the sake of Rita and their son though, more to keep his wrong doings hushed up and to try and protect his so called "clean image."

Before we can even start rolling our cases through the door, a young concierge comes running with his gold trolley. Me and Doreen look on surprised while Rita has clearly had this service many times before. She hands him a couple of notes once he's loaded the bags up, then off he rushes with our cases.

'If you tip well, they will go out their way to look after you.' She turns to say while smiling.

Rita fits right in to these kinds of places easily. But I cannot help but feel a touch out of my comfort zone. I look over to Doreen who must be feeling the same as me, she's looking about with her mouth wide open. It is impressive mind with its huge shiny gold mirrors, little touches of green plants everywhere, the marble floor, which was impressively clean, large dark grey sofas set in the middle, the hotel was immaculate. Although not too big, but big enough so it didn't look crammed. We head to the reception to get checked in. Me and Doreen are still in complete awe as we are walking our way through, my eyes dart everywhere trying to take in every bit of its image, I catch Doreen checking over herself as two stunningly elegant woman walk past us, I feel the same and shift uncomfortably and think that the first thing I will do when I reach my room is tidy myself up. We reach up to Rita who is already standing at the reception area. Even the staff look pristine. Well and truly out of our

35

comfort zone, me and Doreen just look at each other.

'Checking in today?' Says a beautiful young Greek woman.

We leave Rita to take charge. While she manages the checking in, me and Doreen stand back still admiring the hotels beauty and mutter amongst ourselves at how different this is from our Benidorm trip a few years ago. Although Benidorm is great and I love it, this however is something completely different.

Rita struts herself back over then leads us to our apartment. With the tiredness from the journey beginning to kick in, the only desire I have right now is to get showered, eat and get my pyjamas on. But knowing Rita, she will already have the night planned.

The apartment is as beautiful as the rest of the hotel, with the same matching décor, everything just flows perfectly, the black and golds, the huge chunky mirrors, oversized vases. Although the apartment wasn't big it was enough, the living area and kitchen was open plan and is the first room that greets you as you enter, then slotted on either side was two bedrooms, then the opposite was a bedroom and bathroom, which Rita takes as soon as she realises. Meaning I am left neighbouring with a snoring Doreen. Our cases are already here, I grab mine and begin to roll it to my room.

'I'm going to freshen up before we do anything else.' I shout to the others who are now retrieving theirs and leave them to it.

I get into my room and just flop on my bed. "I could quite happily just have a nap." I lay there for another few minutes nearly drifting off to sleep, it's so peaceful here. I force myself up otherwise that would be me for the rest of the day. I fling up my case onto the bed ready to start unpacking, not really having the motivation to do it, but knowing I can't stay in these sweaty clothes, I carry on with the unpacking. Before I can unzip the case, Rita is at my door way handing me a gin.

'I've made you this while you get ready, I'm just heading in the shower, I won't be long then you can jump in.'

'Thanks.' I take my drink and turn back to my case. For some reason it looks different, as it lays there on my bed waiting to be opened, almost newer, I'm pretty sure there was a scuff mark on mine as well. I shake the thought out of my head and continue. I grab a hold of the tiny plain silver lock, which everyone seems to use on their cases. I place the key in, for some reason the key doesn't want to fit properly. I try with all my might, wiggling the dam key to fit. It's no use. I stop and throw the keys across the floor and take a breather before I lose my temper. I lift the glass of gin that Rita brought and take a big slurp. Ready to start the battle again I pick up the keys and try them, wiggling them into the grooves and pulling on the tiny lock, eventually I force it open. I throw the key and the lock onto the floor in anger and slowly begin to unzip my case.

'Oh Fuck!' I shout so loud that Doreen comes rushing in.

'What is a matter?' Her face filled with panic as she launches herself through my door.

'This is not my case!'

'You what?' Doreen comes in to take a closer look. 'Oh, that is definitely not your case.' I feel disheartened, its got to be the worst nightmare everyone has going on holiday, losing your case or getting the wrong one.

'What am I going to do? I have got nothing to wear! I cannot believe this is happening! How has it even happened? I saw my ticket before it completely came off!' I feel the anger rising as I'm trying to work out what has happened. Then a notice a guilty looking Doreen as her eyes fall to look at the floor.

'It must have got muddled when everyone started rushing out, I was certain I picked the same case back up! I am sorry.'

As much as I am annoyed at this inconvenience, I cannot blame Doreen it was absolutely carnage in the airport and it's easily done, it could have happened to any of us, unfortunately though it had to be me! As I watch nervously step from foot to foot, I can't help but feel sorry for her.

'Don't worry it's not your fault, I will take it down to reception, I'm sure they will sort it.' Rita then appears back at the doorway with her tiny towel wrapped around her.

'What was all the shouting about?'

'She's got the wrong case.' Doreen jumps in to say before I open my mouth.

'Oh bloody hell, I'll have something for you for now, let's get sorted and we will take it down to reception.' Rita heads back to her room. Just in that small time, I turn round to see Doreen has already started rummaging through the unwanted case.

'What are you doing?' I say shocked.

'I'm just having a look. Must be a man's case look at these little budgie smugglers.' She then throws me a pair of tiny red speedos. I catch them just before they hit me in the face and storm myself over and throw the speedos back in.

'Put it all back we can't go looking through someone else's case!'

'Why? There probably looking through yours right now!'

The thought hits me and makes me shudder. All my underwear getting inspected, my big knickers, skimpy knickers and my comfy old favourites to sleep in, all on show. The thought makes me squirm.

'Put it all back.' I point angrily. 'I'm going for a shower then another drink before I have to deal with this.' I leave the room in a huff.

I was barely gone ten minutes, but when I open the bathroom door, I'm met by a worried looking Rita and Doreen. knowing fine well that the calming, peaceful shower I've just had, is going to feel like a complete and utter waste of time, judging by the looks on their faces.

'You need to come and see this!' I follow them back into my

room, on the bed lay a stunningly carved cigar humidor. The old dark oak scented the room, the little engravings where perfect gold swirls. The chunky big box sat there looking very expensive and posh.

'It's nice isn't it, I didn't know people still smoked cigars.' None of them answer, instead they just lift the lid to reveal the perfectly lined cigars laying on a red velvet cloth. Now they do look very expensive. I go to lift one of the brown wrapped cigars with a golden stamp attached.

'Just wait.' Doreen says. I look on confused but do what I am told. She then lifts the section where they lay to reveal a hidden compartment. I gasp in horror.

'I told you to put all this back!' I snap at a sheepish Doreen.

CHAPTER 8

'I was doing that until I seen this, I only took a quick look and thought I broke it, then this popped out.' I look back down and see the soft white powder neatly wrapped up into a clear package. There was no mistaken for what this may be.

'I came in your room and caught her with this cocaine in her hands! The silly bugger would have been putting it in her coffee thinking it was sugar.' Rita seems as annoyed as me, maybe the fact if left alone with Doreen we could have been drinking it with our morning coffees, now that would have been different!

'I'm sorry I didn't know I thought it was strange putting it in there, but then I thought it was maybe to stop it spilling all over the case!' Doreen looks disappointed in herself for even being anywhere near drugs. 'I've never seen cocaine before, how was I to know?'

Rita rolls her eyes. 'You are so naive at times. Let's get it all put away and pretend we have never seen anything, whoever this belongs to will certainly be missing it, there must be a fortunes worth here.'

I stand still, looking on completely speechless. I'm trying to work out in my head the kind of people who this will belong to, not thinking of anything good I begin to panic and quickly shake the thoughts and bad images away. 'Yes, let's get it all put back together exactly how it was, and it will look like we have never seen it.' Rita begins to pop the box together and tries to pop the middle section of cigars back in.

'Shit! It won't all fit.' She desperately tries to squeeze the section back in, but clearly seeing that it's not budging, she begins to push harder and harder as more panic starts to set in.

'It must fit! It was all in there, so it's got to all go back together, take it all back out and try it again.' I say with a screech to my tone. Rita does just this, but this time there's a huge cracking sound. 'You've broke it!' My tone getting higher and higher!

'I haven't!' Rita tries to defend herself.

'Well, what was that noise? I heard it crack.'

Doreen has started pacing about in a mad panic while putting her hands to her head and begins to mumble. 'They are going to think it's ours, we are going to go to prison!' The tension in the room is rising rapidly as we all begin to lose our heads.

'Shut up Doreen! No one is going to prison we just need to place it all back.' Rita is starting to get snappy. We all are in a fluster, and with Doreen's mumbles whirling in my head has set off more panic. What if she is right?

'Just put it all back in, who cares if it fits!' I shriek so high that I can hear the squeak bounce around the room.

'We can't just put it back, if someone checks the case before it gets returned, and sees a big bag of coke lying there then they are going to report it, especially in a place like this! We are going to be in the shit, our prints are all over it.' Rita says desperately trying to fit it all back together. Her face is full of determination as she doesn't give up trying. Doreen has set off on a full-scale panic attack. Pacing rapidly up and down the room, her head in her hands juddering about still mumbling away to herself.

'I can't go to prison, what will Phil do? He won't cope without me! Oh my goodness I can't go to prison.' She keeps repeating to herself over and over. We can't help but snap at her hoping to knock her out of her useless trance.

'Fuck Phil, right now, you need to help.' Rita aggression explodes.

'None of us can! We aren't exactly built for prison life Doreen!

Get over here and try to help!' Doreen finally snaps out of it and tries to help, the three of us unpacking and repacking, changing each time how to place it back in, hoping something will give. Just as we feel like we might be getting somewhere, we get interrupted by the biggest knock on our door! We all jump back with shock, along with the squeal from Doreen which she tries to embarrassingly shy away from as we both look at her. We all freeze and stare at each other, wondering what to do next, all while holding a big bag of coke! Another thump hits our door!

'Shit!' Me and Rita say in sync while this time Doreen covers her mouth trying to prevent anymore squeals from slipping out.

CHAPTER 9

Repeated bangs hit on our door; it's starting to sound as if someone is losing their patience. The sweat must be dripping down my face, I can feel it slowly slipping down from my forehead. We all stand looking on in panic, waiting for the person to leave. Which they don't of course, a few more hits on the door appear.

'What are we going to do?' Doreen screeches. Then quickly covers her mouth again with her hands. My gasping breath is getting heavier and heavier, I look about trying to bide a few moments, stupidly thinking that something might pop up and rescue us from this shit show!

'Just put it all back in, I will go and answer the door. Just relax and act normal.' I begin to slowly walk to the door with my heart pounding and the sweat pouring from me, I reach out for the door handle trying to steady my shaking arms, when another thud bangs on the door just as I'm about to open it. I jump in the motion which helps swings the door open.

Standing in front of me is a young gorgeous Greek woman, with natural tanned skin and dark eyes, her long waving brown hair just rests past her shoulders. I smile when I see she is wearing the hotel uniform and relax now knowing that there's no drug lords, or police waiting to jump on us. I stop my stupid thoughts running through my head, realising that I probably watch way too much crime programmes, which isn't helping with my paranoia.

'Sorry to keep you waiting I was just getting out of the shower.'

Hoping saying that will make her see why I'm so hot and bothered, and not because we have a load of cocaine in my room.

'You okay madam you look a bit flustered.' "Oh no, does she know?" My panic reappears its ugly head, a stare back trying to work out if she does know. "Of course she doesn't, how can she? I will just deny everything!" My mind wanders off, only a little cough to interrupt me from the young woman jolts me back. I slowly nod my head and smile.

'It's been a long journey, and when we have finally got here, I've just realised I haven't got the correct case.' I speak so fast that I forget to breathe. She smiles back not noticing.

'That's actually why I am here.' She says politely.

"Oh no!" I think to myself hoping that I haven't said it out loud. She continues to stare wondering with my delayed replied.

'Are you sure you are okay?' I nod back trying to hide the shock from my face, she proceeds on, eager to get the task finished.

'I'm Cora I work down in reception, I've been calling on the few guests that have just arrived today, as we got a report from someone also receiving the wrong case. I'm glad to have finally found it's you. May I come in? I have a few things we need to check so we can verify it's yours. Then we can return your case.'

I can hear Doreen and Rita squabble in the background, I hope that woman doesn't pay too much attention to them. I gulp before I can answer. 'Err… sure come in.' Cora follows me through to the living area then stops to take a seat on the sofa. She pulls out her tablet and begins to read something.

'I've just a few questions then we can get your case back to you, I know it's a hassle but unfortunately it's hotel policy, so we have to do this before we can return them.' I smile back trying to avoid an eye roll. She soon starts with the normal, your name, date of birth, where I'm from, then asked me what was inside my case. Which okay, I can understand that, to verify if it's the right one? Then comes the weird questions.

'Have you opened the case that does not belong to you? If so, was their anything there that can cause harm to you or anyone else? Are there any illegal substances?'

"Shit! She knows." My heart starts beating rapidly. Then I remember my thoughts, DENY! DENY everything!

'No!' I snap too quickly. She must know I'm lying as she looks over me, waiting for another reaction, my hands begin to jitter, so I place them on my knees hoping it will stop them. She soon picks up on this.

'It's okay Lynn, there's nothing for you to be worried about, this is just routine policy from the hotel. It's okay if you did accidently open the case, we won't tell them unless something is reported missing. Which I'm sure it won't be, you look like an honest woman.'

"What the fuck is this kind of questioning, this is rather just stupid routine, or she knows!" I must think for a little too long as Cora coughs again, urging me to answer. I know I need to give some truth away, but not too much. I'm sure that's what happens in the crime programmes I've watched.

'Erm yeah the case got opened, but it was just for a minute I realised it wasn't mine and closed it back up, we were about to come down and report it.' She looks at me not fully satisfied with my answer.

'So, there was nothing illegal that you saw?' She leans a bit closer as if I'm going to spill all my secrets to her.

"Shit, Shit, she really knows. Do I tell her or is it a trap?" In my mad panic I get too scared to say anything. DENY, DENY EVERYTHING! Pops back into my head. I try to hide my panic.

'No, like I said I literally opened it and realised it wasn't mine then I closed it back up again.' I see her do an eye roll, clearly not happy with my answer but realising she isn't getting anywhere, she proceeds on to returning my case. I look to her wondering what kind of weird shit this was all about and hope this is all done with now.

'Okay then, everything checks out fine. I'll just message my colleague to bring your case and I will return this one. Should only take about ten minutes.' She stands up getting ready to leave, just as Rita and Doreen come out from the other room with the case. Clearly been listening in. Rita hands it over to her with ease, while Doreen still has a panicked look on her face and can barely look the woman in the eye. She notices and stares in her direction hoping that she will crack under the pressure and spill some exciting gossip! Rita notices the tension rising and steps in before anything else gets any trickier, and just in time by the looks of Doreen, her face flushing bright red and her eyes darting everywhere trying to avoid the woman, she's starting to shuffle from foot to foot while Cora fixes her gaze straight on to her as if to wait for her to crumble and spill.

'Is that everything? We are going out soon for some food.' Cora looks her up and down and nods showing a little frustration at being interrupted. Doreen finally takes a breath.

'Yes, that is everything.' Just as she is about out of the door she turns back around to speak. 'If any of you need anything, and I mean anything at all, please just ask for Cora.' Then off she finally leaves.

Rita makes sure she is well away from our apartment before she closes the door. I see Doreen has just about melted under the heat of the pressure and has needed to sit down. I on the other hand, have my mind going in over drive wondering why all the strange questions? Like surely, they can't be routine very accurate for what we have just seen.

'Well wasn't she strange?' Rita says while she leans up against the closed door.

'I think she knows! Some of the questions she was asking me...'

'We know, we heard it all.'

'Good job that is it all done with, it's someone else's problem now.' I feel relieved and like a weight has been lifted from my shoulders, I make my way back to finish getting ready, with a bounce back in my step, when I suddenly catch Doreen from the corner of my eye, she's started pacing around again, I can see the beads of sweat starting to reappear on her once again flushed face. She starts to fidget with her fingernails, and I can see she is trying to avoid looking at me.

'Doreen! What have you done?' I've known her many years now and I can spot her guilt from a mile off. She then stops and looks at me, then looks down and then looks at Rita. I look at Rita who is now trying to avoid my stare also.

'It's all sorted now, isn't it?' I ask Rita starting to feel unsure.

'Erm about that… It's not entirely sorted; we may still have, the, err, package!' She stutters out sheepishly.

'What! Why?' I glare at them both, my blood is starting to boil my anger ripples through me and I'm so close to start shouting and screaming at the pair, the boiling anger prevents me instead the only thing I can muster out in a scream:

'FUCK!!!' They both sit there silent for a second, probably hoping that I will calm down but there is no chance of that, I've hit the peak of my rage and it's going to take some calming down. 'How can you be so stupid!' They both take my rant gracefully and without any offence, not that they can be offended, they fucked up! But they carry on listening to me shout and scream before they decide to interrupt.

'We were listening to what she was saying, she sounded like a cop! We couldn't put the drugs in, then you get blamed for it! So, we took them out and hid them in the over head lamp.' Rita says, thinking she has done the right thing, but lowers her head knowing she's fucked up, which has left us still with a load of cocaine with no clue what to do with it.

'You have got to be joking me? She was wearing the fucking uniform; she was the one that checked us in, for goodness sake!'

My rage is burning to the point I can feel the heat pouring out of my body. The thought we could have had all this finished with and ready to carry on and enjoy our holiday, really shits all over my parade. All I seem to be left with is a big hot steaming pile of it, and big bag of cocaine which is as much use as nothing to us.

'We know that now when we have seen her, but we didn't know who it was, we just heard her talking and she sounded like a cop! We will get it sorted don't worry...' Don't worry, how can Rita tell me not to worry! I get the sudden urge to throw something at her but manage to stop myself and just dig my fingernails into my clutched palms.

'You are both stupid! I can't believe this! How we going to get it back in the case, I told her I didn't look through it!' My stress starts to rise and suddenly I start to feel the dull ache pound in my head. Doreen finally speaks after she has sat weighing up the situation and my reactions.

'I've got an idea.' Me and Rita both look over in shock. Just then a huge knock appears again on the door.

CHAPTER 10

'I'm pouring a drink, someone else can answer this time.' I walk off in a huff, livid at the situation and then two, how can they be so stupid.

'Pour me one too please.' Rita shouts after me as casual as ever. I don't even answer her, instead I just give her the middle finger with my back turned while I walk away. Luckily this time it's just someone returning my case. I make us all drinks, then we sit down and wait for Doreen to say her idea. I can see she is nervous to speak as she tries to bide herself time by fidgeting with her finger nails and her stuttering continues. My patience is wearing thin, and her delays begin to aggravate me.

'What's this big plan of yours then? I snap at her a little too harshly as I hand over the freshly made G&T's. My tone must have taken Doreen by surprise as I watch her posture stiffen, she takes a deep breath and starts to explain her plan.

'We could basically just hand it back to reception, say it must have fell out. Rita you must have a biggish makeup case that will fit the cocaine. I've got a lot of panty liners that we could place on top, and a couple pair of big knickers, surely no one will ratch through something as personal as that?' I take a big gulp of my drink while I think if this could work, my brain is too foggy and tired to weigh up all the pros and cons of it. I find myself agreeing without realising, while Rita looks over to me in shock.

'I don't own big knickers so don't ask for mine.' Rita butts in with the only thing she can say, while feeling outnumbered on the matter, I can tell this idea doesn't sit well with her, but seen as

49

though no one else has other options, it's the only plan we have right now.

'Of course you don't!' Doreen says tutting.

'I think this is a bad idea.' Rita says while walking off, she soon returns with a black makeup case. 'This should do.' Doreen stands then goes and returns with a handful of panty liners. (There are loads of them.)

'Will this be enough? I've got plenty more if we need them.' She scatters the pile across the table. Me and Rita both look at each other then look at Doreen amazed at how causal she is unloading the big pile. Don't get me wrong I don't mind panty liners and use the myself at times but seeing all the different shapes and sizes and the amount, I start to wonder if she has shares in them.

'What were you thinking? That you are going to piss yourself all holiday.' Rita can't hold her sarcastic comments in. An offended Doreen just glares back.

'It won't be long before you are, if you don't already!' She snaps back.

'I certainly do not!' Rita is horrified with such accusations. She would never openly admit to having to use them, not even to her two best friends.

'Where's your knickers Lynn?' Doreen asks ignoring Rita.

'Why my knickers?' I get a little fluster thinking of someone gawping at my big old comfy knicks. I start to hope that I've actually brought a half decent pair, and not my favourites which are clinging on for dear life.

'Everyone else has contributed, so hand over the knicks please.' I huff at Doreen's demands and go ratch out the best out of a bad bunch of big black comfy knickers. I return and them over hoping there isn't a much of a close inspection. Luckily Doreen packs them in.

Everything packed and the cocaine covered, we stand back and admire the dubious looking makeup case. We can only hope that no one dares to want to rummage through a bag that is filled with a load of panty liners and a little bit worse for wear knickers. It's got to work, it's our only hope to be getting this mess over with.

'Right let's get this over with.' I march out with the makeup bag pressed under my arm, as I'm trying desperately to hold on to some confidence, but the niggling voice in my head is trying to ruin that.

CHAPTER 11

Making our way down didn't take long, soon the reception area comes into view. We slow down our stride, and I begin to wonder if this is a good idea after all. The thoughts of everything that could go wrong have started flashing through my head. I then realize that I've stopped walking and watch the other two proceed ahead. A little check list now pops up in my troubled thoughts. What we need to do and say, will they notice? Will they look in? I try to rehearse what to say, but it's no use, everything keeps jumbling around as my nerves start to get the better of me. I then remember the note Rita wrote and start to think we maybe shouldn't have put that in. basically pleading for ourselves, telling them how sorry we are, and that this got missed out accidently, and that we don't want any trouble. I cringe to myself knowing that they are going to see right through our pathetic attempt to cover our mishandlings. Who would accidently take out a big package of cocaine? Oh, that's right, Doreen would! Thinking she'd come into a lifetime supply of sugar.

It doesn't take long before the other two realise I'm not there walking with them. I watch as they come running back while I'm stuck in a frozen state. I physically can't move, my legs feel like they are made of lead. Rita rushes back to me first then an ever so calm Doreen.

'I can't do this.' I whisper to them when they reach me, my heart is pounding, my palms are sweaty and my legs and arms are started to wobble which is starting to get noticeable, so Rita gets a hold of me to steady my wobbling body.

'What!' Rita gasps. 'We have to do this, come on we are nearly there.' She says trying to urge me along with a gentle nudge, but legs refuse to take another step. I see Doreen's brows turn into a scowl of determination as she reaches out to me.

'Give it to me, I'll do it!' Doreen grabs the bag out my hand and begins marching off to reception, she's almost there before I snap out of my shocked state, Rita looks on surprised at Doreen striding away with no care, I want to run and shout telling her to stop, as I get the most awful feeling that this isn't going to go well, by the time I've managed to open my mouth she's already there handing it over.

'Come on we better go.' Rita grabs my arm and pulls me along to head over to Doreen. Doreen is already back to us before we even get half way. She's marching herself along looking chuffed. I look behind her to see the receptionist closely inspecting the bag, it's Cora, who collected the case from our room earlier, unsure if this is a good thing or not after all her questions. I'm just glad it's over with. Cora then pops it on the shelf behind her and carries on with her work.

'All done. Come on let's go and get something to eat, I'm starving.'

'How can you be thinking of food right now? I can barely move I'm that nervous, never mind eat.' I say just as my legs start to feel like they belong to me again. As we start to head to the restaurant, I turn round to glimpse back at Cora and see two big burly men, they looked huge and scary and don't look like the considerate type, I instantly know it must be them, and can't help but think of close it could have been for us getting caught. I gulp when I see Cora handing them the black makeup bag. The pressure is getting too much for me, and I can't physically go to the restaurant just yet, I think I'm going to be sick. The other two reluctantly agree but follow me back up to the apartment. No sooner from our door closing I find myself hurtling to the bathroom. The sour tasting bile that was rising in my throat has now released itself, but I can still taste the awful burn that lingers. I clean myself up and touch up my makeup, only now starting to feel the relief.

Coming out of the bathroom I hear another bang on the door. The shock makes me want to be sick again, but luckily, I manage to keep myself composed. I hear Rita shouting annoyed, we haven't even been here 24hrs and the number of times we have had a knock on this door is ridiculous.

'For fuck's sake, who else can be knocking on our door.' Rita storms over and looks through the peep hole. 'It's that woman again!' She shouts a little too loudly and opens the door. Knowing fine well the woman will have heard her, but she doesn't care.

'Sorry, it is me again. We have a thank you note from the owners of the case. They wanted to deliver it themselves, but for security reasons we can't give out guest's details.' She hands Rita a sealed envelope. Rita thanks the woman, then shuts the door before she can say anything else.

We all look at each other, then stare at the brown perfectly sealed envelope. I don't know if to be in shock at their quick response or relieved that it's over with. We watch closely as Rita slowly starts to unseal the envelope. Doreen starts to become a little excited thinking that her work at handing it back over has done the job, she genuinely believes that this is a thankyou note. I on the other hand, is not so sure. I can hardly bare to look, so I keep glancing to the floor then back at Rita trying to work out her facial expressions. Me and Doreen start to bicker as I tell her to be quiet and wait to see what they have to say. I look back at an all too quiet Rita, who now has the note fully out and is reading through it. I know it can't be good news as soon I see her expression change, her mouth falls open and her eyes dare blink. The anticipation is killing me.

'What does it say?' I look at her face and see the colour draining from a nice healthy glow to a stone cold white. Her hands begin to tremble as she begins to read.

'They say it's missing!' She squeaks out then looks back down to read the note.

"We seem to have something missing! This better be returned tonight we will be in the bar in the restaurant at 7pm. Hand it to the two men sitting at the bar. You won't miss us. Do not be late!

We all look at one another wondering how that can be, as we have just handed it over, I seen it with my own two eyes. I gulp and look down at my watch and see it's just passed 6.30pm.

'We better hurry, I seen Cora give them the package, hopefully it's just miss timing and they now have it. We need to get in there before they arrive, we can't be walking in dead on 7 that's too suspicious.' After expressing our concerns and confusion on the matter. We start to accept the fact that it is down to bad timing. However, we need to be sure. We head down and hope that we can blend in just like any other holiday makers going for food.

We start to walk in a hurry, I cautiously check every person we walk past. As we walk through the restaurant doors, I find a table in a quiet corner but with a good view of the bar, I quickly scan the bar area before we take a seat, there's no sign of the two big burly men. We order our food and a nice bottle of wine, hoping that if they do arrive then it will look as though we have been here for a while, so it looks as though we are here just having our evening meal like every other person. I glance at my watch, there's still a few minutes to go before 7pm, and still no sign of them. I start to wonder if they have received the "package." Our food arrives quickly, to my relief. I pour some wine for us all and start to believe this nightmare is finally over. Even Doreen and Rita have relaxed. We start chatting away and enjoying our food as if nothing has ever happened. Me and Rita ordered chicken salad while Doreen orders a mix grill. The mountain of meat piled on to her plate is enough to turn my stomach. The thought of a big stuffy meal after everything that's happened today is too much and could quite easily send me over the edge.

'How are you going to eat all that?' I need to ask Doreen, as I watch her devour every mouthful. It's easy to see that she is enjoying every single bite. Which makes me a little jealous. I'm finding my meal is a bit more of a struggle, instead I find myself pushing it around my plate with my fork. Rita just raises her eyebrow and speaks before Doreen can answer my Question.

'Doesn't matter what happens this woman will never be put off her food.' She points out having placed her cutlery down to suggest that she has finished and has now focused herself on the big glass of wine. I can't exactly say the stress has knocked Rita's appetite, as she has never been a big eater, she basically eats to get by and no more.

'We barely eaten all day.' Doreen blurts with a mouth full of food, forgetting her table manners. She quickly covers her mouth to stop any bit of food escaping and signals an apology with her hand. This is what I love about Doreen. (Not spitting food out at us, of course.) But there's no back doors with her, what you see is what you get and she isn't ashamed of that. I often wish I could be more like that, but I always find myself caring about what others think. We laugh just as the waiter heads over to our table. I see another envelope in his hand. I know before I even look at it who it is from, and a feeling of dread floats over me. I place my cutlery down knowing I won't be able to face any more food. I take a big gulp of wine for a bit of courage and hopefully to steady my nerves before I take the envelope from him.

'Reception have told me to hand you this.' He hands me the note and casually walks away without another word, clearly not appreciating being treated like a messenger, although I don't think he suspects anything out of the ordinary. I feel everyone's eyes focus on me and feel the pressure get it open. I slowly start to tear at the corner, dreading what is going to be laid inside waiting for me. Our table has turned to pure silence, even Doreen has stopped her chomping. Their eager eyes are burning into me.

'It's maybe a thank you note.' Doreen breaks the silence with her positive attitude, I somehow doubt it will be. I look around making sure no one else is watching us before I open it. With the coast clear a begin to read it out, only being loud enough for my table to hear.

"I really was hoping it didn't have to go this way. Your little package you left was still missing mine. You are picking the wrong people to mess with. This is your final chance to return it! if you don't, I will find you, I will find your family, your friends and anyone that knows you and end you all! Do not mess me about again!"

I quickly hide the note in my bag and take a huge sip of wine. My hands are trembling that much, that I need to hold my glass with two hands. Doreen and Rita look in a panic, even Doreen has now placed her cutlery down to show she's finished with her half-eaten meal, which is not like her at all. I start to feel sick once again, as my mind tries to figure out what could have happened. Then I cringe with humiliation, wondering if they have been left holding my big knickers and Doreen's sanitary pads.

'Where is the cocaine? It was packed in there.' Rita cries taking the words right out of my mouth.

'She, she must have stolen it, that, that Cora!' Doreen's lips begin to tremble as she stutters her words.

I push my plate away, not being able to face the smell anymore and pour another glass of wine. Trying to think what we are going to do, but my mind is whizzing with too much panic.

'We need to go!' Just as I say it, I see the two men walk into the bar, my mouth falls open and my wine nearly jumps out of the glass. Doreen and Rita haven't seen them, nor did they see them down at reception when Cora supposedly handed them the package, so I would doubt they would recognise the two big men, although it isn't too hard to spot them, as they stand out like a sore thumb. My heart plummets knowing we can't leave now. Like a trapped animal unsure what to do, I start checking every area of the restaurant, finding every exit, any hiding places and look around at all the other people who is already in here. My eyes are darting everywhere, only avoiding them. I know for a fact if they spot me right now, they will know I'm involved. I slouch down in my chair hoping Doreen hides me from their view. I can feel my sweat starting to drip down my face, my hot flushes spiking with every thud of my heart, I begin to tremble that badly that my knees are bobbing away also. I grab my little black hand bag and place it on my lap under the table, I squeeze onto it hoping the pressure can calm my trembling self, before a full-blown panic attack latches onto me, then I won't be able to stop anything, I'd be hysterical.

'What is it?' Rita notices my reaction. I lean in closer to whisper, darting my eyes around the room making sure that no one can see or hear me.

'They are here!' I whisper and nod my head in the direction of where the two men have now seated at the bar.

I can see them clearly scaling the place, checking out each person that is in here, I dart my eyes away when they look over to our table. The two smartly dressed men turn away quickly and begin looking elsewhere and watching the door. They order drinks and eagerly wait for their package. I glance over and wonder if they have picked anyone out in the room who may have their drugs. I do the same, even though I know it is us that has caused the problem for the two men. I spot a group of young women who must be in their mid-thirties' early forties, likely enjoying a girly break away, and wonder if they would think it's them. I then realize that if they were left holding my big knickers, I'd doubt they would own a pair of them let alone wear them, by the looks of the glamourous ladies, so definitely not them. I then see a youngish couple, a man and woman sitting enjoying a few drinks still very much in love by the looks of things, no it wouldn't be them they look too clean cut to have anything to do with drugs never mind stealing cocaine. Looking around the restaurant to find that no one seems to fit the bill, most folk in here are rather old aged pensioners enjoying their well-earned money or people so rich that if they wanted cocaine they'd easily be able to get their own. Then it hits me! They might blame the staff! which technically is true as it's suddenly gone missing when Cora had it.

'Maybe we should tell them what has happened?' Doreen looks over at them then clenches her teeth realising how intimidating they look.

'Are you serious! Do they look the understanding type to you?' Rita snaps at her with her stupid comment. Doreen shrugs back innocently knowing it to be true, I certainly wouldn't want to be the one to tell them! The two men certainly don't look like the understanding type, both must be over 6ft and well-built with muscles bulging from there tightly fitted t-shirts. You could clearly see they looked after themselves, there tan glowed on their skin, clean shaven with freshly cut short hair. They looked similar age to us, but they looked good with it, you can see that back in their youth, they'd have been classed as hunks, with their chiselled facial features almost model like. I notice the smaller of the two has a scar on his face which is like a slice down the side of his cheek, somehow this doesn't disrupt his good looks. The taller man with lighter hair has barely taken his eyes off the door, he looks angry and focused and much more intimidating, just looking at him makes me nervous. The other man has now sat with his back to us, just casually sipping away at his drink. I wait a few minutes to see other people move from their tables, before I make my move to leave, hoping that it looks casual and normal and not to draw attention on me. I do this without telling Doreen or Rita because I can only imagine the objections turning into a row and make us stand out from the rest of the guests, which is what I'm desperately trying to avoid.

'I need to go and find Cora!' I stand up and grab my bag before anyone can object and stop me.

'What!' Doreen shrieks while taking a drink of her chardonnay, which slightly spills onto her chin. She desperately tries to sip it back up through her lips but fails and needs to grab a napkin to wipe it up. It defiantly took Doreen by surprise, if I wasn't so stressed I'd be laughing.

'We all can't go it will look too suspicious, and we really need to find out what has happened, there's only Cora that has the answers!' I stand up and make my way out knowing the men will see me leave, I walk slowly and as casually as I can. I can feel eyes burning on to my back, but I carry on and don't dare to look around. I can only hope that they don't notice my awkward stiff walk that has suddenly appeared, with a mix of nerves, fear, and the fact that it seems to take ages for me to even reach the doors to get out. Taking each step carefully as to prevent myself from tripping up and drawing any unwanted attention, I finally reach out to pull the handle open. Just as I do someone comes hurtling through unaware that I'm behind it. The big chrome, pipe handle wedges my hand like a trap, sending me flying closer to the door that's being opened.

'SHIT!' I scream unexpectedly. As the frame of the door misses my face by millimetres. The apologetic couple quickly dart off to find their table, leaving me to accidently turn around and see who saw. This was a mistake. Of course, everyone seen. The remaining onlookers wait for another reaction. I glance at my own table and see the horrified face of Doreen, her mouth wide open, her glass still in mid-air, she basically may as well have poured her chardonnay onto her lap. I see Rita muttering the words 'Fucks sake!' As she desperately tries to mop Doreen's spillage with serviettes. I catch the two men at the bar out of the corner of my eye. The angrier fella still looks very angry, the one sitting down however is laughing away to himself at my expense. (Great! So, he sees me as the laughing stock, not a suspect.) I think to myself sarcastically. Hating being the focus of someone else's amusement, but I try and reassure myself that this could be a good thing in this instance. I take my now vanished nerves that's been replaced with embarrassment out of the room. secretly hoping the couple who just came through become number one suspects, then a quick pang of guilt arrives, I know I shouldn't be thinking that.

CHAPTER 12

I dart my eyes everywhere, up and down the corridors round the corners, still no sign of her, I walk over to reception, still no Cora to be seen anywhere. I'm starting to lose patience, which is leading me to mutter to myself under my breath. I catch myself doing this and quickly correct myself into a more approachable manner, before anyone notices and thinks I'm a crazy old woman on the loose. I'm starting to get fed up, searching all the usual places where you might find the staff, with not a single sight of her. However, I do manage to spot another member of staff, so I march up to them, hoping my composure looks a bit better than the manic chuntering, crazy old woman just seconds ago, I'm just about to ask if they have seen her. Then out of the corner of my eye I notice her, she walks down the corridor that leads to the gym and saunas, unsuspecting that I'm after her, which actually really annoys me, how could someone be so calm after they have just stolen drugs, I start a cursing mutter again as I chase after her. I begin my fast walk trying to catch up to her, but she's too quick and disappears round the corner. I hold on to my bag tighter and lift the hem of my dress up and start out in a run, making sure no one is watching. (As that could lead to a difficult scenario to talk myself out of. "A crazy old woman, that's chuntering to herself while stalking and running after a member of staff.") "Scrap that, I'm not old, I'm oldish!" "Oh, fuck I'm talking to myself again!" "I hope I'm not losing it, no I'm not losing it, it's got to be the stress. FUCK I can't stop talking to myself!" I block out the little argument that's erupted in my head and I dart round the corner after her. I find Cora is already waiting for me. It's a good job I don't have the pace like a did twenty years ago or I'd have skittled right into her. Then I feel a little embarrassed as she's probably heard my chuntering to myself. She looks to me with concern and maybe a little shock that I've actually ran, which I find a bit of a cheek! She says nothing, instead she waits until I speak.

'I need to talk to you!' I say pointing my finger to her with my panting breath only just managing to get the words out correctly. An amused look appears across her face, which really annoys me. Then I must stop my urge for wanting to kick the young bitch up the arse!

'Are you okay? Why are you running?' I'm not sure if she's being sarcastic, or trying to make fun of me, so I Ignore her question, and try to control my burning rage that's boiling up inside.

'Where is it!' I snap as I try to compose myself to be taken more seriously. I can see the denial already in her face.

'Where is what?' She tries to look confused, which certainly doesn't fool me. I can feel myself burning up, getting hotter and hotter. Knowing she is more than likely trying to take me for a fool. I step myself closer to her, which leaves her with no room to move, she's now trapped with her back against the wall and me pointing my finger in her face.

'You know what I'm talking about! You better give it back, right now!' I say making sure I form every word correctly and fiercely. Deep down inside I'm a quivering wreck, hating confrontation like this, as it brings back memories of the school girl bullies who once cornered me. I try to hold my ground, praying she doesn't see my newly found aggressive mask slip. (Then that, would be embarrassing.) She begins to stutter but still tries to deny it. I cut her off before she can finish, finding my more aggressive manner to be working.

'Don't take me for a fool! They are not messing about; they are going to kill us if we don't get it back to them!' Cora is now pinned to the wall desperately trying to avoid my shouts, that are now hitting her right into her face, and I can see that the poor young woman looks scared. Realising that I'm probably taking my aggressive manner a little too far, I step back to give her some room. I then grab the note from my bag and shove it in her face. My whole body begins to tremble as I lose control of my composure. Cora grabs the note from me and starts to read it. I see her once smirking face change to horror.

'If you don't get it back, I will tell them it's you that has it!' I instantly regret threating her, but it's too late. Her face has gone white and looks as though she might cry, and then she begins to stutter again.

'I will get it back; I just need a little time; I gave it to my cousin.'

'You better get it back or we are all in trouble! Why would you take it?' I look at Cora, she doesn't look like she would take drugs, but I suppose you never can know who does or doesn't these days.

'I'm really sorry I didn't think I would get caught, I've never done this before, I just got desperate, I've got a little girl...' I hold up my hand to stop Cora talking and can't help but feel sorry for her. From reading the note and me cornering her, the shaking young woman looks terrified. Desperate to tell her that I'm not usually this scary aggressive woman and I'm as scared as what she is. I almost do but stop myself when I think that we wouldn't even be in this situation if it wasn't for her.

'Look, I get it you made a mistake, we just need it back then this is done with, and hopefully no one gets hurt.' Cora begins to nod while she sniffles as she wipes away the little tears that are starting to form in her eyes.

'I will phone him now.' She pulls out her phone and places it to her ear, she turns her back to me, so I move closer to listen in better. I can hear the dial tone ringing but no one answers. She turns back around to face me and jumps not realising how close I've gotten to her.

'Sorry.' I say acknowledging that I'm intruding her space. She doesn't answer but instead takes a step further away from me and frowns.

'He's not answering, I'll leave a message and keep trying, my shift doesn't finish to 11.00pm, I'll come and find you when he answers or give me your number.' I hesitate for a minute not liking the idea of giving a stranger my personal details, but knowing I don't have much choice. I hand it over. Cora takes my details and promises me that she will be in touch, although I won't hold my breath, there's been too much sneaking about and trouble today for my liking and my trust in people has slightly been diminished. We both head in different directions as not to be seen together. I start making my way back to the restaurant, exhausted and disappointed that I'm returning without the "package." My body feels like it's done ten rounds in the ring, my back is aching, my knees throbbing, my shoulders are tense and stiff, the list goes on. The only desire I have right now, is to be at home in my safe place tucked up in bed with a cuppa and a book.

My trembling has almost stopped by the time I reach the doors to the restaurant, I take a deep breath before I open it and walk in. I can't help but look directly forward to see where the two men are. I see that the taller man is still watching the door and spots me coming through, as he instantly straightens himself up alerted, only to look disappointed when he sees it's me. (Normally I'd be offended if a man looked at me like this, but in this matter, I'm rather pleased.) I head over to our table, where Rita and Doreen both look up, their eyes wide and curious, desperate to know what has happened. I smile back at them trying not to give anything away just in case I'm being watched.

'So… You find her? Where is it? You got it back?' An impatient Rita blurts out too many questions. Doreen looks on eager to know but says nothing, not that she can get a word in for Rita, who's practically edging out of her seat. I need to calm the overly excited woman and tell them the news isn't as good as what they are expecting.

'Keep it down.' I whisper to them, seeing that their curious, excited behaviour is drawing attention. 'She's going to get it, her cousin has it at the minute, we just need to wait for her to get in touch.' I place my phone on the table next to me, to be sure I don't miss her call.

'Why does her cousin have it?' Rita says.

'Why did she take it? I knew she was a wrong one.' Doreen says before I can even answer Rita. The questions are getting too much to process, and I'm too on edge thinking someone is going to hear us. Before I can answer any of them, I grab my glass and take a big gulp of wine, which seems to annoy my two best friends, as there far too eager to find out every bit of detail. Knowing I don't physically have the energy to go through it all step by step, particularly avoiding the part where I had her pinned to the wall. So, I shorten it and hopefully it satisfies their needs.

'It's complicated, I don't know the full in's and out's, but for what I can gather she's been desperate and that's why she has took it, but it doesn't matter all that matters now that we are getting it back, then this nightmare can finally be put to bed. Has anything happened with them two over there.' I nod my head in their direction trying to be discreet, but Doreen however swings her body round to see who I'm talking about, which would make it obvious if anyone is watching. She's a subtle as the pharmacist who shouted, repeating my carefully whispered needs for some thrush cream, the whole dam shop heard never mind the ever-growing queue behind me.

'Nothing much, the fella watching the door has been on edge the full time, jumping up every time someone enters, the fella with his back to us has barely moved apart from taking a swig of his drink.' I nod back. All we can do now is wait. Knowing it's already going to be a long night, more than likely a long holiday at this rate. I huff and slouch back into my chair, desperately hoping my phone will ring anytime soon. The three of us sit in limbo unsure what to do, our gossip has run dry, the good vibe that we did have before the last note, has now gone, like a big hot steaming turd that has landed on it. I keep trying to stop myself from looking at the two men, but every time I look in Doreen's direction, I get a glimpse of the two in the background. Not that they have paid much attention to us, we are somehow irrelevant to them, which is kind of comforting but somehow kind of annoying: If there was no missing drugs involved and we were just "ordinary" women enjoying a break, "which is what we were trying to do." Then this kind of insinuates that we no longer hold our looks as power. Are we passed it? Do our bodies show that we aren't capable to endure a hot steamy night of passion? Or has the temptation for men become so easy to get, that flirting and lusting isn't a thing anymore? Of course, I'm not wanting a man in my life just yet, I've just lost my husband 9 month ago and he will never be replaced, he was my soul mate, my best friend and lover all in one. But what really scares me the most, is the thought that I might spend the rest of my life alone, I'm barely 60 so it's definitely not what I expected.

'I'm going to get us some more drinks, I think we all need something, I'm going to try and listen in and see if they mention anything.' Rita jumps up and heads over to the bar with her bag in her hand, before I can say that's a bad idea. Knowing all too well that not many men can avoid Rita's good looks, once they will notice her, it will then be hard for them to ignore her.

'Fuck sake she's going to push things too far; we are out of view and out of mind over here.' I mutter angrily.

'You know what she is like.' Doreen shrugs back. We both watch as she strides her long tanned legs over to the bar, her tightly fitted dress shows off her impressive figure, her highlighted hair is bouncing with the soft curls, she does look fantastic, not surprisingly starts to catch the eyes of a lot of people including the taller fella, who's peeled his eyes away from the door and has spotted Rita at the bar. She's not standing next to them but she's close enough to probably hear what they are talking about.

I watch as she ratches in her bag and pulls out her mobile, she casually does something on it then places it face down on the bar closest to them. The waiter is taking her order. The fella who's had his back to us has now noticed Rita, he looks her up and down and smiles to himself clearly liking what he sees. The waiter turns and begins to make the drinks. Rita looks over to the gawping fella and gives him a smile back, he reaches out his hand as to introduce himself. Rita takes it and answers the man. She then turns to receive her drinks from the waiter and heads back over with them on a tray, her handbag under her arm, and I can tell she's trying to walk as sexily as possible, taking her time, swaying her perfectly curved hips knowing the men will be catching a glimpse of her from behind. I look round and see that she's left her phone on the bar. The man has already turned back around and is speaking to his friend, this will not impress Rita at all. The taller man rolls his eyes and doesn't look happy at what he is hearing, he's leaned in closer to talk to him, he rants on for a minute until Rita's admirer hushing him. "He must be in charge." I think to myself. Rita has already landed back with the drinks and has started dishing out the gins.

'What are you doing?' I snap back at a smiling Rita.

'He's quite dishy that one.' Rita says still smiling as she points out to the smaller man that is sitting down with his back to us. I can see Doreen frowning, and I can tell what she is going to say before she opens her mouth, because I'm also thinking it.

'Oh, you mean the fella who's probably going to kill us if he doesn't get his package back.' Doreen's sharp reply jolts Rita to a stiff pose, and I can almost feel an argument about to erupt as Rita prepares to defend herself.

'Why have you left your phone?' I whisper butting in hoping I diffuse the tiff that's about to start, as a stupid harmless comment could easily lead to an unnecessary argument, especially when there's alcohol consumed.

'Calm down Doreen I was only saying, you are so uptight at

times....'

'Your phone!' I intervene again as the tension continues to rise, Luckily Rita understands now is not the time for a petty squabble and finally answers my question.

'I'm recording them, I'm going to go and get it in a minute, we can see what they have been saying, and if they have any suspicions on anyone yet!'

'What! If they catch us...'

Rita interrupts me quickly. 'Don't panic, I've locked it so they won't see.'

'I hope you have! What did hie say to you?'

'He just said hiya and introduced himself and his friend, He's called Bill and the scarier looking fella watching the door is called Earnie.'

'You're an idiot!' Doreen blurts out.

'You...' Rita suddenly stops talking. 'Shit! There coming over.'

CHAPTER 13

Bill is leading the way with a bottle of wine in his hand, Earnie trailing reluctantly behind, his stare is hard and has the look of a kid being dragged round the supermarket. I notice Bill has Rita's phone in his other hand. A gulp expecting the worst. I try to nudge Rita to get her attention, but she is too fixed on watching Bill walking over. Hoping that it's shock that's got her attention and not the lust for the good-looking man. He could easily catch any woman's eye: His big masculine frame and chiselled looks are almost near to perfection. I nudge her again and whisper that he has her phone. My heart is pounding away as I start to feel the restless shakes in my fingers. I try to hold myself together as they are almost at our table, although I feel I could crumble at any moment. Doreen however is oblivious that they are walking right to us.

'I know, just carry on smiling or they will know something is wrong.' Rita whispers with gritted teeth.

'What's going on.' Doreen has picked up that something is happening, her eyes widen, and her posture stiffens. I'm almost positive she can feel that they are behind her.

Neither of us can answer as they are staring right at us and are only a couple of metres away. I try to smile the best I can, but my panic is flaring up again and I'm sure I'm beginning to sweat. Bill is composed and confident, smiling away, he walks smoothly with ease, almost as if he's floating, which surprises me considering he's such a big man. Earnie however is still frowning away but does manage to muster a tiny smile which shows off how handsome he could be if he smiled more. It soon quickly disappears though. His small dark eyes look almost black, his tanned skin however is crystal clear with no scars or blemishes, just a few small wrinkles starting to appear around the corner of his eyes. His thick short hair has started turning grey. It's clear to see that these two men certainly look after their appearance. Just as they are about to reach our table, Rita speaks, I think this is more to warn Doreen, who's still wondering what is going on, but will not dare to turn look around.

'Hi Bill.' I see Doreen slightly jump in her seat and her mouth flies open in disbelief, still, she dares not turn around, her eyes are fixed on me. I try to keep smiling but my jaw is starting to ache and has more than likely turned crooked. I quickly urge myself to do a big smile. Then a burn in my cheeks tell me that this is too much. 'Fuck it, I can't fake smile any longer.' I think to myself and just grab my drink.

'I Think this could be your mobile? It was left on the bar; the barman said it might be yours.' Bill hands over the phone. The three of us just stare at him, trying to work out if this is a trick or not. I nervously glance over to Rita. She pauses for a second before she reaches out for it.

'Oh, thank you.' Rita nervously laughs. 'I'd lose my head if it wasn't screwed on.' I notice she flirtingly flicks her eyelashes at him, I can't help but scowl.

He laughs excitedly. 'It's no problem.' He hands over the phone to Rita. 'I was going to put my number in for you, but you cleverly keep it locked.' He says far too confidently. I can see Doreen cringing, and his friend rolls his eyes and looks at his watch, not wanting to be here wasting his precious time.

'That's why I have a lock on my phone, to stop strange men from putting their numbers in.' Rita smiles back at him. "Oh no, this is getting worse." I cringe this time. We are left watching the pair as if it was a game of tennis, our heads bobbing round each time the two flirts. I need to take another large gulp of my drink to make this more tolerable. Me and Doreen frown at each other, knowing all too well what usually comes after Rita's flirting, after seeing it many times before. "If she sleeps with him, we are going to be elbow deep in shit! Surely, she won't?" My mind is racing as I pray to myself that he smoothly walks back to where he came from.

'Perhaps I should get you a drink then?' He says lifting the bottle of wine he's carried over, as if he hadn't already planned that. "Fuck!" my sarcastic mind is going crazy, I need to keep checking myself that I haven't left anything slip my lips. I can't help my annoyance, I'm so annoyed with this holiday, Cora, The stupid dam package and him! I think this is the only time I wish I smoked, least then I could get away from this stupid table.

'Well, seen as though you have brought over some wine, one won't hurt.' Rita smiles, but I can tell it's making her feel uncomfortable. I look to Doreen whose eyes look like they are burning with rage. I tell her to move her chair closer to me, hoping they just think it's to make room for them on the table, when in fact I need to tell her to calm down as I can feel her furious rage bounces over to me.

'Is she being serious right now.' Doreen whispers slightly louder than she anticipated. To which the two men look at her, unsure what she has just said but know it was a sarcastic comment. I see Rita start to blush obviously hearing what she has said. I look at Doreen like you'd look at a naughty child playing up in public. She thankfully understands to cool it.

 'Okay then.' He grins but I do think he can feel the tension: Of course, it doesn't put him off. 'Earnie, go get some fresh glasses for these lovely ladies.' Earnie scowls back at him as I notice his

POWDER TOWN

lip quivers into an angry snarl.

'Haven't we got some business to sort first?' I can see the frustration in him as he burns his eyes into Bill, his lips tighten up as he waits for an answer. The table goes silent. My stomach does a somersault as I watch the two men stare at each other. Bill certainly doesn't seem to like to be told what he should do, as he burrows his eyes right back at Earnie, all we can do is watch on as these two alphas battle it out and see who backs down first. This is not an ideal situation to be, and I can't quite work out if they know we are involved in their "business" or not. I can't bear the silence or the frosty vibes anymore, I feel like I'm on pins. My body is ready to break at any point with my nerves jittering away inside of me.

'Oh, it's okay you don't need to do that.' Doreen says eager for them to leave.

'It will be my pleasure; our business can wait! May I join you all for one? As you can see my friend here isn't much of a talker.' He points his head in Earnie's direction with a smile, but also suggests not to object to his demands again. Earnie doesn't, he turns around to head to the bar, his angry stomp away tells me he's not happy. A little tension lifts as he goes, but still there's an atmosphere that's been left. I see Bill give a cold hard stare to his friend as he watches him leave, I just know that he will be having words with him later. His face quickly softens as he turns to Rita waiting for her answer.

'Of course.' Rita waves her hand to the free seats that are around our table. I glare at Rita and then I feel Doreen's leg swing past me to give Rita a kick under the table.

'Ouch' She mistakenly says it out loud leaving Bill wondering what has just happened.

'Sorry I just banged my leg on the table.' Rita glares back at Doreen. We know she didn't really have much choice in the matter, but she could have tried to put him off, or say we are leaving soon, although he does look the type to insist until he

73

gets what he wants.

Just then Earnie returns with some clean wine glasses and dishes them out, He sits next to Doreen, who stiffens up when he gets too close to her. I place my hand on Doreen's knee to try and calm her and to say I'm right here. Although they both look like people you don't mess with, Earnie however sends chills up my spine just looking at him, I don't see any warmth in his eyes, just dark, cold and angry. She starts to relax slightly and squeezes my hand. Rita and Bill have already set off in conversation, Earnie pours the wine for everyone apart from himself. I think he's only done this to try stop the awkward feeling that has crept in on our side of the table. I thank him and take a big drink, before I can muster some courage to speak.

'You not having one?' Earnie manages to pull his gaze away from the doors for a split second to answer and turns straight back to look at them.

"No!" His blunt answer tells me we won't be getting much out of him, and to not bother try to. Even his tone is scary: the deep husky voice grumbles around the table. This makes everyone stopped what they are doing and turn their attention to him, which doesn't seem to faze him at all. I can see Doreen looks in a panic as Earnie adjusts himself so he faces her, but only so, so he can get a better view of the door. His big, long legs are pressed up to Doreen's, not purposely, just there so big they seem to struggle to fit properly under the table.

'Why don't you have one, it might loosen you up a bit.' Bill says over to him more like an order rather than asking. Earnie just grunts but does just that. He stands up and walks back over to the bar. You can see he's frustrated with the stomp in his walk and the clench of his fists. Me and Doreen look at each other as she feels the awkwardness as much as I do. I quickly check my phone to see if Cora has been in touch, only to be disappointed when there's nothing, it's passed 8pm, no wonder he is annoyed he's still waiting for the package to be returned and all his friend can do, is think about a bit of skirt. Bill on the other hand looks like he's more interested in Rita, which is not unusual as Rita does get a lot of attention off men, but considering he's likely lost thousands of pounds it seems to be the last thing on his mind right now. Then a sudden thought flashes through my head. "What if they know it's us?" I quickly shake it out my head. surely not? By the looks of Earnie, he's ready to pounce on anyone who walks through the door holding a package, and Bill is too comfortable and casual, surely if they thought we robbed them of their drugs then they wouldn't be buying us drinks and getting cosy? Or is it a plan to lure us in. "Stop it!" I need to tell myself. Whatever it is I don't like it, I don't like them this close to us, I don't like how on edge they are making me feel and I certainly don't like Earnie! Bill notices the awkward silence on our side of the table, then Earnie arrives back with a drink that looks like a whisky and tries to change the frosty atmosphere.

'I'm Bill and this grumpy fella here is Earnie. How are you finding it here so far? Have you been here long?' Me and Doreen wait a second before answering, thinking it could be a trick question, but his peering eyes insist on waiting for us to answer. I decide to so before Doreen splutters anything out.

'Erm we've not been here long, but it is beautiful? You been here before?' I ask trying to deter any more questions to us. He looks on but thankfully hasn't paid too much attention to me, I try not answer his question fully but enough for him to hopefully be satisfied. Rita breathes again from holding her breath, the three of us dreading each question in case anything leads us to slip up. That would be a disaster.

'We come here often with business, so out here couple of times a year.' Having a good idea what their business involves I resist the urge to ask. Doreen on the other hand does not.

'What kind of business do you do?'

'Sales.' The two men look with an amused smile as they answer at the same time. like a very rehearsed phrase, technically they could probably see themselves as "sales people" if they sell drugs, which I'm pretty sure they must. We all sit waiting for some more details. I see Rita in the corner of my eye on edge, she's starting to fidget and shift uncomfortably in her seat, and I can see Doreen is desperate to ask what kind of sales and I can only hope she doesn't. Bill must notice this and shuts down any more questions before they get asked. I wonder if he noticed when I done that to him.

'It's not very interesting, we wouldn't want to bore you.' He changes the subject quickly. 'You must visit the marina it is stunning and there's a few nice coffee shops and bars.' I do a fake laugh but it's a bit too much and everyone turns round and looks at me. I flush a little embarrassed then take a gulp of my wine hoping it stops the stares and hides my red face. The ping of my mobile moves everyone's attention from me as they carry on with a conversation. Cora has finally got in touch.

CHAPTER 14

Meet me in the ladies toilets that's just outside the restaurant doors, please be quick I don't have long. C. x

I try to catch Rita and Doreen's eye, but they seem too busy wanting to know more about the marina.

'Is it far from here?' I catch Doreen asking, she's getting lured into the chatter now. Even Earnie has loosened up with his whisky and has started mumbling a few words, he's still looking around and watching the door but not as manic as he was earlier. I look round the table to see everyone laughing and chatting away. A ping of anger fires inside of me thinking am the only one that isn't falling for his charms. Acting like a gent isn't going to fool me. Then I wonder if they are playing the part at keeping things looking normal, they must, because Doreen surely wouldn't fall for this. I stand up ready to meet Cora, but this gains everyone's attention. I was hoping I could slip out without anyone taking too much notice, all eyes are on me, and I feel under pressure to give an explanation.

'Sorry to interrupt, I'm going to need to borrow these two for a few minutes.' I point to Rita and Doreen. Finally, they both realise what I'm trying to get at and begin to pop down their wine glasses to stand up to join me.

'Sure, is everything okay?' Bill asks while Earnie looks up suspicious. Deep down I'm wanting to shout, "I don't need to explain myself to you, you smug prick." Then I remember that these fellas are wanting to kill us, so I be nice.

'Yeah of course, I think it's time we went to the ladies room and powder our noses.' I say with a wink.

'Oh of course the ladies room.' He says sarcastically with a wink back at me and a huge grin, likely thinking we are going to gossip good things about him. I force a smile back.

"Wanker." My thoughts keep rolling on. I know I need to keep myself in check or else my thoughts will be rolling off my tongue. "Imagine calling Bill a wanker to his face." I think again to myself and laugh knowing he likely hasn't had many people call him that to his face before. I start heading out of the restaurant, I can hear Doreen and Rita not far behind me, but I don't dare say anything until we are completely out the room, and the door is closed.

'What are you two playing at!' I swing myself round to them when we are all out of view. Which shocks them, then they both look at me confused from my random outburst.

'What you on about?' Rita snaps back. I move in closer to them just in case anyone over hears. 'You both chatting away like there some nice men, you do remember they are wanting to kill us, right?' I know they know this, but I just need to be sure we are all still on the same page, and we are keeping our wits about ourselves especially with more and more wine going down our necks.

'What are we supposed to act like? The more normal we act the less likely they will figure it out that it's us.' Rita whispers back. Doreen nods in agreement slightly in disgust that I would even think any different.

I know I didn't really need to ask and it's probably a cheek to even doubt them, but this whole holiday has got me on edge so far, and probably the lack of sleep and too much alcohol certainly won't help the mix. I just can't shake the feeling that they could be testing us, waiting for us to slip up, it just seems all to coincidental, I have zero trust in the two men what so ever. I apologise for my overreaction to my friends, which they took no offence and understood that it's more than likely the pressure getting to me. We are all now fully in the toilets, but there is no sign of Cora. Feeling annoyed that she has probably decided not to turn up. I look down the long row of cubicles, but they all look empty, the basins and tall mirrors are immaculate, not a single smear or a bit of dust in sight. The toiletry pamper box is fully stocked with expensive soaps and creams, there's even a pamper box for guests to freshen up. Rita spots this and is right over inspecting and trying the luxury goodies. I begin checking each cubicle, pushing each door to it is fully open, knowing fine well there all empty, but I've seen this many times in movies. (Always be sure no one is lurking about.)

'What are you doing?' Doreen says while watches me open each one, as if I'm trying to find the perfect loo to use.

'Shush.' I push my finger to my lips and move back closer to them so I can whisper.

'We are meeting Cora here, she's just messaged.'

'So has she got the package?' Doreen says while helping me check the remaining cubicles.

'I hope so, she just said to meet her in here.'

'She's not here.' Rita huffs as she's finally finished rummaging through the complementary boxes.

'She's just text me she can't have already left.' I start to feel confused. Why would she message to meet here and not turn up?

'Psstt.'

A tiny little voice echo's, we all look round wondering where it came from. Then look at each other wondering if it was either of us.

'You hear that?' Doreen crouches down and looks around the room again, to see if any feet pop down to a cubicle floor, which of course is ridiculous as we have just checked every single one. (But then again, I've also seen them do that in movies, so...)

'Psst.' The tiny voice appears again definitely not mistaking it this time we all start darting about, checking everywhere we can see, nothing catches our eyes.

'Pssstt, over here.' A more urgent whisper appears from a door at the end of the room, then a skinny hand pops out and waves us over.

'There she is!' I point to the direction, relieved that she is here, I march over with the long stride of my legs, far to happy thinking this could be over with.

'What is she doing in there?' Rita says with an annoyed tone in her voice.

'Just get in here and be quick.' She speaks a bit more loudly this time. We all follow and squeeze ourselves in.

'Eurgh, it stinks in here.' Rita says while holding her nose.

'You're standing on my foot!' Shouts Doreen. The four of us cram into this tiny cupboard, almost nose to nose with each other, so close to one another that I can feel everyone's breath hitting me in the face, I notice the smell of the garlic seasoning from my salad filling the small space. I close my mouth shut hoping to prevent any stronger smell coming out, which is no use, it's already taken over. I can only apologise to them, feeling slightly embarrassed, and think to myself the first thing I will do when I get out of here is raid the complementary box for some mints. Rita's bouncy blow dry sticks to my lips when she pushes her hair out of her face, I try to blow it away, but each time i do a big gust of garlic appears, so I just leave it. We all look at Cora wishing she would hurry up with what she has to say, hoping for good news and hopefully before anyone catches us crammed in here: that would be a sight, how would we explain that to a shocked guest.

'I know this isn't ideal, I'm sorry but we shouldn't be seen together. Anyhow, why are they sitting at your table?'

'Don't ask.' I roll my eyes not wanting to explain the stupid situation we have gotten ourselves into.

'They don't know do they?'

'No of course not. Where is the package Cora?' I try to rush things along so we don't have to be crammed in this cupboard for any longer than we need to, the smell of bleach and soaps are making my nose sting and my eyes water. The dimly lit cupboard was already crammed with cleaning products and extra loo rolls, never mind having four women squeezed in as well, it's a hazard waiting to happen if these shelves topple over. I quickly look at the brackets and just as I thought, there not held by much. 'Well?' I rush a reluctant Cora to answer, while having erratic visions flying through my head of these shelves crashing down on us.

'Erm, kind of, see I can get the package back, but it's not going to be till sometime tomorrow.' Cora mumbles her words knowing this isn't going to sit well with us. I need to let it sink in for a moment before I answer not quite believing what I've just heard, Doreen and Rita look as though they could pounce on her.

'You what! Tomorrow is no good. We need it now!' My heart starts to race, and my anger is rising, I feel like kicking her skinny arse. My blood is starting to pump furiously around my body, and I have to put my clenched fist to my mouth to stop myself erupting in a rage and hitting these flimsy shelves.

'You better not be trying to pull a fast one!' Doreen interrupts. Then leans in closer to her which makes Cora flinch, I grab a hold of Doreen's arm to move her back. Presuming these shelves will not stand for a scuffle. The intensity in this tiny room is building up way to fast, the need to get out hits me, suddenly I start to feel claustrophobic. I don't know if it's the heat or the panic, but everything starts to blur and I see everyone's faces start to spin around. I control my breathing and close my eyes for a second hoping to calm myself down. The sound of Cora's voice focuses me back to a steady mind.

'I know, I'm really sorry, but my cousin has got it and said he won't be able to bring it back till tomorrow. I told him we need it now, but he's just said it will have to wait, and now he isn't answering.'

'What are we going to do? They want it now!' Rita now leans in this time, but before she can get too close, Cora raises her hands to protect herself, although this is unnecessary but takes Rita by surprise and makes her jump back.

'Hang on, you can write another note and I will pass it on, if you can go back and keep them occupied, they won't realise it's you. Just go back and finish your night like you would have, and then hopefully by tomorrow morning the package will be here, and everything will be sorted.' "If only it would be as easier as that." I think to myself. Knowing we don't have any other choice and I'm desperate to get out of this tiny, stinky cupboard. I agree.

'I Don't like this one bit.' Doreen says hesitantly. 'What do we do if they start suspecting us, if they haven't already?'

'Well don't stay any later than 11pm with them, as that's when I finish. So till then I can keep an eye on you all and if anything doesn't look right, I will phone the police. I will keep trying to call my cousin also but it doesn't look like he's going to be rushing over tonight.'

'He better bring it tomorrow. Give me a pen and let's get this over with, they are going to be wondering where we are.' Cora hands over a sheet of paper from the shelf behind her and pulls out her pen from her top pocket and hands it over to Rita. Rita furiously scribbles another note.

You will have your package tomorrow.

'Does that sound okay?'

'Well, it's a bit blunt, but straight to the point I suppose.' I let out a slow sigh as I step out of the tiny stuffy cupboard, feeling grateful for the cleanliness of these toilets. I feel deflated and feel in no mood at all to go back to the restaurant to entertain our two unwanted guests. 'I could do with another bottle of wine.'

'Me two.' Says Doreen.

'Me three.' Rita joins in.

CHAPTER 15

We leave the note with Cora and begin to head back less enthusiastically this time. The two men are sitting at the table as we head in. They look to be having a heated conversation. Earnie is wafting his hands in Bills face with a furious look and his mouth moving far too fast, then suddenly Bill holds his hand up in Earnie's face to stop him, Earnie's temper calms instantly, his mouth is now shut tight, but his glare to him is a furious rage. I know this look, it's a look of knowing to keep quiet and do as you are told even though it's killing you inside to do so. Bill leans in to talk to Earnie, he points his finger in his face aggressively. Earnie doesn't react, though his eyes look as though he wants to hit him. He backs down and sits back in his chair. The three of us stand and watch the commotion unfold, as both of them are totally unaware we've entered back into the restaurant.

'Do you think they know?'

'Doreen calm down, there's a chance they might but we literally have no other option, we need to go on as we were, be friendly, and act as if we know nothing.' Rita heads the walk back to the table, I follow, with nerves spiking in every part of my body, I feel Doreen close to me and notice her nervous twitch in her hands.

'They don't look happy.' I whisper to Doreen. A sudden thought grabs my attention, I imagine the fire alarm goes off and the sprinkles come on, then we need to evacuate the building. "Oh, how perfect timing that would be." Although, I wouldn't like a real fire to start mind, but maybe a practice drill, or the chef maybe over cooks some steak?

'We need to keep calm, come on, let's drink this wine then make some excuses to go.' They spot us walking over and quickly stop their disagreement, Bill's raging face now turns to a smile, Earnie however, still has looks furious. I almost sure I see him huff as he notices us, disappointed in seeing that we have arrived back, you can tell he's eager to get on with sorting their "business" out, rather than cosying up and making friends. We carry on walking over feeling the frosty atmosphere that is hovering around our table. I give a little smile hoping to ease the tension, but Earnie just scowls, this makes my nerves worse and now I begin to feel sick. I need to stop myself from turning back around to leave.

'There you are! I was beginning to think I might need to send a search party out.' Bill says with a smirk. I absolutely hate is sarcastic tone already. He seems to be the kind of man that likes to control. A woman must do as a there told, like we are some sort of property to them, or that our only purpose in life is to serve and please them. I could be wrong but that's the kind of vibe I'm getting off him. He pulls out a seat for Rita to sit beside him, suggesting she must sit back again next to him.

'You know what us women are like, we don't rush.' Rita says laughing. He grins but I notice a slight flicker of annoyance in his eyes, unsure if it's from the recent argument we stumbled on, or he was getting impatient waiting for us to come back. I can't imagine he has to wait on many people.

Bill pours the wine and turns his attention to Rita. Earnie is sitting quiet and holds on to his whisky, clearly still furious at his spat with Bill, he doesn't say a word, but the juddering of his knees and fidgeting with his glass looks as though he's trying to stop himself from exploding. The more he hears Bill and Rita laugh the angrier he becomes. The tension is awful and even makes me and Doreen sit in silence, I can't stop looking over at him to watch his reaction every time one of them speaks, I'm pretty sure he is getting the urge to leave. I take a large gulp of wine and as I do Bill notices and looks at the near ending bottle of wine in the cooler, his shouts over to the waiter to indicate to bring another bottle. I try tell him there's no need, but he refuses to acknowledge this and insists on one more. For the first time me and Earnie lock eyes and think on the same wave length. "Oh, great we are going to be here even longer." Rita continues her chat with Bill, and I try to make some small talk with Doreen. Earnie his focused on his phone and doesn't even attempt to join in. Doreen's handbag slips off her knee and onto the floor as she moves closer to talk to me.

'Oh, bloody hell.' Doreen mutters to herself as she bends down to squeeze herself under the table to retrieve her bag. I nudge my chair out to give her more room Earnie however is too busy knocking back the whisky to bother to move for her. I wonder what is taking her so long. Everyone else seems oblivious that Doreen is on all fours under the table. I pop my head down to see what she is doing.

'Are you ok?' I ask as just as she's starting to lift herself back up.

'Yeah, I dropped my bag then everything fell out, it's a bit of a squeeze under there.' She lifts her bag back up but this time places it behind her on her seat. I see her shifting awkwardly in her chair and begin to mess with her wedding ring, then she grabs her wine glass and takes a big drink, her hands are trembling. I look at her and can see something is bothering her, she's starts fidgeting with her ring again, her face looks clammy and white.

'Are you ok?' I whisper in her ear. The rest of the table are too occupied to notice, Rita's listening to Bill, I can tell she isn't interested, but she perseveres and continues to act intrigued, he seems to like to talk about himself a lot. Earnie is typing away furiously with his big thumbs prodding each button with such aggression it's almost as if his phone is going to crumble in his hands. She looks at me and nods her head in Earnie's direction, then looks down at her hand below the table and makes a gun sign from her fingers.

'He's got a gun?' I mouth this time making sure no sound comes out. I look over to see that Earnie's casual jacket is covering his belt so can't see it myself, but the look on Doreen's face tells me she's not lying. She nods her head. We both sit and look at each other our eyes wide with terror. We then both look away and look down at the table, I try to hide my shaking hands, so place them on my lap, Doreen does the same, I look down and see Doreen's leg has started to shake, I reach over and press down on her thigh, her shaking leg stops, but is desperate to move again so I keep my hand there a little longer and move my chair closer. I'm now starting to think of and exit plan, we need to get out of here and as far away from these two crazy people as possible. I notice the bottle of wine is nearly finished, so I start to think of what I can say to leave. As Doreen starts to settle, she composes herself then downs the remaining wine in her glass. (Which is quite impressive for Doreen.) Bill notices this.

'Wow, you must be thirsty, I will order some more.' Bill pours the remaining wine in Doreen's glass then calls to the waiter to bring more, before I can even object, I do however insist that this will be the last, as it's been a long day. Funnily enough he doesn't answer, instead he smirks and returns his focus to Rita, who is clearly now fed up and had enough. If this was under normal circumstances, I'd get up and leave, As there would be no way would I ever give any more of my time to a self-righteous prick, and terrifyingly grumpy mute with a gun. Doreen doesn't speak she just smiles softly and slightly raises her glass to say thanks. I notice the slight jitter in her hand and so does she, as quickly as the glass went up, she places it right back down again.

Earnie sneers and makes a grunt in dissatisfaction. He finishes on his phone and by this point he looks like he's had enough, he purposely scrapes his chair back along the shiny tiles to make a screech, his long legs heave himself up to stand. I can't believe the size of him as he stands there, he looks enormous compared to us, his hands are like shovels, his legs long and chunky, his full body is just full of muscles, though he's not slim, but he's also not fat, just one well-built man, he must be at least 18 stone. I realise my mouth is slightly open while I'm watching him. I quickly close it before anyone notices. Bill turns and see's Earnie standing and waits for him to speak, as if he needs to have permission to leave.

'I'm going for a smoke.' He heads off out the main doors before Bill can answer. His big frame makes him stand out, and you can see everyone he walks past lift their heads to look at him. Bill doesn't bother to watch him leave but I can see the annoyance in his face. I watch him exit and breathe a sigh of relief; I notice Doreen does the same. A sickly feeling has come over me with my nerves still jittering away. All I can do is wonder when he will receive the note. I look down to watch, it's a bit off 11pm so Cora will still be here. I clench onto my stomach hoping to make it ease. Bill notices my discomfort but thinks it's because of Earnie's awkward manner.

'Sorry about him, as you can tell he's not one for socialising, it takes a while for him to soften up and relax.' I just nod unsure how to answer. "So how about you two then, what do you do?' He asks trying to involve us in the conversation. I'd have much preferred to have been left quiet. However, I answer politely and tell him I used to teach in a primary school. I don't know if he was genuinely interested or our conversation was that bad, but he's trying to make as much small talk as possible. Once we started talking more, my first thought of him started to soften, maybe he isn't as bad as I first thought? Maybe with Earnie now gone, has made everyone more relaxed. I need to pinch myself and remember the sort of people that they are. I doubt he would be this friendly if he knew we have something to do with his missing package.

With more drinks flowing and the atmosphere is feeling a lot better, I could quite easily forget the situation we are in. It's been an hour since Earnie was last seen so it's likely he's given up on then night, or he's going on the hunt for his cocaine alone. Everyone is chatting away nicely. I don't think Bill suspects we are involved after the way he's being gossiping our heads off. Telling us how he's divorced and has no children, his marriage ended when his ex-wife had taken off with another man. I can't help but wonder if there still around to tell the tale. He boasts about coming from nothing, and how he's built his business up from the ground, that it takes him all around the world, and that he now lives a luxurious and wealthy life because of it. I would easily be impressed if I didn't know it was from the drug trade. Then again, all his stories he's just told could be complete bull shit! The only good thing about a man that likes to talk about himself so much, is that we haven't had to say much about ourselves. I look down at my watch and see that it's almost 11.30pm. Even with all the wine on board I still have my senses to panic, Cora will now be gone, so no one will be looking out for us if things take a turn for the worst, and Earnie still hasn't landed back. This is our perfect time to leave. I try to catch the attention of Rita and Doreen to signal that we should be going. As I'm just about to call it a night, something catches my eye. It's the huge frame of Earnie! He's marching over and fast! He's eyes glare to our direction. His posture is tense and angry, I notice his fists are clenched tight, and in one clenched fist I see the note. My body suddenly feels trapped and unable to move. With myself stuck in a frozen state, the only thing I can do is watch him as bounds furiously over to us. My chest starts to ache with the pound of my heart, I suddenly feel like I can't breathe, my hands start trembling uncontrollably. I grab a hold of my bag and squeeze, hoping it helps with my shakes. I feel beads of sweat forming on my forehead, as I become thankful for the dimly lit room. My mind is racing with all kinds but the main one that pops up is… "He knows!"

CHAPTER 16

I dare not move my eyes from Earnie as he reaches our table. He glides passed me and I momentarily breath. He marches over to Bill, who is already waiting, knowing something is not right. They both step away from the table to make sure we can't hear. Both Doreen and Rita look to me, there wide eyes full of panic. I try to listen but it's no use they have their back to us. I do however see Earnie hands the note to Bill. I watch as he quickly reads it, then crumples it in one hand and then hands it back to Earnie, who then places it in his pocket. I gulp, but my throat has gone too dry to even do this properly, so I'm left with what feels like a hard lump that's stuck.

They both slowly turn back around, their faces full of anger being unable overhear what they said leaves me wondering. Do they know? Has Cora told them? There long hard stare tells me nothing good, and I can see Bill is deciding what to do. Earnie fidgets with a bulk under his jacket as I realize that must be the gun. A wave of fluster comes over me as debate if now is the time to come clean, explain ourselves about how this mistakenly has happened. Would they understand? Would they believe us? Would we be digging ourselves into a grave? I try to calm myself down by rubbing Barry's wedding ring in my fingers that's now attached to my necklace, hoping to find some comfort. I look over at Doreen and Rita who are now on the edge of their seats, panic setting in, Rita is gulping at her wine, and Doreen's shaking is now noticeable as she looks around everywhere apart from them two. I close my eyes for a moment taking in precious memories thinking this could be the last time I could think about them. A sudden sense of peace comes over me as I try to relish in it as much as I can.

'You all are leaving already?' His mouth turns into a sneer as ne notices me clutching my bag in one hand and sees Doreen and Rita about off their seats. I can't quite work out if his tone is sarcastic or surprised, either way it has us all terrified. Our silence is too long as he waits for our answer. I prepare myself to muster up my answer and pray that they come out correctly and not to show them how much of a nervous wreck I am, but a calm composed voice beats me to it.

'It looks like you have something to sort so we will leave you to it, plus it's been a long day, too much wine and not enough sleep.' Rita says as she stands with me and Doreen. Earnie nods his head and looks relieved that we are finally going. We all begin to say our goodbyes and turn to leave. I get a sense that they know we are making a quick exit. I need to get out and as far away from them possible.

'Erm, not so fast.' A sharp husky voice stops us in our tracks. We all freeze, unsure whether to turn around or run like hell. The beating of my heart pounds onto my chest, I'm almost positive if they come close enough then they would hear it. I try to compose myself, although I think my shaking legs are about to give way. Rita turns first, I slowly follow, then Doreen. He looks amused as we wait for him to speak.

'You're all quick to leave.' His dry tone sends a tingle down my spine and the hairs on my arms stand up. I suddenly feel cold.

'It's been a long night.' I stutter out with my shaking voice.

'It has, now we need our sleep. We will leave you boys to play nice. We might see you about tomorrow.' Rita says with a smile ever so composed and confident.

'Look at their faces Earnie, I think you have upset them.' Bill says laughing. Earnie looks at us and grins. Unsure what to do I just grin back. The humiliation creeps in and I wonder if they enjoy seeing women intimidated and scared, or they really don't have a clue, and are wondering why we look so frightened. Still, we say nothing. I start to shift nervously from foot-to-foot dreading what may come next. I can see Bill is dying to get something off his chest, so I stare waiting for him to speak.

'Before you go how about you leave me your number Rita? We can meet for a coffee tomorrow. Seen as though it looks like we are ready to call it a night, unfortunately I have some business that needs my attention so will also have to leave.'

We all look to Rita waiting for her to reply. I can only hope she doesn't, but somehow, I know it won't be as simple as that. I watch her and can see she is unsure if to do so, Bill's eyes are staring deep into her as he waits patiently for her reply. The few seconds of waiting feel like minutes. His eyes start to narrow as Rita notices she's taking too long to answer, and I can see she is crumbling under the pressure. I dying to scream "no!"

'Oh, sure.' Rita finally replies, a little bit to squeaky than it should have been. Rita grabs a napkin off the table next to us and turns her back to them, wisely, as I see her shaking hand trying to write her name and number. Bill's hard stare eases as a little curl of a smile appears on his lips. 'Call me.' She says handing it to a grinning Bill. Then quickly turns around to head out the doors. Me and Doreen quickly follow. I turn round for a last look and see Earnie glaring at us. I quickly turn away and gulp and speed up my walk.

Finally, out of view and heading for the closest elevators as fast as we can we don't speak a word until the elevator doors close and we all take a deep breath.

'What the heck was all that!' Doreen gasps.

'I don't know, but I don't like being near any of them. I think I was close to wetting myself.' I reply trying to make light of the situation, although partly true I think I nearly did and would really appreciate a panty liner right now.

'I hope he doesn't call me.' Rita grits her teeth. I look round and see that Rita is uncomfortable and playing about with her handbag nervously, her usual dewy glow is now a pale white face.

'You gave him your real number?' Doreen asks shocked.

'Yeah, I dare not, imagine if he tried to call it while we were still there.'

I reluctantly agree knowing that there's not much else she could have done. Everything goes silent for a minute as we all watch the numbers shoot up for each floor. I desperately wait for the ping, just as we are all starting to calm down, Doreen decides to open her mouth and bring some more shock back.

'Did you notice Earnie has a gun?'

'He's got a gun?' Rita looks up and looks truly terrified. 'What if he calls and wants me to meet him, I can't go, what if he shoots me!' Rita becomes frantic, her eyes look watery and her lip starts to quiver. Thankfully the ping of the elevator interrupts and the doors fly open.

'let's just get out of here.' I push everyone out as we all pick up the pace to race back to the apartment. The corridors seem to go on and on until we finally see our door, making the last dash I quickly check behind us to make sure no one is following. Once we are all bundled inside, I slam the door shut and make sure all the locks are on and even debate moving the little side table that sits next to the door across just in case. Then I think I'm maybe being too paranoid and decide to leave it where it is. Safe and secure and all of us in one piece, we all breathe again, I stay propped up against the closed door. Rita kicks off her heels and flings her handbag, Doreen does the same but not as elegantly, as she slightly stumbles while trying to kick her shoe off, which seems to be stuck on her swollen foot, so instead holds onto the side and uses her other hand to fling the reluctant shoe off.

'What a bloody day?' Doreen huffs and throws her shoe; she then heads to her room to get changed. I look at Rita and see her anxiously checking her phone.

'Try not to panic, he might not get in touch he had a lot of wine, and if he does, we will think of something when it comes to it.' She looks at me, not convinced.

'I know, I just feel exhausted, and honestly can't believe this is all happening to us. I blame myself, I'm sorry for putting you and Doreen in this situation, if it wasn't for me pushing you both into this holiday, we wouldn't be in this mess right now!' Rita flops onto the big sofa and places her hands to her head, not caring that she is scrunching up her perfect blow dry. It's not often Rita shows this insecure side of her, so when she does, you know she's being sincere. She looks down at her phone to check it before she gets up and places it on the side. She breathes a sigh of relief when she sees there is no messages. I watch her as she continues to blame herself. She nervously paces around and fidgets with anything she touches.

'It's not your fault, it's just a shitty situation that we have gotten ourselves into, so please don't blame yourself. Anyway, tomorrow is a new day, and hopefully Cora will have it back then this can be over with.' I wrap my arms around her and give her a big hug, her tiny little frame stops trembling as she reaches out to embrace me back. 'let's go to bed and start again tomorrow.'

CHAPTER 17

Waking up the next day with a heavy, spinning head. I try to lift myself up, but my body feels like it's been weighted down. I slightly raise my head up and notice Rita and Doreen are also sprawled out over my bed. I wonder how and when we fell asleep, I was expecting not having a wink of sleep, but exhaustion must have taken over. I stare confused at the two extra bodies lying across my bed, trying to recall when they jumped in, but everything is blank. As I move to sit myself up, I accidently kick Rita, she grumbles at my nudge before she wakes. Doreen however has barely moved, lying flat on her back with her mouth wide open, snoring so loud that I'm surprised that didn't wake me up sooner.

'When did you both come in here?' I whisper to Rita. Rita heaves herself up and rubs her tired eyes, the black mascara she was wearing last night has now smeared underneath leaving what looks like two black panda eyes. She yawns and does a big stretch before she answers.

'When I came in there was only you in here, so I jumped in, I didn't want to stay on my own and there was no chance I was going to jump in with Doreen and her snoring. But looks like she's made her way in here too.' Rita begins to prod at Doreen trying to gently wake her, but Doreen doesn't stir. 'She's like some sort of wild beast sleeping like that, I bet our neighbours think there's a load of fellas in here if they can hear it.' We both start to laugh. Rita jumps off the bed and straightens out her skimpy pyjamas. I also try to stand up but don't quite manage to do it as gracefully as Rita, still feeling the effects of last night's alcohol. 'I'll put the kettle on. I need a coffee before I do anything else.' Rita says heading to the kitchen. I'm surprised to see her this calm after the way she ended up last night, but I dare not prod and spoil the calming mood she has.

I unsteadily make my way behind her, my head is thumping, and my joints feel seized up. I grab a hold of my head hoping the pressure helps to ease it. Just as I reach the kitchen area Rita is throwing me a packet of paracetamols.

'Here, take these it will help your bad head.' She laughs. I smirk hoping these little tablets ease the pounding ache. Rita is making the coffee and soon the fresh strong smell is filling the room. Once we are both seated with ours mugs, I notice Rita is looking back and forth at the sideboard, I look over to see what's making her nervous. Of course, she hasn't forgotten, as she glares back and forth at her phone laying there face down.

'Are you okay?'

'Yeah, I'm just waiting for that dreaded call.' She rolls her eyes and takes a big sip of coffee.

'You know you don't have to meet him if he calls?'

'We will just wait and see what happens. I need to drink this before I make any decisions this morning. We must have drunk a lot of wine yesterday.' I notice she quickly changes the subject, so I follow on to the new conversation.

'We must of, my head is telling me we defiantly have.'

'Well, we needed it I think after yesterday, let's hope Cora comes through today. Then all this crap can be put to bed, and we can enjoy the rest of our holiday.'

'Let's hope.' I nod back. We carry on talking about everything that happened yesterday, when we suddenly get interrupted by Doreen's grunting snores.

'How does Phil put up with that snoring, I cannot believe

someone can snore that loud!' Rita says raising her eyebrows.

'I would say he's learnt to block it out after all these years.' A couple more minutes pass while we are enjoying our morning coffee around the little round table, when we hear the footsteps and groans of Doreen getting up. Doreen walks in yawning and looking ruff, her usually slightly waved greying blonde bob is now sticking up in all directions, her eyes are smeared with mascara, and a remaining soft touch of pink lipstick is smudged all around her lips. Rita's jaw drops when she first sees her then she starts laughing so loud that it makes Doreen jump.

'What are you laughing at?' Doreen snaps.

'Have you seen yourself in the mirror?' Rita says while pointing at Doreen's smeared makeup and crazy hair.

Doreen huffs and walks to the bathroom to see. 'Oh Jesus Christ! That is scary.' She shouts as she plods back through laughing.

'Don't worry we have a coffee waiting for you!' I shout back laughing.

'Never mind asking me if I've looked in mirror, I think you need to.' Doreen says pointing at Rita. Rita just laughs and gives her the middle finger.

'Anyone else as rough as me?' She says reaching for her mug. Me and Rita both raise our hands to agree. Doreen looks over on the side and sees Rita's phone. 'Has he called?'

Rita gets up to grab her phone and has a quick look. 'No thank goodness.' Rita sits back down and plays with her coffee mug before she speaks again. 'Do you think they know it's us?' I knew something was up and her being so calm was just an act, which is understandable we have been thrown into an awful situation, with no idea how it' going to pan out, the only thing we can do is hope everything goes as planned today. Do they know it's us? I have no idea, if I start overthinking things already, I will lose my mind, so I push the dreaded thoughts away. First thing first, we need to get sorted and look for Cora, things have got to go to plan today, they must...

CHAPTER 18

'It's only just gone past 9.00am, but we are all ready to start heading down to the breakfast area. The three of us now freshened up, with all the traces of last nights smeared makeup removed and looking a bit more respectful. We make sure we have things with us so we can laze around the pool, seen as though it looks like it's going to be a beautiful day. The sun is already beaming with no cloud in sight and the heat must already be close to 30 degrees. I keep reminding us that we need to do things as we would normally do on a holiday, so breakfast and sunbathing is exactly that. I've chose to wear a brown v neck bather that looks like a wrap around, not confident enough to wear this on its own, I grab my long white beach shirt that rests just above my knees and slide it over, I match it up with my oversized floppy hat and a pair of cork and white wedges with of course my huge sunglasses to cover my tired eyes. Doreen sports a plain black bather which has a belt around the waist and places a floaty navy-blue t-shirt dress on top of it. We both stand about waiting for Rita, who seems to have been taking forever to get ready, Doreen is starting to lose her patients and starts shouting at her to hurry up, my belly is grumbling away and I'm starting to feel sick with hunger. Then finally out pops Rita. She looks incredible, her hair done in perfect soft beach waves, her cut out white and gold marble effect bather shows off her incredible figure, her brown high wedges make her legs look even longer. I gasp when I see her, then automatically cover myself up more feeling slightly insecure. It's not her intentions to make others feel this way, it just so happens it does occasionally, thankfully we are used to it and do know her true nature isn't what it looks like. Which others have said her to be a self-absorbed, fake arsed snob, I have insisted to others there' a lot more to her than what you see. She does look after herself and cares about what she looks like, but what is so wrong with that? I do however wonder if this is why she only has me and Doreen as girlfriends. However, we know why she spends so much time and effort and money for her appearance. One, she got very insecure about herself when she caught her ex-husband cheating with a co-worker, she vowed never to have a man make her feel like that again. Two, she is desperate to find her prince charming and marry them. Although she would never admit to this, it has occasionally slipped out in conversations with alcohol. Most women and possibly even most men know once your settled in a comfortable relationship you do tend to let your appearances slip, it's not intentionally it just happens, but for Rita however, she's never let anything slip and she's set her standards that high that they'd be no chance she's going to find a man that ticks every single box. I've seen her many times lose good men to this ridiculous perfect obsession, not wearing the right outfit, being too small, being too big, turning up to her house with holes in his socks, his knees where too knobbly wearing shorts. like who really gives a shit as long as they are decent man, but her obsession with finding the perfect man has made her lose sight of what is actually important, which is quite sad to see, but still she is determined to keep ticking them imaginary boxes.

'You can't go down for breakfast in just that! You will finish the poor old fellas off!' Doreen laughs and chucks her a long beige beach kimono. Rita rolls her eyes as she puts it on.

The elevator pings open to the lobby, we step out and check everywhere hoping we don't bump into Bill and Earnie on our travels, that is the last thing we need right now. Considering it is prime time for breakfast the place seems quiet, which makes it easier for us to scan around. Then I gulp realising that we must be easier to spot too. With no sign of either of them we carry on walking. The reception area is free with just one man standing behind the desk. Which I see to be the perfect opportunity to try and track down Cora.

'I'm going to go and ask if Cora is in.' I don't wait for a reply instead I rush off towards the desk. I can hear the clopping of Rita's sandals upping the pace just right behind me, but I don't slow down. The young man spots me rushing over, he stops typing on his computer and looks up, wondering if a complaint is coming his way, the tall stylish man tenses up. We all reach the desk together. I try to hide that I'm a little out of breath, so I casually fix my hair to give myself some time before I speak. He looks down to us and raises his eyebrows. "Shit, he can tell." He Doesn't wait for me to speak first.

'Good morning, ladies, how can I help you today?' He patiently waits for our reply, while we get our breath back.

'Is Cora here, we need to speak to her?' Rita asks making sure she doesn't say her name too loud.

'Cora? Her shift doesn't start till 11.00am. Can I help with anything? I am the assistant manager!' He points to his shiny gold assistant manager tag on his immaculate light blue shirt.

'No, sorry, we need Cora. We will call back after breakfast.'

'Are you sure? I'm sure I can help with anything you need?' He insists a little more eagerly this time.

'Thank you but we will call back later.'

'Very well then.' He sharply says then turns his attention back to the computer. We walk to the breakfast lounge feeling a little deflated, I was kind of hoping we could have got this mess sorted before breakfast, maybe I was being too optimistic, of course with my luck things wouldn't get sorted that easily.

As we enter the breakfast area, I do a quick scan to see who's already here. With the tables starting to empty we find a nice quiet table in the corner, that looks out onto the fresh green grass with colourful blooms of flowers, and in the distance, you can see the warm sandy beaches. It really is a beautiful place when you manage stop and look at it. With no sign of any trouble lurking about we take a seat and begin to scan the breakfast menu. I didn't realise how hungry I am until I could smell the freshly cooked breads and croissants, they smell delicious, and gives off the holiday vibes, continental breakfasts are always a winner in my book. I look over to the breakfast buffet and see all the fresh fruits bursting with beautiful bright colours. I place the menu back down knowing exactly what I'm going to get.

It doesn't take long before I'm placing my fork down after taking my last bite of melon, but I do debate grabbing another croissant, feeling my full bloated tummy I decide I best not. My hunger has finally vanished along with my thumping headache. Doreen is still eating away at her breakfast and Rita has finished and is taking big slurps of coffee. She suddenly turns to me her eyes wide and alert as if something as just clicked like a switch being turned on.

'I'm a nervous wreck, I'm constantly checking my phone, dreading if I get a call.' Her jittering panic is easy to see as I try to calm her. I notice she's not eaten much and is fidgeting with her mug and toying with her phone. A huge smash comes from the kitchen area and makes Rita jump out of her seat, and Doreen's breakfast jumps off her fork and falls on her lap as she was just about to take a bite. I look at us, to see we are all complete nervous wrecks, anyone else in the restaurant has barely flinched and here we are, almost dropping to the floor.

'Bloody hell, it was just someone dropping some plates. Look at us all we need to pull ourselves together. We can't be like this the whole time. Rita, no one is going to force you to meet Bill, if you don't want to go simply say no. Doreen, I need you to keep calm and stop thinking about that.' I whisper it so no one else can hear 'Gun! We need to remember that we need to act and carry on as normal, like we would do on any other holiday, if we keep ourselves busy hopefully it will take our mind off things, and hopefully keep us out of sight of them two. Let's finish up here and we will go and see if Cora has landed in so we can get this over with!' The two of them look at me a bit shocked at my bluntness, but nod in agreement. I know it was harsh and we are all edge and scared, but the more I see them jumping and flinching the worse it's making me.

'Your right, I don't know why I'm worrying myself so much with him, I need to treat him like any other man that wants to take me out, and I've told plenty of them of them no before.' Rita says sitting herself up looking more confident. Until Doreen speaks.

'But did they have guns?'

'Doreen!' I shout back at her. She holds her hands up understanding that her sarcasm isn't the time or place for it.

'Sorry, that was meant to be a joke.'

'Well, it's not funny.' I snap.

'Your humour is shocking if you think that's funny.' Rita crosses her arms and slumps back lower down in her chair with a sulk.

'I'm really sorry, I won't say it again.' Doreen flushes then carries on finishing her breakfast.

It's just a little after 10.30am when we finish our breakfast, so we decide to grab a couple of sun loungers and relax and soak up some sunshine while we wait, Rita has a huge floppy hat and oversized sunglasses, knowing this is her kind of style anyhow, I can't help but wonder if it's also is an attempt to disguise herself. Doreen is doing some sort of puzzle in a magazine, I grab out my book and begin to read my soppy romance novel. We seem to be finally relaxing. The sun is blaring down on us making it incredibly hot, until every so often a little blow of breeze cools me down. I look over to the other two and wonder if there managing to relax as much as I am. Rita looks flat out, I'm unsure if she's fallen asleep or just making the most of the peace and quiet, I can't quite tell with the floppy hat and oversized glasses covering most of her face. Either way, we all seem to be enjoying it, it must be the most we've relaxed since the start of the holiday. I could lay here all-day listening pepples chatter in the background and feeling the cool breeze wafting over me every so often, my mind is suddenly at ease as my eyes begin to close.

An hour passes without me noticing. The three of us have barely moved, Doreen is still fighting on with her puzzle book, Rita is there somewhere hiding under her floppy hat. I sit up and place my book on the side hoping I haven't lost my page from dozing off. The heat of the sun is starting burn on my skin, it's got to be at least 32 degrees. I take a sip of my mojito that Rita ordered. The cool mint and lime hits the back of my throat with just enough rum to taste, the classic cocktail never seems to disappoint. I lick my lips to take in every bit of the bursting citrus flavours. I could sit here all day drinking these, but looking at the time, I realise that Cora should be in work by now.

'That mojito was amazing.' I say making sure I get every last drops out of my glass.

'Aren't they just fabulous darling.' Rita speaks without moving but still hides under her hat. Doreen looks up from her book and agrees, then looks down at Rita.

'Are you trying to hide under there? You do know it makes you stand out more?'

'I'm not hiding!' She quickly snaps back and jumps to sit up. 'I don't like the sun on my face.' She pleads.

'Yeah okay.' Doreen tuts and returns to her puzzles.

I wonder if now the time is to disturb the peace and mention that we should maybe go and look for Cora. Feeling slightly guilty having to remind them while there clearly enjoying this moment without any worry. I slowly open my mouth to speak then close it again. Something has caught my eye in the distance, I lower my sunglasses down to the edge of my nose to get a better look. Walking along the poolside, his white teeth gleaming along with his bronzed toned body, his dark shorts revealing his muscly legs, with no care in the world is Bill. 'Oh no it can't be!' I mutter to myself. He hasn't seen us yet, but he is looking everywhere, and every woman he walks past looks at him. His casual stride is so smooth that the peers from everyone staring don't interrupt him. He looks like some kind of God. He looks good and he knows it.

I fly myself back into my sun lounger and grab my book to cover my face hoping he doesn't see us. I try to whisper to Rita who is now hiding back under her hat. I must look like a school girl trying to spread gossip, keeping my book in front of my face while trying to get Rita's attention.

'Psstt.' She doesn't hear my first call, so I do it louder. She finally lifts the edge of her hat up to look at me.

'What?' She snaps annoyed at my interruption.

I mouth the words while trying to point my head in Bills direction still hiding behind my book. 'Bill, is over there.' Rita doesn't understand what I'm trying to say, and this time lifts her sunglasses up to look at me closer.

'What are saying?' She whispers back noticing that it's a secret conversation. I go to repeat it again.

'Hello ladies, I almost didn't see you there.'

Shit! I think I almost die when I hear his voice! Rita's still staring at me but this time her eyes are wide with shock. I look back and shrug as if to say. (Tried to tell you.) We both slowly sit up, I lower my book and stood in front of us smiling away is Bill, wearing nothing but his shorts, he's that close that I can see tiny little specs of sweat rolling down his toned stomach. My mouth falls open. I look over to Rita and Doreen. Rita now has removed her sunglasses completely, I'm not sure if its shock or she's impressed but she doesn't remove her eyes from him. I see Doreen in the background has now, lowered her puzzle book, she doesn't remove her sunglasses, however she makes an obvious gawp, and peers over the top of them, her pen suddenly falls out of her hand, which makes her jump and breaks her gaze, she fumbles about with embarrassment trying to retrieve her pen. There's a moment of silence before any of us can reply. I see the other women around the pool looking at us whispering and wondering why he's stopped and talked to us and not them. (If only they knew what his business involved.) We must be the only woman around the pool that dreaded this hunk of a man coming over to us. Rita takes a deep breath and gives a big smile before she answers, as though she's preparing a character for a role.

'Hi there.' She says nothing else and continues her fixed stare on Bill. Which I think he likes. A grin appears on his face, and if I didn't know any better, I could have sworn I see little nerves jump through him, he twitches his stance and his big strong hands clench then release just as quick, quickly enough for no one else to notice.

'I was going to call you, but seen as though I've bumped into you now, you fancy going for a coffee, there's a great coffee shop just on the front near the marina.' He straightens himself back up as if relieved to have gotten his words out without a jitter. "Surely he can't be nervous?" The thought leaves me wondering. This man is full of surprises. I look round to Rita, I'm eager to see what she says, surely, she's got to say no! She carries on looking at Bill, leaving no hint to what she is going to do. The long pause has everyone on edge. Doreen's eyes are darting back and forth between the two, my heart is pounding waiting for her answer, "Please say no" I keep repeating in my head. Bill also eager for his answer tries to say something but instead scratches his head just as he does Rita answers.

'I'm not sure I think we have a lot on today?' She looks round to me and Doreen waiting for us to back her up, we quickly nod our heads.

'Yes, we've got a pretty hectic day ahead.' I answer furiously nodding my head. Bill raises his eyebrows and takes a good look at us, sitting about soaking up the sun with our books and puzzles. Clearly not looking so hectic.

'Mmm... Well you don't look too busy now. He makes a point of noticing that we are in fact not too busy right now. 'We won't be too long, I promise I will have you back this afternoon so you can, carry on with your hectic day.' Bill insists, and I can't help but notice the hint of sarcasm in his tone. Rita shuffles a little uncomfortably in the lounger, she looks right over at me again, and I see that she's cracking under the pressure.

"Don't you dare say yes!" My thoughts are bouncing in my head I look back at her with an angrier stare, hoping she can read what my eyes are trying to say. She looks back to Bill with a fake smile appearing.

'Sure, let me freshen up and I will meet you in the lobby in 20 minutes.' She answers with a big, cute smile.

I close my eyes in frustration. "Fuck! Why would she do that!" I smile nervously while Bill is still lingering about. I turn to look at Doreen who looks more horrified than I am. Her jaw has fell wide open and her head swinging back and forth in all directions desperately trying to get one of our attentions. Doreen catches my glare and gives me the look to say, "What the fuck!" Bill however is too pleased with the answer to notice our shocked faces. All he seems to be able to do is grin back at Rita. I can imagine as soon as he is out of view he will be jumping for joy, he stands for a moment longer soaking in the glory of winning a date with Rita before he answers her back, he then casual walks away as smoothly as he came.

Once he is out of sight, Me and Doreen both have our eyes burning into her, she must know this as she tries to not acknowledge our stares on her. Instead, she sits herself up ready to stand without saying a single word, she begins to gather her things ready to leave! Doreen is furious and getting more and more frustrated at her ignorance. She burrows her eyes and blurts out in anger.

'Are you crazy!' Doreen snaps. 'I thought we agreed that you wouldn't be meeting him!' Rita huffs back and immediately stops what she is doing and turns to face Doreen.

'What was I meant to do?' She says with sharp tone, I can't help but think that she might be nervous, which of course she should be. Rita never normally gets nervous before dates, she's very experienced with dating and multiple dating that it never really bothers her, it's just normal in her life, especially never being short of admirers. However, this is a totally different kind of date and I have a very bad feeling about it.

'You say no! that's what you say!' Doreen is just getting started on the telling off, when Rita holds up her hand and cuts her off in mid-sentence.

'Then what do you think would happen?' She now finally turns her attention to the two of us. 'What happens if he starts watching us because he's got curious as to what we are up to? What happens if he catches us chatting with Cora and his drugs! What happens if he starts wondering why suddenly I've gone frosty with him, after telling him last night that I would go out with him! Do you think he looks the type that takes things well, when he doesn't get his own way? We also agreed to try and act as natural as possible, so they don't suspect anything!' Rita's rant leaves her breathless as me and Doreen sit silent unsure how to respond. 'Have you even considered the difficult situation that I have been put in?'

Once she has finished, she looks at us, her eyes become watery and I notice the slight shake in her hands. Of course, we didn't think of the pressure this puts on her; I also wonder if she is putting herself in this dangerous situation to help with her guilt from all this. I can clearly see now that she would rather not be going on this date. She hasn't put herself in this situation to cause any upset, but she has done it to help us. Now I understand why she has said yes, although I'm not happy with this choice, she does have a point. We don't know how things could have turned if she said no, at least when she goes, we know Bill is out of the picture for a few hours, we can hopefully retrieve his goods in the meantime. Just as things are settling down and we all understand what is happening, Doreen can't help but have one more last say on the matter.

'Well, you still could have said no!' Doreen mutters quietly under her breath.

'Oh fuck off Doreen!' Rita snaps harshly her eyes glaring at Doreen. Doreen sits debating to react and just as she is about to, I decide to intervene before there's a full-blown argument again.

'She's right, you have been put in an awkward situation, I think what we are trying to say is that you don't need to go if you really don't want to go.' I try to soften the icy atmosphere that has now surrounded us. They both thankfully back off from this escalating any more than it needs to.

'Thank you Lynn, I think this is the best option for us, I'll just go for a coffee for a couple of hours and then hopefully when I'm back everything is sorted.'

'Pass me your phone?' I hold out my hand waiting for it, she doesn't ask why, instead just hands it to me. 'I'm putting a tracking app on, then we can see where you are, and if you need us, call.' I grab her phone and make sure everything is connected and that the tracking is working so I can follow her on my phone. We say our goodbyes and Rita heads off to get ready to meet Bill. I take a gulp as I watch her walk away.

CHAPTER 19

After listening to Doreen for ten minutes telling me how much of a bad idea this is, I have to shush her up, my nerves are already on edge, if she carries on, I'm going to lose it. We head off to the reception area to find Cora. Hoping this refocuses us on what needs to be done in the meantime and take our fretting minds off Rita for a little. I must have looked at the app ten times already and she has only just left. The closer we get, I see the same young man standing behind the desk but no Cora, I give a quick look round to see if can see her anywhere else, but nothing, I do another quick look behind me making sure there is no Earnie in sight as I get near to the desk. The man notices me coming, and sure I've just seen a little eye roll from him, I march a little faster. The annoyed man doesn't wait for me to speak.

'Cora has not turned up for her shift! She is meant to be starting the preparations for the dinner duties. This is going to put the whole shift behind! So please if there is anything I can help you with, do say so now as it's going to be a very busy day.' The flustered assistant manager sneers.

'Is she sick?' Doreen asks innocently which seems to annoy the man even more.

'What is it with Cora? She hasn't turned in for her shift, I don't know why, but I can help you with whatever you need?' He stops his typing and looks right us in the face. The determined look makes me uncomfortable, and the attitude he has, has surely got to be out of character for his job role. I'm eager to prod for a little more information but decide not to. Doreen however isn't bothered by his terrible tone and continues asking more questions.

'Does she often not turn in? Is this unusual for her?' Doreen persists on with questions. The assistant manager doesn't bother to hide his eye rolls this time and begins to tut before he answers.

'No, she always turns up for her shift, I don't know what problem it is you have, or what the need for Cora is? But if you are not willing to let me help, then I'm sorry but you will have to step aside, there is other people to tend to!' He points behind us to the growing queue that is now forming. We smile politely back and leave quickly. My mind starts racing with all kinds of things as we are storming away, I feel irritated by his poor manner, but mainly where the hell is Cora? We are no closer to sorting this shamble of a holiday out. The drugs are still missing, Rita has gone off with Bill, Cora is nowhere to be seen. Things are just going from bad to worse. We walk far enough away so the man is out of ear shot before we stop to talk and figure out what we are going to do next.

'What are going to do now?' Doreen huffs and places her hands on her hips. I don't know how to answer just yet, I need a minute to think some things through, but I feel the pressure from Doreen's stare, looking at me waiting for the answers, so I turn my back to her slightly while I try to figure it out. Surely this can't be a coincidence Cora not turning in today when she promised to get the package back! All kinds of thoughts start whirling through my head, is she part of it? has she stole it? Or has something happened to her? Losing a few moments in my thoughts, I see Doreen is speaking cause her lips are moving but can't hear what she is saying, behind her in the background I watch the assistant manager. His gaze is fixed on us even though the waiting queue of people are waiting on him, his eyes never move from us even as he picks up the phone and is talking to someone on it. He must not notice that I can see him as Doreen is standing in front of me with her back to him. I interrupt Doreen even though I don't have a clue what she is saying, but I cannot take my eyes off the young man behind the reception desk.

'Now isn't that strange?' I nod my head into the man's direction. Doreen instantly swings round to see what I'm talking about. The man becomes shocked when he knows we have noticed him, he slams the phone down and quickly turns to focus on the growing queue in front of him as if trying to disguise the fact that he was watching us.

'He is strange, isn't he? He couldn't wait to get us away; I think he was offended that we didn't want his help too.' I slowly nod keeping my eye on him to see if he looks back. He doesn't but I think he must sense that I'm looking at him.

'We need to see if Rita has left?' I start a fast-paced walk to the lobby entrance. 'You try calling her.'

'What...' Doreen unsure what is happening dashes to keep up with me while trying to phone her while on the move. I pick up my pace when I see the lobby doors, not caring that I'm bumping into people in the process, I hear Doreen's heavy pants close behind me. I bust the big heavy doors open, and the heat of the afternoon air hits me suddenly, no cool blast from the aircon like inside just pure hot air surrounding every part of me. I dart my eyes round frantically looking, she's nowhere to be seen, I go further out to see if I can see her in the distance but nothing. My heart fills with dread, and I get a niggling belly ache telling me something is not right. I turn to a breathless Doreen.

'She's gone!'

CHAPTER 20

'She's not here.' I repeat again in a frantic haze. Doreen looks at me confused.

'We know, she's gone for coffee with Bill.' She notices my panic. 'What is it Lynn? You're scaring me now!' I try to slow down my panic breathing so I can explain, but my words start mumbling out not making any sense. My body starts shaking as I'm pretty sure I'm just about to start with a panic attack.

'I've got a bad feeling, a really bad feeling!' I finally manage to muster some words up. 'Have you called her?' Doreen looks at me concerned as the fear rises in her eyes.

'I've tried there's no answer.' She holds out her trembling hand to show me her phone.

'Call again, we need to find her.' Doreen looks at me panicked and tries to call Rita again. She's starting to pace around listening to the dial tone ringing. She shakes her head to let me know there's no answer. She walks back closer to me unsure exactly where to put herself.

'What is going on?' She softly says as she wraps her arm around me trying to calm me down.

'I don't know, there's something not right I can feel it, it's just seems too much of a coincidence Cora not coming in, Bill insisting Rita goes for coffee with him, and how the night ended last night. Then the man at reception. Do you not think it's all strange?' I look up at her and wonder if my paranoia is getting the better of me, or I'm going crazy, I'm not sure.

Doreen takes a deep breath. 'This whole holiday has been strange so far, I agree there's something strange going on and I'm not just talking about..' She whispers so no one else hears. 'The drugs. Maybe we should call the police?'

I debate this for a moment, then I remember about the tracking app I put on Rita's phone. 'The tracking app, il check this first before calling the police, you keep trying to call while I do this.' Both of us desperately typing away on our phones become oblivious to everything else that is happening around us. A man comes rushing out of the hotel and bumps right into me. My phone flies out of my hand and crashes to the floor. I look up to a see a young frantic man in a fluster, he looks more in a panic than I am.

'I'm really sorry.' The young man repeats himself in a panic. He can't be any older than 30, with dark olive skin and almost jet-black hair. His big dark eyes looked like they were about to fill up and burst into tears. I could feel his stress bouncing off him, his erratic tone and jitters were obvious to see.

'You okay love?' I ask the handsome young man. While Doreen is still on the phone unaware.

'Yeah, I'm fine, thank you, and once again I'm really sorry I didn't mean to.' He didn't even finish his sentence when he turned round, he only got a couple of feet away from us when he put his phone to his ear and holds onto his head with his free hand. You could see the young man really wasn't fine at all. Knowing I've got my own things to worry about, I turn back to Doreen to see if she had any luck.

'Rita! Rita you there? It's me Doreen.' Doreen shouts loud enough that it's attracted the attention of people passing by. 'Bloody dam voicemail I thought she answered.' Doreen then begins to shout into her phone. 'Look Rita, you need to call us back as soon as you get this!' She hangs up and turns to me and shrugs to say still no answer. Once Doreen is closer to me, I check over my phone, there doesn't seem to be any damage, so I carry on to find the tracking app, I'm just about to open it, when in the distance, the young man who bumped into me just seconds ago has completely stopped what he was doing and is staring right at us. I flash of anger comes across his face. I can't help but wonder what his problem is, so I look behind me thinking it must be someone else he's looking at, but no one is there. Doreen spots him too and looks at him confused. He starts marching back to us with a finger pointing in our direction. His pretty face is now filled with anger as he charges right to us. I tense up as he comes hurtling towards us, wondering what could be going on? I try to think if I've seen this man before, but I'm pretty sure I've never met him, he must have the wrong person, or he's crazy? Have I met him before? No definitely not! Is he even talking to us? I look round to check again, yep, he's definitely meaning us. The furious man is just inches away from me, and all I can do is gasp in shock.

'Where the fuck is cousin!' He is that close to me I can feel his breathe and spit hitting me in the face. I notice the shocked people passing by start taking a wide birth around us, but do not dare to intervene. Completely taken by surprise I can't seem to do anything, but just watch as this man keeps getting closer and continues to shout at me. Doreen however doesn't shy away from his confrontation and intervenes immediately.

'Excuse me young man!' Doreen says pumping her big chest up to move him back away from me. He moves back a couple of steps as Doreen moves forward. Slightly taken back by Doreen's outburst. His rage begins drop, and he becomes slightly nervous. Doreen is now confronting him and moving him back from his powerful march. Still pointing his finger although it becomes a little bit shaky rather than the sturdy arrow shape he had. I watch on as the overly confident man starts to crack under Doreen's pressure.

'You're the gangster granny?' He stutters out slowly, he notices that his finger is shaking, so he moves it down by his side then moves his hand to his hip, trying every position to keep his composure, he tilts his head up and points his chin more squarely to us desperately trying to keep his masculinity. 'You two' he waves his finger at me and Doreen, then realizes he shouldn't and quickly puts it back down to his side. 'I heard her on the phone to a Rita, that's one of the names my cousin had got in trouble with, and now she is missing. What have you done with her, and where is she? I've got your drugs here, but you're not getting them until I know she is safe.' Sweat is starting to pour out of the young man's forehead. I can tell he is scared, but the determination in his face tells me he's not messing about. I Figure out that this must be Cora's cousin, I breathe a sigh of relief, we really don't need anyone else gunning for us.

'You have got this all wrong, they aren't our drugs.' He rudely interrupts me before I can finish explaining.

'I don't care who they belong to, give me my cousin back and you can have them!' He steps back another step and clutches on to his man bag that he has across his body, like as though we are going to pinch it off him. I can see Doreen is losing her patience with the screeching, erratic man and walks a bit closer to him. Desperately trying to keep his distance from us, he jumps back in a flinch and holds onto his bag even tighter. 'Keep back.' His husky voice comes back rather than squeaky tone he had seconds ago. He rummages in his pocket and pulls a pepper spray can and aims it right at us. This time I flinch back, wondering what the hell to do, this man must be crazy. 'I'm going to give you one chance, where is she?' The eager in his eyes tells me he will start spraying if he has too. The shake in his hands has now vanished as he lines up the aim ready to spray. I can't quite work this fella out, one minute, he's scared and on edge, jittering all over the place, the next minute he's ready to attack us with pepper spray without even a flinch. "He must be on the bloody drugs!" I think to myself. I don't take any chances, so I take a step back, he notices me back away and eases his tense stance. Just as everything is cooling down into a more composed manner, I start to think of ways how to explain what is going on.

Doreen on the other hand sees her opportunity and lunges at the desperate man, taking us all by surprise.

'Oh no you won't.' Before we know it, she has his arm bent behind his back and is pulling it tighter, the more he struggles to break free. The poor defenceless man yelps out in pain. I can't believe what I'm seeing, and neither can the young man, as he hopelessly watches the can roll on the floor by his feet and I'm sure I see a flicker of regret creep over his eyes. Doreen keeps a hold of her tight grip keeping the young man's arm pinned.

'Doreen what are you doing? Let him go, it's Cora's cousin.' They both look up at me in their tussle, his eyes pleading with me to help him like a lost little puppy. Doreen's big boobs are pressed up to him keeping the man's arm pinned behind his back! I don't know if she just can't hear me, or she is too focused on keeping him pinned as she ignores my demands. I shout as loud as I can this time. 'Let him go!' Doreen snaps out of her trance and steps back dropping his arm, she holds both her hands up to show she no longer has a hold of him. I wonder if all this tension is getting to much for us, and that's why we are starting to act weird. I look at Doreen still in shock at her ninja skills, but also impressed at how fast she sprang into action. The young man steps even further away from Doreen and begins to massage his tender, stretched shoulder as he scowls nervously at her.

'Sorry about that, I'm a bit on edge these days.' Doreen says while giving a big pat on the back to the already sore man. The nervous man flinches from her touch. I don't even try and work out what I've just witnessed from Doreen, but that's not the normal Doreen I know! "I must have a word with her when I get chance, the stress, yes I'm going to blame the stress, it's likely getting to her too." We all take a second to calm down. Passers are now completely avoiding our area, not that I can blame them, we must look like a pack of nutters. I bounce my mind back into the now knowing time is running out, thinking of ways how to explain everything to this man, so it makes sense, although nothing much is making sense at the minute.

'I'm really sorry about that, but you need to listen to me very carefully.' The man looks at me curious but still very much on alert as I notice he darts his eyes to the pepper spray that's still laying on the floor. 'We aren't who you think we are in this.' The man straightens himself up and looks over his shoulder at Doreen, making sure he's out of her reach. Clearly still a bit uncomfortable to be that close to her I shout her to come and stand over by me. A reluctant Doreen does so but keeps her eyes on the young man, who watches her every move also. I wonder how she learnt such moves but know this isn't the time to start asking. When she is far enough away from the man I begin to explain quickly and as briefly as I can.

'I don't know what Cora has told, you but them drugs aren't ours, we picked up the wrong bag at the airport. The bag we so happened to get had the drugs in, we panicked, Cora got involved and here we are. We really aren't the bad guys here. We are looking for Cora too, but she hasn't landed in to work she was meant to meet up with us at some point this morning. Now our friend Rita is out with one of the lunatics who the drugs belong too!' I try to get the words out as fast as I can without anyone else hearing. The young man's expression changes to be more serious, and the confused look vanishes. I try to figure out if he believes me or not, as there is no hint in his face. 'I promise, I'm not lying to you. We are really trying to find our friends also, so if you don't mind hurrying this along, I've got an awful feeling that things are going to go terribly bad if we don't find them soon. You can help us or move out of our way so we can carry on, I'm tracking Rita as we speak.' I look at him waiting for an answer. He stands up tall and looks us both over then gently nods his head.

'Okay fine, but make sure you keep that crazy woman away from me!' He glares at Doreen.

'Oh behave darling, I'm harmless.' She says with a grin. They both stare at each other. He doesn't bother to answer her. I break up the frosty glares and start introductions.

'I'm Christos, Cora's cousin.' He points to himself suddenly his nervous expressions have completely gone, and a professional confident persona appears. 'I think you are right Lynn, something must be wrong Cora wouldn't miss work and wouldn't tell anyone know. She takes her work seriously and she needs this job.'

'Where is Cora's child if she's missing?' I remember that was one of the excuses why she had taken the drugs in the first place. Christo's looks at me with a confused look on his face.

'What? Cora doesn't have a child?' Me and Doreen raise our eyebrows at each other and tut. I start to wonder if this is another ploy or set up, I quickly shake the thought, we have no other choice right now, my main concern is to find Rita.

'She makes a habit out of lying that girl!' Doreen rolls her eyes.

'That was the reason why she stole the drugs, wanting a better life but needed the money.' The young man knows he's messed up with something and doesn't try to keep up with the charade.

'Woah, I don't know what she has been telling you, or what kind of mess she is in. she really isn't a bad person, she's been working every hour she could these past few years, so she can save to study and make a better life for herself. She's certainly no drug dealer! And she doesn't have any children.' He keeps calm as he tries to explain what he knows. Doreen is miffed with the back and forth stories and stops him.

'She actually led me to believe you're a drug dealer!' Doreen takes a step closer to him. 'You both aren't lying to us, are you?' Doreen moves even closer to Christos, I don't think she is trying to intimidate him, but it is coming off that way, Christos steps back and holds his hands up in defence.

'Wait, wait! I'm certainly no drug dealer she didn't even tell me what it is, I looked and seen what it was. I'm not lying to you I swear.' The shock in his face shows me he's being genuine. I'm getting fed up of wasting anymore time, the fact is we are all looking for someone, we need to concentrate on that, regardless of the messed up stories we all have.

'Give the man some space Doreen, we need to stop this now and focus and finding them.' Doreen steps back but doesn't take her eyes off Christos. She's not normally like this, I think this whole situation is messing with us.' I begin to apologise for her aggressive behaviour. He nods but keeps his distance from her. 'I'm tracking Rita on my phone, and it looks like they are by the beachfront if we hurry, we may find them there. Have you checked if Cora's home?' Christos looks at me as if I'm stupid.

'Of course, I've checked, there is no sign of her being there all night, her phone is now off so the only clue to where she could be, is now with your friend. They must be at one of the beach café's there's a few along there. Let's go I know where it is at.'

We all sort our differences to head off to the beachfront, waving down the nearest taxi that passes. Me and Doreen clamber in the back, while Christos takes the front, our eyes fixed on the red dot that's showing the location for Rita.

'To the beachfront please.'

CHAPTER 21

The beachfront is now in view, and the sight is breath-taking. The row of cafés and bars all line perfectly facing the beautiful clear blue sea. Each one having their own outdoor area with many tables and umbrellas protecting people from the strong rays of the sun, that's now beaming down on us, there's not a cloud insight just the open blue skies, the smell of the ocean fills the air as I inhale the salty scent. It really is stunning here, and it would certainly be the place to come and relax for many hours. I can't help but feel a ping of envy of all the people sitting enjoying the views, without a care in the world, while we are here desperately trying to find our friends and family and avoiding drug dealers that want to kill us. There is far too many people about for us to easily spot them, my eyes are darting everywhere looking for Rita's floppy hat, but everyone seems to be wearing them. I pull out my phone hoping it gives us more of an accurate location. As I do this Christos comes over and grabs it out of my hand.

'Let me check your phone again, so we can see where she is!' Although he had already grabbed my phone out of my hand before he finished asking, I let him carry on hoping he can understand it more than me. He begins scanning it then looking up at the row of cafés and bars then checks the phone again. 'It looks like they are over the other end.' He points in the direction. 'You see the one with the black and gold umbrellas?' Both me and Doreen follow the direction of his pointed finger, and nod when we see them. 'I think that's the one they are at so if we sit at this café.' He then points to a closer café. 'Then we might be able to get a good view of them without being spotted. Then we can see if she is okay first and then figure out what we should do.' I agree with him, knowing this is the best option right now. If Bill isn't suspicious already, he certainly would be if we rushed over "all guns blazing."

Doreen interrupts us not liking the sitting and observing plan. 'We need to go and get her now! We can't be waiting sipping coffee!' Doreen is getting flustered; I can see the heat of the sun is making her sweat and her cheeks are slightly turning red.

I'm about to answer when I'm interrupted again, this time by Christos. 'We can't just march over to her and drag her away; he will know something isn't right and if they do have Cora then we might never find her! We need to sit down watch and think what we are going to do next.' Christos and Doreen are now sizing each other up as I brace myself for another showdown between the two. This time Christos doesn't have the nervous behaviour he once had, if out he seems to be thriving in the action and gaining more confidence, so he doesn't back away from Doreen's objections, and soon a heated discussions erupts as they both fight on with whose plan is better.

'Stop this!' I shout determined not to be interrupted for a 3rd time. They both stop and look in my direction. 'Christos is right we can't just barge over, we need to be careful, he might also have a gun!' I try to finish my what I was saying when Christos interrupts me again.

'They are armed. You're sure you seen they had a gun?' Christos stares seriously into my eyes.

I look at him wondering if I should have maybe mentioned this before dragging him along with us, it does kind of change the whole dynamic of things. Oh well, too late he knows now. 'Erm yeah the other one had a gun with them last night, hidden under his jacket, Doreen was the one who spotted it.' He looks over to Doreen who is now nodding and telling him that its true. His whole posture changes into a more serious manner, I can see in his face he's taking a minute to think things through.

'This changes everything.' He mumbles as if not to say it out loud, but me and Doreen hear him, we look at each other unsure what he is going to do.

'You're not going to leave us now, are you?' I ask softly but it's enough to break Christos's deep thoughts. I know we have only just met him but for some reason having a man coming to help us makes me feel a bit more secure, so the feeling that he could maybe bolt on us is filling me with dread.

'No, but we need to get sat down and carefully figure out what we should do next. There is going to be no rushing over to get her, there's too many people here who can get hurt if things go wrong.' We all agree on this. I look round and see the masses of people floating about enjoying their day as normal, then a vision of a crazed gun man on the loose sends a shiver down my spine, I quickly shake the thought out of my head.

CHAPTER 22

We follow Christos to the café, being careful not to get noticed and look to see if we can see them. We watch on as he carefully inspects the tables then takes a seat with a view of Rita and Bill. Close enough to see them but far enough to be spotted easily. He sits at the seat that faces in their direction, which leaves me and Doreen having to twist round to be able to watch. It wasn't until we all sat down and order coffees that I began to wonder about Christos. I looked over to him, he is now rapidly texting something on his phone which seems to be buzzing a lot now. He looks at his receiving message and just looks at it for a little while, then looks over in Rita and Bill's direction then back down at his phone. His eyes seem to light up as he does this. Placing his phone back on the table next to him. I couldn't help but think that there is something more to Christos than he's letting on. I Glance over to Doreen to see if she has noticed, but she is too busy stirring her coffee and looking at the food menu and every now and then turning round to have a glimpse of Rita and Bill. I turn to face Christos again, who's still casually starring at them, I don't think he's even blinked yet. I look round to Rita, who's sitting there oblivious that we are here watching her. Instead, she looks rather relaxed with their lunch that has just arrived, too anyone else who could be watching you would think they were a couple, and likely would never guess the situation she was really in. I look back over to Christos and was about to begin to question him on how he knew who Rita and Bill are without us pointing them out. When suddenly his gaze changes elsewhere and a scowl comes across his face. I turn to see what has his attention.

I can only see the back of him, but I knew it was Earnie right away, the big bulky frame and the slow casual walk right up to Bill. I watch as Bill moves his chair out and stands away from the table, Earnie is now whispering in Bill's ear, Bill turns and looks at Rita and gives her casual smile and holds his finger up to say. "I'll be a minute." Earnie then slips a few notes to Bill, who then looks at them, then looks at Earnie, anger spreads across his face. I could read the words from Earnie's lips saying, 'I told you so.' Bill then nods his head to Earnie; Earnie then walks away leaving Bill and Rita. I look at Rita who is shifting nervously in her seat now, also unaware what the two were talking about but having an idea that whatever it was isn't good for her. Bill goes back to the table with what looks like a big grin on his face. He says something to Rita, Rita looks at her watch then nods. They must be finishing off their date. Dread begins to spill over me and knowing what them notes could be fills me with panic. I look over to Christos who now has his phone in his hand and is secretly pointing it over in the direction of Rita and Bill.

'What is he doing?' I mumble to myself having had enough of his strange behaviour. I start wondering who he really is, then I start feeling stupid at spilling everything to this man that we know nothing about. I see his phone laying back on the table and can't stop my urge at grabbing it to have a look to see what he is up too.

'What are you doing? Give me that back?' Christos scrambles trying to retrieve his phone, I however hold it up above my head desperately trying to keep it out of his reach. Doreen finally peels her eyes from the menu and looks at us confused, she says nothing and just watches us fight over his phone.

'What am I doing? More like what are you doing? You're up to something. Are you and Cora in this together? Or you on their side? I nod my head in the direction to where Bill is without taking my eyes off Christos.' Doreen has now put her attention fully to us and places the menu flat on the table, I see her hands now clenched into a fist ready to pounce. Christos looks shocked and darts his eyes back and forth between me and Doreen, unsure what he should say next. People on the next table look on unimpressed that we are carrying on and disturbing their peace. I notice that we are drawing to much attention and decide to tone it down. Christos realises this too and calms himself down. We both bicker in a whisper.

'Stop! It's not what you think.' Christos pleads trying to explain himself.

'I knew there was something not right with you the first time I laid eyes on you! You better start explaining.' Doreen says as she moves herself closer to him, she then picks up the fork that was set out, but keeps her other arm laid on the table, so anyone around would not notice, she then slips it down under the table and must have moved it pretty close to Christos's private area. Christos bolts upright and gulps. 'I've about had enough of this holiday now we really don't need any more surprises, what is going on?' Christos shifts uncomfortably in his seat. Doreen keeps her eyes focused on him and doesn't move.

'Okay, okay!' Christos raises his hands up. 'Please remove the fork away from there and I will tell you everything. Me and Cora aren't the bad people here.' He gulps while he waits for Doreen to remove the fork. I look on wondering if I should intervene, but I don't we need some answers.

'You keep saying that, but why should we believe you?' I look at his phone and see that he was recording Rita and Bill, I ratch further through more of his images and see pictures of us all from when we checked into the hotel, photos of the suitcases, us in the lobby, pictures of us at dinner with Bill and Earnie the list was endless, basically from the time we touched down till now he had images of us all. 'Why do you have pictures of us? What is this?' The anger is raging through my body now. Doreen must have prodded the fork closer to his man parts, as suddenly he stiffens up and lets out a squeak.

'It's not what it looks like, I can't tell you everything just yet just trust me. This is a lot bigger than......' He then cuts off what he was saying and jumps to his feet quickly and looks over in the direction where Rita and Bill are. 'Where have they gone? They've fucking gone! Did anyone see where they went?' We both look over to see the empty table. We shake our heads in shock. I can't believe we missed them going I stand up to my feet to help get a better view, but I can't see them anywhere.

'Give me my phone back.' He snatches it out of my hand and rapidly starts dialling a number. As he walks away for some privacy. He shouts back over to us. 'Try calling Rita again, you don't realise how dangerous that man is she is with.'

My palms are sweating, and my hands begin to shake as I open my phone to begin calling. Doreen still holding on to the fork, her mouth open and her head turning in every direction trying to find which way they went. 'There's no answer.' I stutter out. My head is starting to spin, and I can't help but think this could be my fault. Did the fight over the phone alert them? If I didn't do that then we wouldn't have taken our eyes off them. All kinds start running through my mind. The panic rushing in sharply is making my body heat up and my head begins to swirl. 'You don't know how dangerous that man is.' His words keep flashing in my head.

'I can't see her anywhere!' Shrieks Doreen who now stands up for a better look around.

'We need to move now.' Christos urgently says while still having his phone to his ear.

'Wait, stop! What is going on? How do we know we can trust you? You could be with them?' Deep down I know he isn't with them, you could just tell the way he acted and sprang in to action when they disappeared, the concern in his face looks sincere, but I can't help but wonder what the hell is going on.

'Lynn, we don't have time for this now, we need to go and find her, you don't understand the danger she could be in. You are just going to have to trust me on this' Christos strides over to the table where Rita and Bill where, before I could answer him.

The three us inspecting around the table looking for some clue, there is nothing. I look closer around and even underneath the table in case Rita has left anything. A Waiter comes over and ask's if we are dinning today but doesn't ask what we are looking for, instead he raises an eyebrow not wanting to know anymore. "More than likely thinking, here we go again with some more weird customers."

'Sorry not today, but the couple that were sat here just now, which way did they go?' Christos asks politely. The Waiter looks up wondering why we are asking.

'Sorry I don't know.' Shrugs the young waiter.

'Okay.' Christos pulls out his wallet and begins to roll out some notes, 'How about now? You any idea where they went to?' The young waiter's eyes light up seeing the cash, he quickly grabs the notes and pops them in his pocket before anyone else could see. Me and Doreen gasp at the quick exchange and look around to see if anyone has noticed, which they don't, everyone seems to be too interested in sipping their coffee's and tucking into their fancy salads to be bothered to even look up. We move in a little closer to the waiter, who now is cleaning down the table and trying to secretly give out the information without making it too obvious to anyone who may be listening.

'Listen.' He edges closer as if he's going to tell us some classified information. 'I don't know exactly where they went, but I overheard the man talking about showing her a boat he has in the harbour. That's all I know.' Christos nods and thanks the young man. He quickly heads out of the café area and is back on his phone, I follow more closely to try and hear what he is saying but can only manage to pick up some of the conversation. I try to sneak up a bit closer.

'Check boat owners on the harbour, and if there are any possible sightings.'

'Boat owners? Sightings? Who is this man?' I must have gotten too caught up in my thoughts that I hadn't realised that Christos had now stopped walking. He suddenly hangs up and halts his walk and turns around to face us again, only for me to slam right into him. I try to play it down and hide my embarrassment of being caught snooping. A shocked Christos on the other hand is glaring at me with his eyebrows raised. Waits for me to explain why I'm snooping. Of course, I ignore this and carry on as normal.

'So?' I say sharply taking a step back to give him some room. He seems to appreciate this, but not enough to tell us exactly what is going on. Doreen catches up to us still with her phone to her ear.

'Still no answer. Let's head down to the marina we might be able to catch them.' A panting Doreen ushers up beside us. As I start to agree with her and head to the roadside to wave a taxi down, Christos stops us before we can go any further.

'You both need to go back to the hotel now and nowhere else!' Before I can object Christos jumps in front of a passing taxi which comes to a hurtling halt just a few inches in front of him. He peers his head in and speaks to the driver, then turns back to us and demands we get in the taxi back to the hotel.

'We aren't going anywhere without Rita!' I snap at him. A frustrated Christos opens the taxi doors trying to urge us into the back seats. Of course I put up a fight and refuse, I see Christos is starting to beam redder and redder, not quite sure if it's with anger or the sheer embarrassment, as the once oblivious coffee drinkers have now focused their attention to us, while they casually still sip away.

'Please just get into the taxi!' Christos says through gritted teeth. I Still insist on making it hard for him. I cross my arms like a tantrum toddler and refuse to move. 'It's safer for you both to go back, you can't do anything more.' Christos is now gently trying to usher me into the back of the taxi, he manages to move me to the open back door. He gives me one final desperate push; my body finally moves with the momentum. I'm just about in, but I'm still reluctant to get pushed in that easy and grip a hold of the taxi roof with both hands, and try my hardest to push my body out, though anything below my waist has been nudged in. Willing not to give up I try my best to hold the top half of my body out, my fingers are now sliding away from the burning roof of the car, I can't help but notice the little whiff or sweat coming from my armpits, which my face is now fixed snugly under. "I inconveniently think to myself that I must wash as soon as I can." This however makes me lose my focus for a second making my grip become weaker and weaker. My last desperate pleas from my loosening grip, knowing I'm going to be pushed fully into the taxi any second was to start shouting and hope that a passer-by intervenes. I know that this is extreme and very, very embarrassing but it's the only thing I can think to do, with one hand gone and the other clinging on by a fingertip. I begin to shout.

'Get your hands off me I'm not going anywhere.' I screech a little too loudly which now has caught the attention of people passing by as well as those sitting trying to enjoy their coffee. I look around feeling the embarrassment, but I'm still determined I'm not getting in that taxi. Christos gives a little harder nudge; this time and I end up losing my grip and falling into the taxi seat. He quickly moves my feet, that I'm trying to stick back out, out of the way and slams the door shut and leans on it so I can't open the door. Doreen still eagerly trying to get in contact with Rita, can't be completely aware what is happening as she takes to the other side of the taxi and pops herself into the seat willingly next to me. Feeling betrayed I give an angry scowl at her but receive no reaction back, which is unusual for Doreen, she normally likes a little confrontation. Christos then tells the taxi driver to take us to our hotel and to make sure we only get out once we are there! He's extremely adamant that there will be no extra stops or turning back around. The driver agrees and holds his hand out waiting for the extra cash for his demands. Christos hands over some notes then stops, the taxi driver continues to hold out his hand insinuating to hand over more. Christos huffs but hands over the extra notes. This seems to be the way to get things done round here, I note this down in my head in case I ever need to do it. As the taxi begins to set off, I quickly pop my window down and hang my head out not being able to contain my anger anymore, I begin to shout like a lunatic at Christos.

'You won't get away with this Christos, I will find you! You bastard!' To my amazement Christos just grins back and casually waves. I notice the crowding people looking on in shock, their peaceful afternoons interrupted, then I hear Christos say to the concerned people.

'My mum. She's getting on and gets easily confused.' He shrugs his shoulders innocently at them. I see the pity appear on their faces and some begin to laugh. I can't seem to control my anger, I don't know if it's with all the stress lately or lack of sleep or I am turning to a crazy old lady, but I pop my head out of the window once again and begin to shout as loudly as possible as the taxi turns round to head us back in the direction of our hotel. Even though I'm no longer on the facing side of him, I still must shout.

'I'm not that old! And I'm not your mum you're a cheeky sod!' I hear the roar of laughter coming from the crowd. Embarrassed, I slowly slide my head back into the taxi. I look out the back window of the taxi and see Christos still casually waving with a big grin across his face! I sit myself back in my seat and let out a huge huff of frustration.

'Who does he think he is? He's only just turned up on the scene and he's dishing orders out!' I start mumbling out, waiting for a bit of support from someone but no one replies. I look up to see the taxi driver who is cautiously staring at me through his mirror, he notices me staring back and quickly shifts his eyes back to the road. Clearly thinking I'm a mad woman. I catch a glimpse of myself in the reflection of my window and can understand the judgement I've just received. I do look crazy; my cheeks all flustered, my hair puffed out in all directions and my eyes blood shot and sharp, and the thought of me hanging out the window screaming at him… I cringe to myself and begin to wonder if I am losing my mind. I turn my attention to Doreen who is now chuckling to herself. She seems me and instantly stops and pretends to ratch in her bag that's on her lap.

'What are you laughing at?' I turn my anger to Doreen. Who looks at me and casually winks.

'You need to calm down Lynn, we are nearly here now, look there's our hotel.' I follow her pointed finger. 'See we will be back in time for the bingo!' She starts rapidly winking at me now. I look at her muddled, wondering what the hell she is talking about, then think she's maybe joining me in the crazy gang.

'What are you talking about?'

'Look we are here now, come on let's go.' She smiles at me and jumps out the taxi that's now stopped. I wonder if I should speak, then don't bother instead I try to work out who lost their marbles first and when. 'Come on Lynn we don't want to miss the first round.' Doreen's standing there holding the door waiting for me to follow, still winking away. I slowly slide myself out without taking my eyes off her. I wonder if I should be concerned by her strange behaviour, she's maybe got a stress twitch and that's why she is winking so much.

Once we are stood out in the fresh air and being rather worried about Doreen my temper starts to fade. The driver zooms off as soon as the door closes, no doubt making sure we don't jump back in. As soon as the taxi is out of view, I look to Doreen. 'What are you playing at? We can't just leave Rita!'

'Calm down. We aren't.' Doreen hushes me. 'We weren't going to get anywhere with Christos, but we don't need him, we know where he's heading.' I look at her with a confused look and wish that I could start this day again.

'But we don't know who he is or what is going on. Why are you so calm?'

'I'm not calm I've tried calling Rita at least 60 times since and nothing! Her phone is just going right to voicemail now. So, let's calm down this erratic state.' Doreen wafts her hands over me as if trying to wave my craziness away. 'Let's go and find ourselves a taxi!'

Feeling quite relieved that we haven't lost the plot and the quick clever thinking from Doreen, a smile appears on my face. 'So, you don't have a twitch?' I have to ask. Doreen looks at me confused.

'What? No!'

CHAPTER 23

The ten-minute journey seemed to drag as we sat admiring each hotel we drive passed. Asking the driver to put his foot down so we can get there more quickly seems to be a mistake, he doesn't take this lightly and soon puts his foot down, leaving us pinned to our seats. The blurred scenery is whizzing past us at some speed now as he weaves in and out of traffic. Making my already anxious body more tense, I find myself trying to use an imaginary break peddle, while closing my eyes praying, we don't crash. I peep over to Doreen and see her clinging onto the overhead handle with one hand and her other hand keeping a grip on her seatbelt, she's puffing away through gritted teeth and her eyes bulge with terror. (Note to self: never ask a Greek taxi driver to go faster!) I eventually see the sea coming into view. I start thanking all my lucky stars that we have made it here in one piece. The hurtling taxi starts to slow as we enter the marina, and eventually comes to a halt in the parking area. Even though we have come to a complete stop, I find me, and Doreen have stayed in our tense positions. I'm pressing down that hard with my foot that I can feel shooting pains racing up my leg. Doreen is still clutching on to what I like to call, "The Holy fuck handle." Which is very fitting in this scenario right now. The driver chuckles to himself through his rear-view mirror amused with our horrified expressions. Doreen slowly turns her head to face me her mouth falls open and her eyes still wide, she slowly releases her grip from the handle.

'Well. That was some journey!'

We pay the chuckling man, and slowly lift our stiff, tense bodies out of the car. We watch as he races off out of view leaving us with sprays of dusts lifting from his spinning tyres.

Finally, we are here, dusting ourselves down as we try and regain our composure. Doreen is chuntering to herself while blaming me for the terrifying journey. Which I do take full responsibility for and imprint it, in my brain to never ask that again!

We both stand looking over the marina. It was beautiful, all different kind of boats and yachts littered everywhere. This place must be loaded with money. You could see it, possibly even smell it. Everything was pristine even the paths leading down were immaculately clean, everything just looked in its place even all the boats and yachts were lined perfectly in order, sectioned by sizes in each part of the marina, the flowers even seemed to bloom brighter, the air seemed fresher and the sea calmer it really took your breath away. The two of us just gazed out unsure what we should do now. The place was huge, far too big for us to search every part of it. I quickly scan all around the marina seeing if there is any sign of Rita or Christos, although it wasn't packed with people there was still too many people around for anyone to stand out. There are people sitting on their own boats enjoying the sun, having a few drinks with a late lunch, there was some working on them and making them more perfect than they already are, there's even some with cabin crew milling about waiting for their captains to return, then there are people like us just wondering around admiring these gorgeous things. We are almost to the first section of the marina where the smaller boats seemed to be docked. They were certainly still beautiful even if they are tiny compared to some. I look at them all pristine and shiny and think even these smaller ones must cost more than my home. I look over to Doreen who is gazing in sheer amazement, but can also see her edging frown creeping over, she doesn't take well to the fact that some people are so stupidly rich while some others are so unfortunately poor, which I do understand, but on the other hand I wouldn't be complaining if I was so rich that I didn't know what to spend my money on. I might have two boats, one for weekends and one for weekdays. I laugh to myself at the thoughts. If only...

'Just look at this place.' Doreen says taking in every bit of the perfect view.

'It's marvellous, isn't it?' I reply dreamily, thinking what it would be like to be a part of this kind of life.

'I suppose, if you like this kind of thing. No one should be this rich, it's stupid!' I wouldn't say its jealousy slipping into Doreen's tone but there's certainly a hint of envy. Who wouldn't be envious of this place it's absolutely stunning, sitting out on your deck with the mid-afternoon sun beaming down, while sipping on some wine watching the world go by... definitely got to be close to perfection.

'This place is Rita all over, she would relish in living this kind of life daily.' I can't help but say. She would fall right into place here and wouldn't stand out as an average working person would, probably like me and Doreen are now. I remember back to the glimpse I caught of myself after my crazy episode with Christos, if I still look like that now I will stand out like a sore thumb. I quickly ratch through my bag to dig out my small makeup case and apply some lipstick and smooth out my hair, I luckily have a miniature deodorant spray in there and rapidly spray my underarms before anyone sees. Knowing fine well it won't cure my desperate needed to wash, but it will have to do for now.

Doreen catches me trying to titivate myself up, and rolls her eyes, then holds her hand out for a spray of the deodorant also. She sniffs each pit and pulls a face to suggest the smell isn't pleasant. She doesn't hide her sprays but quite openly spritzes each arm pit in view of couple sitting on their deck that has been watching us. I see the woman shaking her head and can almost imagine her saying: "Bloody commoners!" Her husband screws his face up in a look of disgust. In my embarrassment I drag an unfazed Doreen out of their view.

'Wouldn't she just? She's probably sitting on one of those big things right now.' Doreen points to the bigger luxurious boats in another section. 'Sipping on champagne having the cabin crew run round after her, forgetting about the situation we are in! living a life luxury.' I hate to agree under the circumstances, but Doreen is probably right. Rita would soak this right up and make the most of it while she's there.

'I can't see her or Christos anywhere?' I look round while trying to shield my eyes from the blaring sun that's sneaking in around my sunglasses.

'Me neither and her phone is still going to voicemail. Why don't you check the tracker?' Almost forgetting about this, I quickly snap my phone out and open the app. I little hope excites me, only to be left disappointed a few seconds later. The tracker is off but does have the last place to be at the marina but doesn't tell us an exact location, so we are no further on to finding her. I look out to the huge, beautiful marina and realise this is going to be a long day. Be like finding a needle in a haystack.

'Well good news, her last known location is here, but that was over an hour ago and there's no more readings likely because her phone has been turned off! Why would she turn her phone off?' I take a deep huff and start looking round again hoping there is some glimpse of her somewhere, desperate to see her floppy hat and hear her la de da tone.

'Surely she wouldn't switch it off with what is happening right now.' Doreen's face turns white while she tries to process it all and I can see her mind is going into overdrive. 'He must have turned it off. What if he knows? What if he has taken her out to sea, we might not see her again, they could be anywhere by now!' Doreen starts to panic pace up and down the path and places her hand to her forehead, as though to try to ease her racing thoughts.

'I think it's time we phone the police.' The awful pit in my stomach begins to appear again making me feel sick. My hands start to tremble as I think through what Doreen has just said.

137

What if Doreen is right? What if he's taking her out to sea? What if he's holding her hostage? I find myself pacing up and down alongside Doreen. Giving in to the madness of the panic. 'What are we going to do? This is just getting to much I can't bare it anymore.' I carry on pacing trying to avoid the rising panic attack that's about to erupt any moment now. Doreen stops her pacing grabs hold of my arms.

'Snap out of it Lynn! keep focused!' She squeezes me tighter which makes me concentrate on what she is saying rather than my wandering thoughts. 'We can't phone the police just yet she might be fine, and we could possibly put her in danger doing that! I think we need to check around first and if we can't find her, then we should call them?' I agree what other choice do we have. We start scanning round and asking people if they have seen anyone who looks like Rita and Bill. Although most of the people don't understand what we are saying because they don't speak English or they are making out they don't, so they don't involve themselves, some are brushing us away with their hands, while some say they haven't seen her, even though they barely look at the picture we show them. We head further down where the posher bigger boats are. Some of these boats are huge, and must cost a fortune, but the beautiful boats all seem deserted. We quickly scan the first row but nothing and no one is to be seen, this part of the marina is defiantly a lot quieter than the ones near to the front. We begin to stroll down further where there is another deserted row. Feeling like we are getting nowhere anytime soon, I see an empty bench, so I walk over and take a seat, trying to gather my thoughts and decide what we should do next, is it time to phone the police or are we going to put her in danger if we do? Wandering around hopeless with no signs of her, is driving me insane with frustration and panic. Doreen joins me on the bench. We both just sit quietly with only a disheartened sigh to be heard. Chilling thoughts begin to appear, we will we ever find her? Is she okay? Is she still alive? I quickly shake the extreme thoughts away desperately trying to avoid letting them in. Doreen must have noticed and moves herself closer to comfort me, wrapping her arm around me to hold me tightly. Which makes me feel more secure, unsure if to hug her back or burst out crying, instead I do both. Before I know it, my tears are coming down fast and hard spilling down my cheeks. The salty tastes have now reached to my lips, and no matter how much I try to stop my flowing tears, they just seem to come thicker and faster, and now I'm losing all control of myself, even the thick gooey snot has made an appearance, I must look a mess, but I don't care. Doreen squeezes me tighter.

'Come on love, we will find her, and like we said earlier she's probably sat somewhere like lady muck sipping champagne with her feet up having someone running after her, and no doubt fanning her if she can get away with it.' I try to picture Rita doing the things Doreen has said and it almost works, until an image of her trapped and scared flashes in, and just about sends me over the edge, my body starts to tremble, and my lips are quivering with the tears continuing to flow. (I've finally lost it; the stress has broken me.)

'I think it is time we call the police.' I sniffle to Doreen who looks down to me and nods her head. She pulls out her phone and starts calling. Hearing the dial tone ringing, I wait for a voice to appear on the other end. Then I hear something in the distance. I prop myself up and turn and face Doreen, who has her phone to her ear, still waiting. Almost sure I've just heard something; I sit myself up a bit further to see if I can hear it again. Another soft mumble appears, but not loud enough for me to hear what is being said, I turn back to Doreen, but I still can hear the dial tone, so it's not that. Realising it's not coming from the phone. I quickly scan round to see where its coming from, but still, I can't see anyone here. Then I hear it crystal clear, and louder this time. I stand up and look around to check again.

CHAPTER 24

'Hello there, is everything okay?' A frail voice of a man takes shape. I'm Still scanning around with no idea where it is coming from. I hear Doreen now on her phone giving out our details but curiously wondering what I'm searching for. A little voice pops up again, this time in a shout!

'Behind you!' Me and Doreen swing our heads around at exactly the same time. Behind us, standing on the deck of his boat, is a slim skinny old man with a long grey beard that reaches down to his chest, where he wears a white and pink flowered shirt, his sand-coloured shorts reveal his knobbly knees. I look at him amazed, is this real? Or have I lost it and my mind is playing tricks on me? He speaks again. 'You ladies okay?' He shouts, wafting his straw hat as a signal. I wave back shyly, unsure if he's talking to us. I look around again to see that he can't be talking to anyone else, as we are the only ones here. He begins to shout over again. 'I've seen you ladies wondering about for a few hours now, are you lost?' Doreen stops the conversation on her phone and listens in to what the old man is now saying, I can hear the voice on the other end calling out, 'Hello, are you still there?'

'No, we are looking for our friend we can't find her anywhere, she went off on a date and hasn't been in touch since, we believe she could be down here but have not found her.' The old man listens patiently, and a creeping concern appears on his face, understanding that he could have stumbled upon a possible missing person's case.

'Argh I see, well I see a lot of things go on down here and I see some dodgy characters too.' Okay, well that doesn't help my situation right now, I think to myself, but continue to hear the man out. 'There was a young woman around here last night, young thing she was as well didn't look right with him, she was walking with one of the brutes who have a boat down there.' He points towards the bottom end. 'I'm telling you them two fellas look shifty mind, they've had a boat here for years, but never speak, I've told my wife for a long time that there's something not right with them, my wife tells me I'm just too nosey and should mind my own business.' Doreen slams the phone shut mid conversation. Realising that this must be where the boat is. I try to edge closer to the man desperately wanting to hear more. 'What does your friend look like?' He asks as I edge closer to him so we aren't shouting over the barrier, making sure that no one else can hear our conversation, being especially careful in case that is Bill and Earnie's boat.

'She's slim, perfect hair with blonde bits through. Probably looked classy, with oversized sunglasses and a huge floppy hat, about our age.' I try to muster as much information in one sentence as possible without trying to confuse him, as he already seems a bit eccentric. He stops and thinks about it for a minute. I shout back to get his attention again. 'She was with a man, who's tanned good looking, tall, oh and he has a scar on the one side of his face!' The old man's face lights up.

'Oh! Now then, I don't think I've seen your friend pass by, but that man sounds like one of the brutes I was on about. You better come over here so I'm not shouting, for preying ears might hear.' He glances all about as if someone could be listening in. Me and Doreen rush over to the old man. Unsure if he's maybe lost the plot or if he is telling the truth, but either way this the closest we have come all afternoon. As we get there, we hear another tiny voice shouting from inside his boat.

'Who are you talking to dear.' Then out pops a little old lady, looking very elegant, she must be in her 70s, but she looked good and so fresh. With a long white maxi dress and arm full of big chunky bangles, sporting a small white floaty hat, which her golden blonde wispy hair pokes out from under it. Her tiny frame shows she looks after herself, her slightly tanned skin made her soft pink lipstick stand out. Her skin glowed and you could see she looked after it, no doubt using plenty of suncream over the years protecting herself from sun damage. I suddenly begin to feel the burn of the rays on my skin and think I must apply more sunscreen as soon as possible before I turn cherry red.

'Oh, hello there.' She says warmly but surprised to see guests. 'He isn't bothering you, is he? He sometimes can't keep his nose out of other people's business.' Her tone was soft and pleasant, but suggests she has heard what he was telling us as she looks at him with a disapproving stare.

'No, he's not, he's actually trying to help us find our friend.' I reply softly back to her, hoping we aren't being an inconvenience to them. She notices the swollen redness in my eyes from me crying and looks at me concerned. For some reason women seem to notice the look of worry before you can even say anything, we just seem to have that instinct of knowing when things aren't right. I would spot this on my husband when he came home from a long stressful day at work, I soon spotted it when my daughter first found out she was pregnant, before she even told me. We just know that genuine look of concern. The look she is giving me right now.

'I see.' She answers. 'Well not many people are often down this end as you can see this part is usually very quiet.' I look right down at this almost deserted section of the marina. 'Are you okay pet?' The woman moves a bit closer and takes a hold of my hand showing she's truly concerned.

'I'm okay thank you.' Realising that we are intruding on this couple and would hate to think we would get them tangled into our mess, I decide we should probably leave. 'Sorry to bother you both, we will get on our way. Sorry.' The little old lady gives us a warm smile, understanding and a little relieved not to be having any hassle turning up at her door. Her husband however isn't satisfied with just leaving things like this, So, he turns to his wife hoping for her to offer some more support.

'They said that their friend is with a man with a scar on his face. Doesn't he have one like that down there?' He looks eagerly at his wife waiting for her to answer.

'Okay.' She looks a bit more curious this time, but slightly huffs in annoyance. 'Yes, he does but so do many other men, you seem to have a problem with them two down there, you're always talking about them!' She scowls at her husband, likely tired of hearing his wild stories on them two. She turns back to us again. 'There is a man down there with a scar on his face, but I haven't seen him with a woman walking down there. I only ever see him walking with another man, there both big fellas you know. I think they might be, together. You know like a couple.' She whispers not to let anyone else hear. I see her husband pull a face at his wife.

'There not a couple!' The old fella blurts out completely dismissing his wife's accusations. 'I'm telling you now, the two down there are wrong ens.' He nods his head to the direction of their boat, his face being totally serious. 'I have a good sense for these things, and I'm telling you they are trouble, you need to stay away from them, and tell your friend that too.' He still points his skinny long finger, to the annoyance of his wife as her face turns to a scowl, she's probably heard him saying the same thing far too many times. She turns to face her husband. Her Calming soft tone now changes to anger, the next thing we know a squabble has erupted between them.

'How the hell would you know their trouble? You wouldn't know trouble if slapped you across the face.' His wife shouts getting more annoyed at him. 'You don't half talk utter pants at times, have you taken your tablets today?' The poor old man starts to mumble to his wife who's now eagerly trying to usher him back inside. 'Don't take any notice of him, he's started to lose his marbles. Sorry we can't be of any help. But if you want to go and have a wander down there and have a look for yourself, it's just the big boat on the left, the very end one, I think it has gold and black letters on it. You probably won't find much, like I say nothing really happens on this end of the marina and its usually quiet, especially this time of year.' The women guides her husband back inside the boat, all while he's still chuntering away to himself, then everything goes silent as me and Doreen are left standing there.

'It's got to be them.' Doreen sounds hopeful. We both look down towards the other boat there is no one in sight, so now would be the time to go and check it out ourselves.

'It defiantly sounds like them, even if they haven't seen Rita doesn't mean she isn't there!' As we start walking along to the boat, I get surprised at far down it is from the top, although it didn't look it. It sits neatly at the very end, and I can't help but notice how deserted and quiet it is, with no neighbouring boats near like the rest, just theirs sitting elegantly on its own. Was this area to dock specifically chosen? It would seem that way if you wanted to kept out of sight and have more privacy, I gulp knowing exactly why these men would chose this area. Me and Doreen finally reach it. My heart is thumping away, and my anxiety flying all over the place, dreading what we are going to find or who may bump into. It would certainly take some explaining if Bill and Earnie catch us. I start to think of a cover story just in case. "We came for a stroll looking at all the beautiful boats!" Wouldn't it be too much of a coincidence to end up at theirs? I shake the thoughts out of my head and decide to deal with that if or when we are faced to. Doreen has started doing her pacing up and down again, I can see she is thinking about what to do next. We can't see much from down here the boat is too high, do we quickly climb aboard? The steps are right there, willing inviting us on! No, we can't! Or can we? We will only be a second. The niggling voices in my head seem to be arguing with one another, one full of courage, the other totally not. I look up at the boat, it is huge, and it absolutely must have cost a fortune. Knowing all too well that their job in "sales" isn't likely the only thing that has helped pay for it. (If so, I certainly took the wrong career path.)

All sparkling white, with chrome bars running along the edges, finishing off the expensive look with oak floors, and white leather seats on the deck. The black and gold words said Charlton, presuming that must be the name of it. There didn't seem to be anyone about or any crew members like some of the other bigger boats had, and there was no of Rita, not even a floppy hat in sight. Although the main living area seemed to be on the other side of the boat. So perhaps Rita could be in that part. I stand on my tip toes and try to peer over but it's no use, we need to go up to get a proper look.

'What should we do now? Should we go up there?' Doreen says as she edges closer to climb aboard, while peeking around making sure no one is watching her trying to sneak on, which obviously makes her look more dubious. I hesitate for a moment knowing that is probably the only way we are going to find out for sure. I almost say let's go, but then my objective thoughts pop up and discourages me.

'You can't just walk up there? We don't know if Bill or Earnie is in there or if Rita is there, we might caught, or It might not even be their boat.' I start screeching as quietly as I can to not attract any unwanted attention, bearing in mind there is absolutely no one around to hear, apart from the old couple way up at the top, but still, I try to keep quiet. Doreen carries on trying to scuffle up ignoring my pleas. 'We don't need breaking and entering to be added to the list of crimes from what this holiday has brought already.' I hope to distract her from going any further, but in fact it spurs her on. Doreen quickly looks round to me when she reaches the top and smiles.

'If we are already going down for something, what's one more added to the list going to do?' Then just like that she's away, sneaking closer towards the doors on the deck, I've now lost sight of her, my legs are wanting to go, and they almost take the step after her, but my conscience holds me back and makes me place my foot back to the ground.

'Doreen!' I shout but trying to keep my voice low. There is no reply on my first call, so I shout out again, still nothing. I begin to worry; I start thinking someone could have been waiting at the top and has snatched her. 'Shit!' I snap at myself knowing I'm going to have to go up there and find her. I quickly scan around to see if there is any weapons I could use just in case someone is waiting for me at the top. The only thing I can find is a stone, not a brick that could have been handy right now! A tiny, piss poor stone, it's about the size of a small tea light candle. I pick it up hoping it weighs more than it looks. It certainly doesn't! I throw it out into the sea in frustration, knowing it's about as much use as my lacey thong that's sticking right up my backside right now! Least with that I could maybe choke someone with it! The thought is horrifying and totally unachievable. By the time I would be able to take my long shirt off and pull down my swim suit to retrieve this thong, I'd be dead and buried somewhere. I don't always wear a thong with a swim suit, but going down for breakfast and pottering about it seemed fitting to wear one, although now, I'm not entirely convinced, and no doubt the red sore chafing marks will agree. I carry on with the task in hand and place one foot on the step, then the next, and the next, until I reach the top. I step on board and gasp. It really is beautifully finished, the smell of the rich leather hits me, the citrus polish making everything gleam and smelling amazing. I look round I notice not one thing is out of place, considering this belongs to two fellas I'm impressed. I find Doreen with her ear pressed to the tinted glass doors that would seem to be the entrance to the inside of the boat. She hasn't noticed me just yet, so I walk over slowly hoping that the wooden floors don't creek. Tiptoeing until I get to her, I reach out my hand and touch her gently on the shoulder, trying to be as quietly as possible. This however makes

Doreen jump and sends her pressed up face to bang on the glass. We both jump back in shock, then freeze waiting to see if anyone has heard us. The only sound I can hear is my heart thudding away and Doreen's heavy pants as she squeezes her tender nose. Doreen presses her ear to the glass doors again and holds her finger to her lip to tell me to be quiet.

'Do you hear that?' Doreen whispers. I lean my head in closer to listen, everything is silent.

'I can't hear anything. I don't think anyone is here.'

'Shh. There is someone here, I've just heard them.' Doreen adamantly says, slightly offended that I'm doubting her. I lean in closer and press my ear up to the glass alongside Doreen. Still not hearing a thing, apart from Doreen's heavy pants that are now hitting me in the face. I go to stand up fully and suggest we leave before some catches us. When I hear it. It's like a tiny little clank, it sounds very faint and could easily be missed, but it's definitely a sound. I press my ear to the glass again, this time the clanking is getting faster and louder. I start wondering what it could be, my mind fizzes with excitement and relief that it could be Rita.

'I can hear it!' I gasp back at Doreen, whose eyes are wide and alert.

'Rita!' She shouts out and without a second thought she tries the door. It opens and before I can stop her from darting in, she's entered and vanished from my view. Leaving me alone to look through the darkened doorway.

flat screen tv that's hanging on the wall beside it. Doreen reaches me and starts closely inspecting the well laced book shelf, slowly moving each book out and placing them back.

'Hello?' Doreen speaks into the book shelf. I try to work out what she could possibly be trying to do, when nothing happens, I begin to open my mouth to ask. When suddenly a frantic burst of banging appears from behind it. The shock from the loud bursts makes us jump back.

'Oh shit!' Doreen shrieks. I move closer back to the bookshelf as a scared Doreen slowly begins to back away from it. 'It's coming from in there?' She points her shaking fingers in the direction. We both stare at it waiting for something else to happen.

'Is someone there? Please, please help me!' The faint voice of a woman shouts out. 'Please help.' Then is followed by hopeless sobs.

'Shit! Someone is in there!' I yell to Doreen with a high-pitched squeak. 'Rita is that you?' A tiny bit of hope pings inside of me, As I'm already looking for a way to get her out, we could do this before anyone arrives back, we could get our things and head straight to the airport and get away from this place and the crazy people in it, in fact let's just leave our things, we will get her out and go! My racing mind starts getting ahead of itself.

'No, please get me out of here. Before he comes back.' The words crush me instantly and my imaginary plan is shattered. I listen to the desperation in her voice, it's piercing, the hope of it being Rita vanishes and my heart sinks. 'Please help me.' The tiny frail voice begins to cry. I know we can't leave her, no matter how easy it would be to do so, I just can't. Suddenly my body is pumping with adrenaline. I begin to search frantically on the book shelf for some clues, with the constant reminder of words ringing in my ears "Before he comes back." The words make me shudder, and then panic, if we get caught, we will be joining her.

'Listen love, we are going to try and get you out, but you need to be quiet, while we do so.' Doreen whispers back into the book shelf hoping to try and calm her desperate pleas.

'Doreen!' The tiny voice shrieks. 'Is that you?' We both freeze, who is this? How do they know Doreen? Doreen stops searching and we both look at each other. The unknown voice must notice our silent confusion. 'No, it's me Cora. Please don't leave me here! You need to get me out. He's going to kill me!' Cora's panic starts showing as she rattles on the other side trying to get out. Her outbursts become that loud that the sound is echoing around the room. I fix my eyes on the doors waiting for him to burst in and catch us. Cora has completely lost it now and is screaming, shouting and frantically banging. I now recognise her voice, it's Cora the one who stole the drugs and landed us in this situation. Her panic escalates and I wonder if she thinks we have left her, I could never do that, however the thought crosses my mind for a split second. 'Get me out of here! He will be back any minute!' Her cries bounce around the room. If you've never heard anyone plead like their life depends on it, then you will never truly understand the desperation, the shrieks, the chill it sends over your body, the ache it causes in your heart that becomes pure agony. I've never felt anything like it and hope I never have too again. I fight the panic in my body as it tries to tear me piece by piece, I can rather let it consume me and risk losing this trapped woman forever or I can fight it and give us all a chance of walking out of here. I chose to fight, knowing I'd never be able to live with myself if I walked away and left her.

I start helping Doreen search the bookshelf, row by row, book by book we raid each section. Nothing seems to work or stand out. Cora's cries become frantic as she realises time is running out and we might have to leave her. Each thud she lands starts to sound like she's losing hope. Defeated like a wild animal finally accepting it's deadly fate from its predator. The thuds slow down to almost a complete stop.

'Cora stay with us, try and keep calm, we will get you out. I promise we won't leave you. We just don't know how to do it yet.' I talk to her hoping to get a reply and to reassure her we aren't going anywhere.

'Lynn! You are here too! Oh, my goodness, you need to get me out of here, he is crazy! He kidnapped me and chucked me in this room, you need to hurry he's going to kill me I know it! There was something behind a book that he used to open it.' I feel relieved to hear her voice, although her cries are calmer, I can hear the shake in her tone. I carefully but quickly begin to start searching behind each book. Doreen follows suit and starts at the other end. My hands are trembling with fear, there is too many to search behind in so little time we have. 'Please hurry, he will be back soon!' I stop being so careful and start chucking each book off the shelf, not caring where they land or even if they can tell someone has been in searching. We need this young woman out and now, I quickly glance at my watch and notice we have been in here for a least 15 minutes already, how much longer can we get away without being caught in here!

'Is Rita with you?' I ask already knowing the answer. She can't be or she would have said by now.

'No, there just me in here. Get me out!' Her cries become shallow; she slowly bangs on the other side. 'They are going to kill us!' Me and Doreen both stop searching and look at each other, the hairs on my arms stand up, my throat goes dry, the sickly panic rises in my stomach.

'What do you mean us?' Doreen snaps back.

'They know! Just get me the fuck out of here.' I hear the fear in Cora's voice.

'Did you tell them it was us?' Doreen asks as I carry on searching.

'No, please help me.' Cora's cries are getting heavier and heavier, I can hear the start of a panic attack coming, she repeatedly thumps the other side and begins to scream. 'Help! Help.'

'Cora be quiet.' I try not to shout too loud, but with the panic rising it's hard not to. Listening to Cora's desperate screams sends a shiver down my spine. Not caring where the books land now I begin throwing each one off the shelf. I race on trying to find a button, which is a lot harder than expected when under so much pressure. My nervous consciousness keeps making me glance to the door, checking for the dreaded sight of someone catching us. So far, the coast is clear, deep down I know that won't be the case for too much longer.

'Found it!' Doreen shrieks and pushes down on the hidden handle, with a big heavy creek of the door, it opens slightly. Me and Doreen lean our full weight on and push as hard as we can to fully open it, finally the door gives in. We nervously peer inside. Everything has fell silent and the air goes cold. Sat on her knees facing us was a beaten Cora. Her tiny frame cowering down looked so fragile and shattered, she was almost unrecognisable, her once glowing appearance is now tarnished and broken. Her nose is bloodied, her puffy swollen eyes have turned black with mascara running down her face, her nails are torn, and her fingertips are bleeding from desperately trying to claw open the door. Her usual pretty, and confident self has completely vanished all remained was a defenceless, scared woman. It's heart-breaking to see, as my eyes start to well, the aching agony rips through me. (How could anybody do this!). Still in her work uniform she freezes when she sees us and I can see the hope in her eyes wanting this to be real. Suddenly relief floods over her, she tries to smile but her split lip prevents her doing so, as I watch her wince in pain. We rush over to pick her up, unsure where to grab her without causing her too much pain, we juggle around her, but everywhere we touch brings her pain. My mouth becomes so dry, and I can feel the bile rise up in my throat. The thought that anyone can do this to another person, let alone a strong man do this to a woman makes me feel sick to the pit of my stomach. Seeing her so frightened and beaten, I try my best to hold back my tears. Doreen begins to lift her up, but Cora's is too weak to climb to her feet, I grab hold of the other side of her and wrap her arm around my shoulders while I hold her round the waist. We lift her to her feet; she murmurs a small groan through gritted teeth. We now have her fully up and are trying to guide her out. I see the hurt in Doreen's eyes, this woman is in a bad way, physically and mentally.

'Sorry, but we need to get you out of here.' I feel a pang of guilt at giving her more pain with every jolt I make.

She looks at me exhausted and mouths the words. 'Thank you.' Her cracked lips rip open adding more wounds to her already bloodied bruised face. One eye is already completely swollen closed as the purple, black bruising has formed around it. She yelps out in pain when I accidently nudge her in the side. I apologise immediately and look down to see her lifted shirt reveal more bruising covering the side of her ribs. I gulp, this young woman hasn't just been held and beaten, she's been tortured!

Me and Doreen hold her up on either side and begin to make our way out of the hidden room. We try and move faster but surprisingly the young women was heavier than she looks. I give a glimpse round the room just as we are about to step out of it. lined with shelves full of art and locked boxes, supplies and booze, it looked like a hidden pantry, but at the far end was huge safe fixed into the wall, beside that was a single chair with what looked like rope tied round the arms and the legs of it, on the floor laid a small pool of blood. I look at Cora and see her wrists are marked with rope burns. In the corner next to that laid a couple of blankets and a bucket. I understood then, that they were planning on keeping her trapped. The bile that was sitting in my throat has now risen into my mouth, I quickly swallow the acidy taste back down. This confirms my suspicions, the poor woman was kidnapped and tortured. A sudden image flashes, Rita being in this same situation. The thought makes me just about fall to my knees. This time though I can't hold the acidy bile and it flies right out and lands on the floor just in front of me, leaving my throat burning with pain. Everyone stops and looks to me, Doreen, gives me a warm smile but her eyes urge me to keep going. Cora's not fully aware of what is happening, with her sheer exhaustion and dehydration she tries to muster all her strength she has to get out. I quickly wipe my mouth for any remaining trace and procced on, knowing it's only a matter of time before someone lands back here.

'We are almost there, keep going.' Doreen urges us on.

The two of us holding the limp weight of Cora push on seeing the daylight bursting through. I look up to see we are almost at the big leather sofas. My panting breathe has got heavier and heavier, I push the sick thoughts out that keep trying to pop up in my head, I need keep my focus on getting off this dam boat. My body aches, my head is thumping but seeing that we are almost there pushes me on.

The already dimly lit room goes darker suddenly! My first thought is that the clear skies have filled with clouds. As I slowly look up, I realise that I couldn't be any more wrong. I take a huge gulp and study what is blocking the light. It takes a second for it to register in my head, not sure why as the whole time we've been in here I've constantly thought about it. It must be the shock, but it throws me off balance. The light from the door that's leads to our freedom is now blocked by huge dark frame. It says nothing nor does it move. The cold dark figure just stands facing us. It didn't need to reveal itself to tell me who it was, the bulk of his frame was easy to identify along with the gun that is now in his hand. Me and Doreen freeze, the only thing that seems to move is my thudding heart and my eyes darting searching for another way out. There of course isn't one that I can see. Cora soon realises what has made us come to a halt, her body suddenly drops as me and Doreen struggle to keep her upright. Her soft cries start pleading. 'No, no, no.'

CHAPTER 26

'Going somewhere ladies?' A cold husky voice calmly speaks. He didn't need to speak, for me to know it was Earnie. He doesn't move from the open-door way, instead he just watches us, waiting for a reaction. My mind starts to race, I try to think of ways of how to get us out of here, the thought that this may be the last place I see burns into me. I start looking for anything to use as a weapon, but everything seems to be too far, and I know he would catch me before I even got a hold of anything, I seem to think he knows this, he knows we are trapped, we aren't strong compared to him, he knows he's got us. Although we can't fully see him as the light trying to Shine through behind him, disguises him, but I can see the smirk that has appeared across his face, his crooked smile bares his white teeth, his eye sharp and hungry, knowing we have done him a favour by being here for him to catch us all together. He moves his arm to point the gun in our direction. He slowly steps in from the doorway, each step he takes starts to reveal more and more of his features, his eyes dark and serious, his mouth in a cruel grin, he's got the power and he knows it. I let out a shriek and jump back, he is now almost in touching distance. Cora begins to cry knowing what fate awaits us, I've got a rough idea what that will be, but still I can't move, my body is paralysed with fear. I can only hope what he does have planned is quick, I somehow doubt that, he's enjoying it too much. He is going to break us down piece by piece until he has had enough. The thought makes my whole-body tremble, starting at my knees going upwards until my full body is dithering. Cora starts pleading with what little energy she has left in her body.

'Please no, just let us go.' Me and Doreen hold on tighter to the quivering Cora, not that our bodies are much steadier, I desperately try to stop my knees from giving way, I can't fall, I can't give up, I can't end like this!

'You are not going anywhere, none of you are! Now sit the fuck down and shut up!' He ushers us with his pointed gun to the sofas. We all slowly ease ourselves into the sofa that his facing him. I never take my eyes off him or that gun, that I can now see right down the barrel of, a black pit of nothing. Nothing is said for a moment, as we wait in silence for what is to come next. I watch as Earnie is deciding what to do with us, he starts pacing back and forth but never leaving enough room for us to run. One thing for sure is, he isn't planning on letting anyone leave. The panic that's bolting around my body is making my head spin, I'm not sure if I'm going to be sick or pass out, I cling a hold of Cora's hand even tighter. Cora sitting in the middle notices and returns a gentle squeeze. I can hear Cora's soft sniffles as her tears begin to flow down her cheeks. I turn to look at her and try to give her some comfort. Doreen also moves in closer, we all huddle up dreading what is to be next. I almost think about screaming, would anyone hear? I doubt it we are too far from anyone, the closest people to us will be the old couple we spoke to earlier, I highly doubt they will be aware we went inside the boat. How can we be so stupid? Why didn't we phone the police? I start to get angry at myself at being so careless, I never thought that if I was in this situation that I'd be this stupid! Hindsight is a wonderful thing until it's upon you.

'Stop fucking crying! You brought all this on yourself.' Earnie snaps, his voice is deep and angry. It sends the three of us to jump. He laughs when he notices it has made us even more terrified. You can see the thrill he is getting from this; he starts to relish in it, absorbing all the mighty power he holds. He stares right at us with no glimpse of compassion he doesn't care, he has three hostages trapped, terrified, one already beaten, and he's ready to go again. It's becoming clear this isn't the first time he's done this sort of thing. It's too natural for him, he's too calm and most of all he's enjoying it. His movements are slow and smooth, the grin he has across his face tells me he thinks he's untouchable, which against us he's probably right. I start to despise him, from the moment I first seen him I knew he was odd, his behaviour now confirms it. I start to wonder what drove him to be like this, was it childhood trauma? Or was he just born with a dark soul, either way I have no sympathy for him, I hate him, I hate how we were put in this situation, I hate how he can scare me so easily, for what he has done to Cora, what he might do to Rita and most of all I hate him because he's going to be the one that ends my life! I start to play with my husbands wedding ring that's tied onto my necklace, hoping it brings some kind of comfort, it does not. 'See you lot have caused me a lot of problems and cost me a lot of money. You almost got away with it too! But your Dolly bird friend slipped up!' He smirks even more. I try to think what has happened for her to slip up knowing deep down that she would never put is in danger unless she was forced, the thought sends a shudder through me. Is Rita trapped somewhere? Is she still alive? Everything starts flying through my mind. I dart my eyes to Doreen, and hers dart to mine, she looks worried thinking exactly what I am. Then anger rises in me. I've never wanted to kill anyone before, but I do him, I want him to die, I want him to suffer, I want him to vanish off the face of this earth!

'You better not touch her!' His laugh is cold, as he starts wandering back and forth absorbing every bit of this moment, making sure he keeps us trapped on the sofa. He's comfortable in this situation and he's only just getting started.

'Don't worry she's perfectly safe with Bill, for now!' He laughs once again. 'See I knew there was something up with you three at the bar, but Bill wouldn't have it, I think he took a liking to Rita too much to see past it, he talked about her all that night. Obviously, his views have now changed!' He grins and shakes his head. He wants this attention, he's loving it, then I wonder if this is the only thing that can make him feel like a man, if so it's a pathetic one at that. 'See not only did you steal our drugs, but she made a fool of Bill, he does not take well to being made a fool of. I can only imagine the fun things he's going to have in store for the lovely little Rita.' His laugh sends chills over me and I can feel every hair on my arm begin to stand. I feel the sick rising in my stomach at the thought, then I feel my lip curl up angry at him. I dig my nails into the side of the sofa trying to stop my urge to leap up and getting myself killed. I feel Cora squeeze my hand tighter to hold me in place, sensing I'm about to do something stupid.

'You're a maniac! You will never get away with this!' Doreen shouts back her anger starting to erupt. Unfazed by her outburst, he just shrugs and carries on.

'Well, you see, we kind of already have! No one knows you're here. There are no cameras down this end of the marina, and as you guessed walking down here there is no one about. It's one of the reasons we chose this place to dock. We like our privacy you see. I was already out looking for you two.' He points to me and Doreen. 'I almost had given up for the day, so you can imagine the excitement I got when I found you both here already.'

I try not to give him a reaction no matter how much I want to shout, scream, hit! I sit as still as I can, hoping it takes some joy away from him. The thought of the room rushes in my head, we probably aren't the first people to be held here aside from Cora, and I doubt we will be the last. I Start wondering if Christos is on the marina, have they tracked down which is their boat? I don't care who is anymore, I pray for him to find us before it's too late, then I remember he thinks we are back at the hotel, another stupid thing we done, I curse at myself, we were warned how dangerous they are and we still didn't listen. "I'm a fucking idiot!" I try to swallow but my dry throat seems to be stuck together, a flash of another two chairs added to the room jumps into my mind. We are doomed!

'First of all, we thought it was just this pretty young thing, well she was pretty until I got hold of her.' He places the end of his gun under Cora's chin to lift her head up making her look at him. She closes her eyes tightly and jerks herself away. He removes his gun from her chin and carries on talking with it swinging in his hand by his side. Teasing us, reminding us he has the power to do whatever he wants. 'She was so quick to give us that last note, that I knew she must have had something to do with this, or she knew who did! So, I waited and waited until you finished your shift. You really shouldn't walk alone on dark late nights; anything could happen to you!' His laugh is pure evil as it roars out of his mouth. I've never wanted to slap someone across the face as much as I do with him. He's a predator and he loves it, the thought of him hiding waiting to pounce on a woman doesn't surprise me at all! 'She was loyal to you ladies though, she never once gave me your names, even after beatings, she remained tight lipped.' This time Earnie uses his free hand and slowly cups her face and wipes his thick thumb across her cut lips. Cora flinches out of his grasp, he doesn't seem to mind, he's too eager to carry on with his story.

'This young pretty thing can certainly handle the pressure, I tried to be nice at first and gave her the chance to come clean, she wouldn't give nothing away, so I had to drag her into the room which looks as though you found.' He points to the open hidden door as we all follow his finger. Seeing all the books scattered along the floor, I look further in and see the chair he used to tie Cora to, her blood lingers on the floor. I quickly snap myself back round to face Earnie, then look at the open door that waits in front of us. I desperately want to run, could I make it? I need to stop thinking someone is going to come and save us, there not! We are here and no one knows, if we don't fight back, we are going in that room and surely, we won't be coming out alive! I gulp at the thought, but start thinking what I can do, and wait for my chance. 'As you can imagine she put up a fight, so had to tie her down to the chair, after the first hit she laughed, can you believe that? She soon stopped laughing though when a few more followed.' He chuckles to himself, while we look on horrified. He's clearly insane, he must be. 'Anyway.' He proceeds on. 'I had to stop her punishment when she stopped answering back, I've been strictly told not kill anyone until I'm told to do so, and she looked like she had enough, so she got untied and a little piss bucket threw in, can't be having a mess over our nice clean boat can we.' He sarcastically teases her and squeezes her cheeks with one hand. I look over to Cora and can see she is bubbling with rage. Not only is he wanting to hurt us, but he also wants to humiliate us. I start to understand his pathetic behaviour. It's not just about the drugs, or being made a fool of, he hates women! It makes sense now, no man in the right mind would treat a woman like this unless they truly despised them. He doesn't respect a woman, women are worthless to him, he can't have ever truly loved a woman, it's just all hate. I start wondering who may have turned him like this, his mother? Girlfriend? Rejection from an admirer, the list could go on, whoever it was, has certainly made him into this monster.

'You're a fucking animal!' Cora spits at him! He laughs again. I hold my breathe dreading what is about to unfold and know things are about to take a rapid turn. He's not going to take that lightly, not if I'm right about him!

'She's feisty as well.' He pulls out a tissue from his pocket and slowly wipes the spit away ever so casual which I find more unnerving. I uncomfortably shuffle in my seat; we all look at him waiting for his reaction so far, it's too calm, like a storm waiting to brew. Then just as we don't expect it, in a split second he hurtles his body to her, and this time grabs her by the throat and pushes her back on the sofa, holding the gun up to her temple. 'Don't fucking tempt me!' His puffing grunts echo down my ear along with the choking sound of Cora, desperately trying to breathe. I don't even realise that I'm screaming until everything goes silent. I peer through my hands that are covering my face dreading to see what is happening. Just as fast as he pounced on her, he lets her go and steps back to finish what he was saying. He's let her go, something is not right, I just know this isn't going to be forgotten about so easily. I look at Cora as she carefully holds onto her neck, I can see the red imprint of his big fingers where he's squeezed her too tight. She coughs trying to get her breath back. 'Me and Bill had a long night trying to figure out who took it! Wasn't until we landed back at the hotel, we were sitting there convinced it was just this little minx involved.' He points at Cora who jumps back scared, half expecting another assault. 'We come to this hotel quite often and for many years, never had any issues. But you, Cora, seem to be always sniffing about when we arrive, but this time you were more determined at getting involved with us. I noticed you made sure to be checking us in even, when you were in the middle of sorting some other lovely customers. I thought at first it was maybe because we are long returning customers, and we do tip well.' He smirks proudly to himself. 'But somehow your always there, when I noticed it was you delivering all the notes and sorting the cases also, it started getting me thinking. You must have known more than you were letting on. The last note though was the final straw, even if it wasn't you, you sure knew who it was, and that's why you're here now.' He stops pacing and stands to face us all. 'I could have sworn you had taken it. Until now this is where your little dolly bird friend pops in.' He waves the gun towards me and Doreen, my face barely moves, my throat is getting dryer and dryer to the point I feel like I have a huge lump in my throat, my eyes stinging with the urge to blink but somehow, they won't, I can't, I need to keep focused, we must get out of here! 'See, when all the notes were lined up in front of me, it got me thinking. As you can probably guess, I don't trust a lot of people. I just happened to glance at the number your friend Rita wrote down for Bill, and surprisingly they are very, very similar!' He stops talking for a second to see if we would give a response. His glare cold and dark eyes wait for a guilty plea, but we say nothing, I try to keep my eyes focused on him even though I'm desperate to turn away, unsure if he's testing us or toying, I'm too scared to move, too scared to breathe to scared to wipe my watery nose. Then suddenly Cora breaks the awkward silence. His focus shifts to her, as I finally breathe again.

'It was all me! They had nothing to do with this, just let them go. Do whatever you want with me, but please just let them go, they are innocent in this!' Her pleads are powerful and sound genuine. I'm shocked that she is putting herself on the line for us after what she has already endured at the hands of him. I look round and her stare is fixed on him, she isn't scared this time and she doesn't blink. I begin to admire her courage and determination, but I know she can't take all the blame for this, it has just been a messy misunderstanding, and no one should be beaten or tortured or even killed for such thing. It seems so ridiculous as I think about it, then I remember he's not such a normal person, he's a psycho who hates women, so given any opportunity to cause harm, of course he's going to! It doesn't matter how much she pleads, he's letting no one go, that's never been his intentions, his only thought is on how he's going to make us suffer and then who he will kill first.

'Stop it Cora!' Earnie begins to laugh teasing her which angers her, she jumps to her feet and moves closer to him. I knew instantly that this is going to end badly, Earnie tenses his body ready for what Cora is about to do, you could have easily missed it, but I saw him flinch, is he scared? No of course not, she's surprised him, I bet he's not used to women standing up to him. As she moves closer to him, close enough that they are just inches away from each other. Cora stares right into his eyes, her fist clenched, even with an already bloodied and bruised face, she doesn't stop. I watch the shock sweep across his face, he's confused, he's never had to deal with a woman squaring up to him, why would he? He's huge and strong, most men won't even stand up to him, never mind this skinny half beaten woman.

'It was me!' She says right to him without blinking, her teeth gritted together, she stands her ground and doesn't move an inch. I see this infuriates him, his eyes turn almost black as the rage is bubbling inside him, but she's caught him off guard, and he's not so sure how to react. Earnie stops laughing as he shuffles from foot to foot, unsure how to handle her outburst. He is the first to move his gaze and he looks over Cora's shoulders to me and Doreen. We both continue to watch on in horror, scared to see what is about to happen. He notices our fear and adjusts his posture and confidence and stares right back into Cora's eyes. His dark eyes are focused. Just in that spilt second, Cora doubts her courage and glimpses back to us, which becomes a huge mistake. His reflexes are sharp, with the momentum of Cora turning around, he smashes the gun to the side of her head. She flies back into the sofa. Clutching her head, the blood starts to seep through her covering hands. I scream so loud I feel the burn in my lungs. Me and Doreen lean over her to try and protect her from any more blows. She was barely conscious, her groans becoming weaker, her body starts to flop lifelessly. The blood was pouring right over her. Doreen grabs a cloth that was on the table and presses it to her wound, I hold her heavy head back and try to remove her blood-soaked hair out of her face.

'You are going to be okay, just stay with me. Don't close your eyes.' I keep whispering to her not caring if he hears. I'm covered in Cora's blood; her eyes look at me desperately trying to stay open. Me and Doreen both trying to put pressure to her wounded head and keep her awake. Earnie comes rushing over screaming. He's lost all control of himself.

'You think I like doing this sort of thing to a woman!' He comes over frantic and wild. 'I have to do this don't you see?' I don't know if he is trying to justify his actions, or he is just a complete psycho! I stare back at him desperate to jump up and hit him. He steps forward to us, grabs a limp Cora by the hair and pulls her up off the sofa. I jump up to try and protect her from him, trying to cling on her body as she slowly groans out in pain, this time I can't hold my outbursts of rage anymore. This is it, the time to strike while he's already been taken by surprise, if we don't fight back now, we will never see the outside of this boat again. The adrenaline pumps through my body as I prepare myself.

'You leave her alone.' I shout trying to hit him as hard as I can with my fists. He lets go of her hair, pulls his free hand back and slaps me across the face. The power of his slap sends me flying, I land on the floor in a heap. In total shock I just lay there, my hand pressed on my face. The searing sharp pain rising a long one side, the ringing in my ear is pounding through my head. I'm sure I lost a few seconds. I look up to see Cora slumped over on the floor. I try to pull myself up off the floor but my weak knees and dizzy head from the hit I've just received has wiped me out. I see Doreen darts up, the anger in her eyes as she tries to jump in to help but he's too quick for her too, he swirls the gun round and points it right in her face just in time before she reaches him. Doreen halts herself to a stop and places both hands up in surrender. I look on helpless the gun is just inches from her face. It's no use, he's won!

'Don't you even think about it, you really thought you could take me on, look at you all, your pathetic!' He begins to laugh in Doreen's face, his face twists with excitement as he regains control. His teasing laugh halts and his dark gaze freezes on her. Doreen's face now looks scared. She says nothing and hasn't moved an inch her hands are still up in surrender. I try to heave myself off the floor, but nothing seems to move, I dart my eyes back over to Doreen. Her stare still fixed on the gun that's still pointed at her. Earnie eases his stance and begins to lower the gun. 'Well, you've made my decision easier, I know who I will kill first.' Doreen's eyes shut tight for a second then opens them as she composes herself to face him.

"Fuck you!" She sneers.

Earnie mocks her and tries to diminish her courage. 'You all have some balls on you, I'll give you that much.' In that instance he grabs her by her hair and yanks her down to the ground, so she is now on her knees with him standing over her. His huge body blocks most of my view, I begin to panic, he's going to shoot as he aims the gun to her head. I start frantically shouting, trying to do anything to take his attention off Doreen.

'No!' I shout, 'You piece of shit! You're a coward, you're not a man!' Still unable to move fully I just lay struggling trying to distract him. Earnie has the gun pointed to Doreen's head still. He hears my shouts but never turns his attention away from Doreen, but it does hold his finger from pulling the trigger. I shout more. 'You fucker!' 'Have you got to do this, so Bill doesn't get his hands dirty? You're the one that goes down for murder while your boss walks away!' I see his stance tense up, and the slight turn on his head shows me I've hit a nerve.

I finally gain his full attention! He swings his full body around and storms over to me.

'I've told you to shut up!' He now starts shouting in my face, I feel every spray of spit hit me. His anger has reached to boiling point, his face flames red, he bares all his teeth and I can see the beads of sweat forming on his forehead. He now points the gun to me, his steady posture has vanished, he tries to steady his shaking hand, but his anger is too far gone. He's going to pull that trigger, I can see it in his eyes. His screams are piercing my ears. Doreen looks over to me and we just stare at each other, knowing these are going to be our final moments. Doreen starts to scream at him.

'Look at you, a pathetic excuse of a man. What is your boss going to say when you kill us, he won't be happy you've disobeyed his orders!' She shouts knowing it's going to belittle him and uses the words that fuels his rage hoping to distract him. I watch as his blood shot eyes start to twitch, I can see he's thinking of a reaction as he stops his screams at me and lowers his gun from my head, I close my eyes in relief.

'He is not my boss! We are business partners!' His lip quivers as he screams back at her.

'Really? Why are you here doing the dirty work and he isn't? I bet it's always you that does these kinds of things, while he's nowhere to be seen.' This completely freezes him; I see him thinking it through in his head which makes his guard fall. Suddenly the barely lit room goes even darker. This takes everyone by surprise, unsure what else is happening, my eyes begin to dart around the room, someone else is here, I can see them coming closer, my heart skips a beat. Is it Bill? I gulp as a look back to Earnie. He is totally unaware, which makes me think that it is him. He maybe has noticed him or is he expecting him. Panic pulses through me as I try focus my eyes on the unknown figure. It's racing over fast.

CHAPTER 27

'I can do whatever I want!' Earnie growls has he spins around and points the gun to Doreen. The rushing figure raises something high above their head. Earnie finally notices and spins around to face it.

'What the...' Earnie begins to say when suddenly a swoosh of something hits over his face, the draft of the swoop brushes across my face. Timed perfectly for him turning around just as he was pressing the trigger. The gun goes off with a loud bang. I scream out, terrified to see if Doreen has been shot. I watch as if in slow motion the big lump of his body flops to the floor beside Doreen. I can't fully see her as she's lying on the ground behind him. I frantically scream her name, desperate to see movement. Nothing moves for a second, I feel my frantic screams burn everything inside of me, She can't be dead! Please don't let her be dead!

Finally she gasps out and lifts her head above his bulky lifeless body. We both stare to each other shocked, scared and trying to figure out what has happened. I'm too scared to look anywhere else. Then I hear a little familiar voice speak out.

'You girls okay? I knew these two where dodgy characters! My instincts never fail me.' The darkened figure steps closer and helps Doreen her feet. He then finds a light switch and flicks it on, the room lights up, and reveals the shocking states inside. 'Oh, my goodness, what has he done to you all, looks like I've just got here in time.' He takes a look around, his mouth falls open when he sees the hidden room. 'I seen him coming back to his boat and got a little worried when I didn't see you both walk back up.' Doreen stands in shock unable to speak but instead just shakes uncontrollably. The little old man comes over to me and helps me to my feet. With his help I finally managed to get up, still a little wobbly, I grab the little frail man from the boat and squeeze him so tight, that it makes him almost topple over.

'I'm so glad to see you.' I thank him relieved to still be here, well I think I am, I pat down my body making sure everything is still intact. I quickly glance over everyone else, wondering where the bullet strayed too. I see a small circle hole that makes the light pour in on the wall behind Doreen, it must have missed her by inches. We will never be that lucky again.

'No problem at all, I always knew there was something off with these two, I'm just glad to find you all safe. We better get going before he wakes up.' The old man bends down to pick up his walking stick that he used to hit Earnie with. There's a little moan that comes from Cora's fragile body. The old man notices her crumpled over. 'Oh my goodness what have they done to this poor woman!' He almost looks like he could cry as he sees her fragile bloodied body on the floor, he rushes over but Doreen beats him to her and steadies her to her feet. She mumbles something.

'It's okay love you are safe now.' Doreen reassures her.

'Phone!' She mumbles more clearly this time, and points in the direction of the cabinets where the decanters lay perfectly in position. I debate taking a drink of one, I certainly could do with it. I peel my eyes away to search for her phone, there isn't one in sight.

'Here.' I quickly hand over my phone to her not wanting to waste any more time. Without another word she snatches it and begins to dial a number. As we all begin to gather ourselves up, ready to leave quickly. My body has almost stopped shaking but can still feel the stinging thud on my face, I catch a glimpse of myself in the mirror, the raw print across my cheek is bright red, my eyes all blood shot from crying, I stop and look at myself for second trying to recognize the woman looking back at me. When a thud of the door makes me jump, everyone gasps unable to take any more shocking surprises we look at the door ready to pounce.

'Arthur! What are you doing in here.'

'Bloody hell Betty! What are you doing creeping up on us like that!'

'What the hell is going on here.' Betty spots the carnage in the room, then looks over to the lifeless body of Earnie still laying on the floor. 'What have you done Arthur?' She the looks round to see the blood-soaked Cora. 'Oh, dear are you okay? Tears just roll down Cora's face as she nods. The little old woman rushes over to her to help her walk. Betty's face turns white as she begins to understand what has been happening in here, she quickly tries to usher everyone out into safety, she totally ignores the lifeless body of Earnie as she steps around him to get to us, but I can see a sneer of disapproving look when she looks at him.

'I told you they were up to no good these fellas.' Arthur stumbles over to his wife with his walking stick. Betty is horrified at what she is seeing ignores her husband and begins to urge us out even more quickly while checking that the man on the floor hasn't moved.

'Come on we need to get you out of here and somewhere safe before he wakes up. Has anyone phoned the police?' We all start rushing out, making sure the injured Cora gets safely out first. Doreen and the old woman help an unsteady Cora to her feet, keeping her propped up from falling back over. A wobbly Arthur follows with the help of his walking stick. I start to follow the rest out, getting closer and closer to the beams of the sun that waits outside from this dark, musky boat. My thoughts are going crazy as I try to process what has just happened. This must have distracted me from hearing waking groans of Earnie, I only notice when a see a flicker from the corner of my eye. Something has just moved. This stops me dead in my tracks. I listen as my brain tells me to run, but I can't move. I need to run! My delayed reaction starts to kick in as finally my leg lifts to move, but it doesn't move the way I want it, it feels trapped. There's only me left in here, the rest have made it out. I'm glad of this but then quickly realise that there is no one here to help me, I start to panic. I look up to see the brightly lit doorway, I'm so close I can feel the cool breeze of the sea air drifting in. Then I feel it, the tightly gripped hand that is pressing sharply into my ankle. I let out a huge yelp, which makes his grip go tighter. I turn to see Earnie slowly regaining his consciousness, although he was still half kneeling on the floor and still injured from the blow to his head, his grip was solid. I look at his cold dark eyes, he wasn't about to let me go, not for a second time, his grin shows his teeth as I suddenly fix my eyes on the slaver that is escaping from his mouth, he looks like a monster. He is a monster, and he is determined to kill me. I try to jerk my leg free, but it was no use, his grip just got tighter and tighter, he pulls his strong arm towards himself, with one swift move I end up stumbling over and falling on the floor just in front of him. He begins to crawl on top of me, his huge frame pinning me to the floor. I look at the doorway, no one has come back, I'm alone pinned to the floor. I listen to is heaving panting grunts has he moves himself to be fully on top of me. My legs and body are totally pinned by his weight. He lines his head up to be opposite my face. His nose almost touches mine. He looks deep into my eyes and I stare right into his. I see no resemblance of human being, his angry eyes are like dark pits of nothingness. His heavy grunts and flared nostrils bounce into my face, leaving me with the smell of his stale cigarette breath. I don't notice he has his hands around my neck until I start to feel him squeeze. It starts of soft as if he is trying to get his hands in the correct position. Then once he's done that, he starts squeezing tighter, I suddenly feel my airway close, I panic unsure what to do. He sees this and gently releases his grip, but not fully just enough so I can gasp a little air back into my lungs. Then he squeezes again, tighter. I watch him laughing as he sees me struggling to breath. I manage to free my arms enough to be able to start hitting him in his face, but it's hopeless they barely touch him. He squeezes tighter.

'Don't fight it, it won't be long now!' He sniggers to me.

My airway is completely blocked, I start to feel the pulsing pressure flood to my head, I feel my eyes have started to bulge, the more his notices my struggle the more excited he gets. I desperately try to hold on, surely someone has noticed I'm not there. It's getting too late, my body has stopped fighting, my arms lay slumped beside me and I feel my eyes begin to close. I know this is the end for me. I flood my mind thinking of my daughters, my grandchildren, my husband, everyone I love bar him, I can't have his laughing face be the last I see, I won't give him that. I make sure to keep my eyes closed not to see him.

'Open your eyes, fucking look at me bitch!' He screams in my face as I take away the pleasure of his kill. I don't open my eyes, il never open my eyes for him. He loosens his grip just enough to let me breath again. I still dare not open my eyes. This infuriates him enough to let me go, instead of choking me, he begins to slap me across the face. Each powerful hit sends shooting pains through my body. I still keep my eyes closed. 'Look at me!' He screams and fires more slaps at me, my face has gone numb on one side and I can't hear anything apart from the ringing in my ears. I don't feel anything. I can't feel anything and I can't see anything. I start wondering if I finally died. There's no one here to guide me if I have, there's nothing, it's just dark, cold and lonely.

As I'm giving myself up to the nothingness. I hear it, it's like a shimmering echo. Unsure what it is, in fact I'm unsure where I am, but I try to focus on it, I try to follow it, desperate to make out what it is. I'm getting closer to it, I hear it more loudly, it's starting to become clear, losing its shimmering echo, I start to notice words being formed. Where am I? I push the thought out of my head, I need to keep my focus. I find myself wondering in a pit of black, I stop as I notice the light, although it's tiny I can see it shinning in the distance. I must get to that light. I start running to it now. I'm almost there, if I could just reach my hand out to touch it...

My body bolts up without my say so. My lungs suck in as much air as possible, relieved to be tasting such freshness. I finally slowly open my eyes. My whole body doesn't feel trapped anymore, it's just my legs they won't move. I can hear the echo, I can understand what it is saying now.

'Lynn, Lynn wake up.' I listen carefully and notice it isn't the deep angry voice that was screaming at me just seconds ago. His voice is soft and gentle. I let out a groan as I start feeling the searing pain that thumps in my head. I hear the voice repeating itself. My eyes start adjusting from the darkness. I'm not met with Earnie's snarl. Instead, I see the scared wide eyes of Arthur, he's looking down on me. I blink a couple of times hoping it helps adjust my hazy sight. It's defiantly Arthur, I see he still holds his walking stick above his head. I notice he shakes nervously.

'What's happened?' I mumble the words out as I try to understand what is going on. I look down at my legs and notice Earnie lays unconscious across them. His head and hands lay on the floor just at the side of me in front of Arthur, while the rest of his body has my legs pinned. I try to wiggle free, but I don't have the energy. I look up to Arthur, He's in shock, he hasn't moved, he's now staring at the lifeless body waiting for it to move. I try to speak to him, but before anything can leave my lips, I hear the rushing of footsteps running across the wooden floor.

'No one move, it's the police! Drop the walking stick!' The man panics even more his whole body begins to jitter uncontrollably while he still holds his stick over his head. 'Drop it and get on your knees!' Arthur looks at me, clearly traumatized I try to help him, but the burning pain in my throat and neck won't let me shout.

'Do it Arthur, it's okay.' I whisper to him. The old man understands as he slumps to his knees shaking so bad that he can't get any words out to speak. The police rush over to him and kick his walking stick away and try to forcefully cuff him. The old man screams out. I lay there helpless; I can only watch on as they forcefully pounce on the old man. His terrified eyes never leave mine.

'It's not him he saved me! Get this man off me!' The sharp pain in my attempt to scream makes me wince, but it's enough the grab the attention of the policemen, he looks over in my direction to see Earnie slumped over me he then looks to see the marks around my neck then slowly releases Arthur. Another policeman comes into view as he slowly walks to me. I see him smile. I try to recognise the familiar face, as I begin to cry. I wouldn't have recognised him at first now he's wearing trousers with a shirt and tie, he looks far more professional than he did earlier on. I watch as he starts ordering the other officers about. Soon a rush of officers come to my aid and help lift the lifeless body of Earnie off the top of me. I instantly start to feel the blood rush to my legs, which soon turns to pins and needles. The familiar face bends down to my level. I watch as he offers his hand to help me up. I hesitate for moment not sure if I'm able to do so. He realises this and places is other hand gently around my waist and lifts me to my feet. As I unsteadily stand waiting for my body to come back to life, I cling a hold of him to steady myself. I try to speak but as I do so I feel the burning pain stabbing me in the throat. My hand quickly grabs a hold of it as it's my first reaction to make it stop. I wince in pain. He looks at my swollen bruised neck and I notice his disappointment. He knows he almost failed, if it wasn't for Arthur, I would certainly be dead! My throat feels like sandpaper as I try to speak, he notices my struggles and hands me a bottle of water. The first sips burn, but soon the water lubricates my dry throat.

'Don't worry your safe now.' He still holds on to my trembling body as he slowly begins to walk me out. He stops and turns to the other officers who are racing about trying to secure the scene. 'Get the old man out of here and make sure he's fine, I want every inch of the place searched and searched again, we can't miss anything!' All the other officers rush to his demands without any hesitation. More and more officers are flooding into the place as we try to squeeze out the tiny doorway. I look up at him and smile, my feelings of something not being right about him, where correct. As I now understand why!

'I know you?' I mutter to him in a raspy tone.

'You certainly do.' He smiles 'You okay Mam?' Christos laughs. 'Come on let's get you out of here.'

CHAPTER 28

It soon turns to the next early morning by the time we all got some hospital treatment and checked over, we were then given the all clear to head to the police station, where we could be kept safe and to give statements. Cora was still in the hospital to get some treatment on her wounds and slight concussion, but other than that we are told she is doing fine and coming round quickly, so should be soon on her way. Me and Doreen are left in a plain room waiting to be interviewed, although we have already been through this, with what seems like to be a million times, we are being pressed even more, unsure if they are trying to make us slip up or being overly cautious. I feel drained and sore, all I want to do is find Rita and go home. We are being looked after well though and have had a specialist come to us to talk about the trauma we've just received, no doubt we will be needing some therapy when we get home, which I can't bare to think too much about yet, I can't go home without Rita, what am I going to tell my family, her family? Should I tell them? I push the niggling thoughts, I need to keep focused on finding Rita, then I start thinking about the rest.

There's still no sign or call from her. I feel helpless and don't even know where to begin to start looking, we've been pressed that many times to think back if there was ever a place Bill and Earnie might have mentioned, but nothing springs up, there was only the beachfront and marina, which of course Christos knows about, he was there. I clutch on to my neck, the pain is still throbbing away but thankfully some painkillers have eased it, the purple blue bruising is clear to see and wouldn't take a genius to work out that I had been strangled, almost to death, a shudder runs through me when an imagine of Earnie on top of me with his hands around my neck, his eyes cold and dark the sneering teeth hungered for a kill. I quickly shake the image away and look over to Doreen, who in her own traumatic experience has barely said a word. They said this could happen, it's the shock. I walk over to her and wrap my arms around her as I hold her cold shivering body. Still, she says nothing but instead has snuggled herself in closer to me.

'We need to find Rita and get out of this place.' I say softly knowing I won't get much of a response, but I know she is listening. The door creaks open, as Christos and a cleaned-up Cora enter. I'm shocked to see Cora out of hospital and looking so well, apart from the cuts and bruises you would realise that this young woman had been held captive and tortured.

'How you both doing? I'm Detective Hamas, and this is Detective Peters.' Christos introduces them both. My mouth drops open in surprise, the amount of twist and turns this holiday has brought already, makes me struggle to keep up. I knew Christos was in the police when he turned up at the boat but had no idea that Cora was too. I start thinking back over the previous days, trying to make sense of it. How she dealt with the accidently swapped cases, the questions she gave me before I got my case back, they were weird but now they make sense, The notes, the missing package, the things Earnie said about her on the boat, the list goes on. Piece by piece things start to fit, although I still don't fully understand why everything happened the way it did, it does start to make more sense. When things calm down and when we get Rita back, I will press them for an explanation, surely most of the things that has happened could have been avoided, especially with them being the police! Or are they corrupt? No that's my paranoid voice trying to doubt me again, I'm not even going to let that lead me down the twisted roads, not right now, I can't it's too much, my head can't keep up with all the information being bounced around as it is.

'No, get out!' I reply out loud to my paranoid voice accidently. Then quickly apologise to a shocked Christos and Cora, who are now looking at me confused. I feel my face flush red as they wait for me to reply. 'Shouldn't you still be in the hospital?' I mutter hoping it distracts them from my paranoid outburst.

'Yeah, I probably should be resting up a bit, but I'm just as eager to get all this finished with, as you probably are. So, just light duties for me for a while, plus I wanted to come and see how you two are holding up.' She gazes over to us, I notice she's trying to read our expressions, although you don't need to see it, you can probably take a good guess at how we are! Christos interrupts wanting to get on with the business.

'Yes, we are the detectives on this case and have been for a long time now. This might be confusing, so I do understand your frustrations with not having the full answers from us, but we don't have time to explain it all just yet, unfortunately you three stumbled on a case we have been investigating for many years. We've been trying to catch Bill and Earnie for a long time now. This, however, is the closest we have ever gotten to catching them. We do have Earnie in custody now and is likely not to be released for a very long time. The trouble is we still don't have a clue where Bill or Rita is at. It's urgent we find them, there's a very good chance Rita is in danger. Now we are so close to catching them. With Earnie already in custody, it will no doubt add pressure to Bill, we don't know what this could make him do, so as you can understand it's crucial, we find her, sooner rather than later. Has she tried to contact you since we left each other at the café?' My dreaded thoughts are coming true, is she being held somewhere? Is she being tortured just like Cora? Is she even still alive? My head feels like it's going to explode, I don't know how much more I can take, the stress and panic is killing me. Doreen sits up and listens carefully to every word, she shakes her head to say no, but still won't say a single world. I know she is still in shock, but I can tell what Christos has just told us, has completely terrified her. I answer more clearly to a waiting Christos.

'No not a thing, we tried calling when we were at the marina. And her last known place on her location was there, but nothing since.' I try to speak without my voice shaking and stuttering but fail, my nerves and panic are all over the place. Cora notices and tries to reassure us.

'Try not to worry, we are doing everything we can to get Rita back to you.' Her bruised face warms with her smile, but her eyes show that she has doubts. I even have doubts, I was seconds away myself from being killed and I had other people around me, Rita is alone, she won't have anyone be able to come to her rescue just in the nick of time, like I did, like Cora did. She only has Bill, now he knows the truth, he will surely kill her, especially now he has to with Earnie out of the picture. I start wondering if Bill is still playing along with the date, or has he confronted her already? I try to take comfort knowing she could be still entertaining him on the date, then realise it's now the next morning the date should have ended hours ago. I start to get angry at them not believing the genuine accident, because this is all it is, two cases accidently got muddled up at the airport and it's ended up spiralling out of control. People have nearly been killed and have gotten hurt, over such a stupid, stupid mistake.

'Do you mind if we look at your phone so we can check also.' I don't hesitate and hand him my mobile. Christos quickly scans through then walks out the room with it. 'I won't be a minute.' He says while leaving the room, I don't even bother to object, I don't have the energy to do so. Cora stays behind which leaves an awkward silence that fills the room. We find each other just staring around hoping that someone speaks first. All I can hear is the little clock on the wall just tick, tick, ticking. I get lost counting each one, until finally the silence is broken.

'Can I get you both anything to eat or drink?' The thought of food makes my stomach turn, but knowing I haven't eaten for a long time I should probably try so I nod ask for a coffee to go with it. Doreen nods in agreement. Cora leaves the room and takes the awkward atmosphere with her. I wonder if there's any guilt or regret from her, not only has this turned into something far bigger than it needed it to be, the amount of people that has been placed in danger or have gotten hurt is far too many for my liking as it stands, never mind the fact that Rita is still missing.

She's only gone a few minutes and re-enters with two large mugs of coffee and a few biscuits and a couple of packed sandwiches, it's not until I see the food that I realise how hungry I actually am. I snatch up one of the sandwiches and take a bite as quickly as I can, eating like I've never eaten for days. Surprisingly, the fresh bread and ham salad tastes so good, or I'm that hungry that anything could taste good right now. Doreen must feel the same, after she watches my first bite, she quickly reaches over for the other and begins to ravish into it. It's the most action I've seen out of Doreen for a while, she's eating and sipping away at her coffee, I watch her becoming more brighter with every bite. The much-needed food certainly has perked both our energy levels up as I feel the sluggishness start to disappear. Christos arrives back shortly after and hands back my phone.

'We haven't gotten much joy, but we have found Rita's phone it was on the verge at the top of the marina. However, there's still no sign of her, but that doesn't mean we need to worry just yet, we have many officers checking the surrounding areas. We are also going to check every inch of the hotel in case they are back there. We have the upper hand at the minute as Bill shouldn't have clue that Earnie has been caught yet, or at least we don't think he will know, but it will only spare us a few hours before Bill notices something isn't right. That's why we must get moving quickly. Detective Peters is going to stay with you at the hotel and we will also have undercover officers all around the hotel as caution, we will be discreetly searching the place as not to alarm Bill. I'm afraid we must ask before we part, it may seem offensive, but please understand we need to ask.' He looks to us slightly embarrassed as I notice a his cheeks turn to slightly red, but he asks anyhow. 'Is there any chance that Rita may have been lured into working with them?' His question feels like a slap to the face, the cheek of it. How can they ask that they are partly to blame for some of this mess anyhow!

'Certainly not! How could you even ask that!' I scowl back at him trying to hold my temper.

'How dare you!' Doreen is disgusted, but hearing her speak finally, somehow calms me.

'I'm sorry, we had to ask. We thought you might be working for them when we first seen you involved. Like I say we have been watching them for some time, and they never make any mistakes, well until now that is.' Christos looks sheepish, even Cora has put her head down in embarrassment. I try to keep my anger under control from the outrageous accusations, I know it's probably routine and they must go through every scenario, but come on really? After everything that's happened so far. I jump to my feet still holding my warm mug of coffee, ready to burst at any moment.

'Please stop wasting time and find Rita!' Although I don't shout too loud, but the screech in my voice burns down my throat and the pang of pain seers across my bruised swollen neck. I squirm and clasps my hand there to try and ease the pain. The detectives flush red and they quickly dart their eyes from looking at me. Christos nods and backs himself out the door. Cora stays and starts to explain what will be happening when we get to the hotel.

We basically are going to be trapped in our apartment until everything is safe. We finish our coffees before we head back to the hotel. A driver arrives to take us, which doesn't too long to arrive. Desperate to wash the remaining blood and dirt away and hope to finally erase the smell of Earnie's stale cigarette breath, I follow Cora out to the car, Doreen seems to be coming round more to her normal self, but I can see the worry written all over her face as I watch her step into the back seat. I sit beside her while Cora takes the front passenger. Noting much gets said as the car hurtles us back to the hotel.

CHAPTER 29

Back in the apartment everything seems in its normal place, no sign of Rita ever being back from yesterday is like a little salt to our wounds, I was really hoping we would get back to find her in here, but of course that was wishful thinking. Cora is watching over us a little too closely or just being concerned I really don't know but the pacing about we are doing isn't helping anything, only so many cup of teas and coffee can fill the time, I decide to go and have shower and freshen myself up a bit, with a desperate need to wash and put on fresh clothes, I can smell my sweat stained into my shirt and makes me slightly gag. Doreen has already been and done this, and has now came back out looking fresher, though her tired eyes are starting to give in, so she goes to lay down. It's late afternoon now, time seems to be ticking by to fast, all the while we still don't have any new updates on Rita. It's just over 24 hours since the last sighting of her, which was at the café on the beachfront. I'm trying to find comfort with the old saying "No news, is good news." Is it though? Not one single sighting since then, nothing, it's just like she has vanished into thin air. I know with every hour that passes by, pinches a little bit of hope of finding her alive. I hate this, I hate the fact I've watched to many programmes, read too many books and see too much news on missing people, to know that the first 24 hours are crucial to finding the missing person alive. Here we are over that time scale, with nothing!

Feeling the warm sprays of the shower flowing over my aching body calms my manic mind just for a few minutes. I get the sudden urge to want my daughters and grandchildren. The pain in their voices when I told them, although only part what is happening, felt like a knife stabbing me through the heart. They pleaded with me and wanted to come out to us, I wouldn't allow it even if the safety regulations said they could, I couldn't bare for them to get caught up in this, or worse, least having them stay at home I know they are safe. Having to make the call to Rita's son was horrendous, I could hear the broken young man fall to pieces as he screamed from the other end of the line, the pain he must be feeling... A bang on the bathroom door wakes me from my wandering thoughts.

'Lynn! Is everything okay in there? You've been a little while.' Cora's voice echoes outside the room. I know she is trying her best to look after us and manage what is going on, but I can't help but roll my eyes at the persistent woman. I'm feeling angry at so many people right now, that I'm starting to lose sight when people are genuinely being concerned, instead it's being replaced by irritation. Irritation I'm feeling right now as Cora bangs on my door. She bangs again waiting for me to answer. This time I shout a little too harshly which she must be able to easily notice my annoyed tone.

'I'm fine, can I just have five minutes peace!' I snap. As soon as the words leave my lips, I know I was too harsh, guilt creeps over me, I know I'm not normally this rude person, but I start to doubt myself, has this whole situation changed me as person? Am I always going to be rude and impatient now? Has the trauma completely stripped a part of me, have I lost a bit of the human conscious? Have I taken a step closer to becoming heartless empty vessel? Like Earnie! The calming shower has now lost its peaceful magic, so I step out and wrap the towel round me, I stand in front of the mirror and just stare at myself, trying to recognise a little bit of me. My once fresh-looking face now looks pale with one side swollen from the vicious slaps, my eyes are hollow and dark, and the bruising is now covering right over my neck. I look horrendous and feel it.

Stepping back into the main room, I find Cora is still pacing around, continuously checking her phone and making sure the doors are still locked, she must have checked at least 20 times prior to this. I wonder if being held hostage is affecting her more than she is letting on, it's got to be, no one can endure what she did and not be affected by it. Doreen has joined us again as she wakes from her nap, she however looks a bit better, but I can see she is still exhausted.

'Did you manage to sleep?' I ask as I join her on the sofa.

'No, not really.' I don't press her for anything else, instead I just sit closely beside her.

I look at Cora and ask if there is any more news, even though I already know the answer to this, there isn't. I see Doreen is starting to get agitated and has stepped and walked over to the kitchen area, I can see she is trying to find something to take her mind off things, but there is nothing. I feel her agony, I've tried for the last few hours to do this, and every single time I do, my mind jolts me back to Rita, then Earnie choking me, then the gun pointed to our heads. I'm pretty sure all this trauma we've received isn't going to be fixed with a couple of gins sitting round a table discussing how much of a fucking disaster this holiday has been!

'We can't just sit here and do nothing!' Doreen blurts out. 'We could at least be out helping to look.' Cora looks up and gives Doreen a pitiful smile, knowing fine well that would never be allowed to happen.

'I know this will make you feel helpless, but we really can't let you out of here it's too dangerous. You've only just had a lucky escape you might not get another! The best thing you both can do for Rita now is to stay here and be safe. We will do our best to find her trust us we are good at our job!' I can't help but feel patronized by her, how can she expect us to be this calm, when in fact they put us in more danger by taking the drugs when they could have been handed back to them and we wouldn't be involved like this, and Rita wouldn't be missing. The more I think about it the more I feel my burning anger rising, I know it's only going to be seconds before it explodes.

'Really!' I snap. "Here comes that heartless, empty vessel." 'If you were good at your job then why are we even in this mess? You took the drugs when they could have been handed back to them and we wouldn't have been involved! You would certainly still be locked up or worse if we hadn't come to the boat!' My anger is erupting, and I can't seem to stop myself from speaking. 'You're the reason Rita is missing! and the reason we were held at gun point.' Cora looks straight to me, I can tell she is reliving the terrifying moments. Her eyes well up for second, which she quickly brushes away, and straightens herself up.

'I can't thank you enough for saving my life, but right now we have to focus on getting Rita back, I understand how you can think it's my fault she is missing, perhaps that may be true to an extent, but I promise you we are doing everything we can to find her.'

'So why take the drugs?' Doreen repeats my question hoping to get a direct answer. Cora shuffles from foot to foot a little nervous at what to say, I wonder if she has been told to keep certain details quiet. We both fix our gaze on her and wait for an answer, we demand it, surely, it's the least they could do.

'You see, we didn't know if you were involved or not, for all we knew you could have been smuggling the drugs in, the misplaced suitcases could have been planned. We had to make sure that they were drugs to be able to use that against them, so they had been taken to get tested, that's why they went "missing" and if you all were involved, we couldn't exactly tell you this. like Christos said earlier we've never been so close to catching them so everything had to be checked and double checked, we couldn't risk any mistakes.'

'Really! We are three grannies; do we really look like drug smugglers!' Doreen huffs then continues. 'No mistakes! Rita is missing that's a pretty big mistake!' Doreen finishes off breathless. Cora looks down at her feet and considers it. When she has finished mulling things over, she composes herself. She's not going to have all the blame pointed to her, she doesn't even have to say it, but I know she is thinking it.

'You will be surprised what dealers will do to get drugs moving, nothing is off limits to them. But anyhow when we searched through the suitcases before handing the correct ones over, we noticed that there were no drugs to be found.' Doreen now does the shameful stare at the floor knowing she removed them from the case first. 'So, as you can imagine, that made us think that you were involved and threw us off guard. When you came back down with the make-up bag of course it got us curious and i found it very strange, but I somehow knew that must have been the drugs! We had two ways to play it out, one let it ride out as you were planning, but it left things a bit sketchy as to who the drugs belonged too, which was a risk for us not seeing them again! Plus, you weren't the people we were after really. Or two remove drugs and test them, hoping apply pressure which could lead to mistakes, to finally catch Bill and Earnie on something concrete to charge them.'

'You used us as bait!' The anger is burning inside of me ready to explode at any minute. Cora flushes. I feel exploited, used and what for, their case?

'You've got to understand we haven't even been anywhere near to catching them for years, this was our one chance to try, we would probably never get this chance again. Bearing in mind we still weren't 100% sure you all weren't involved, so please don't see yourselves used as bait, that wasn't the case.'

'You nearly got us killed! We still don't know if Rita is alive or not!' My face feels on fire as I shout. Doreen stands with her eyes fixed on Cora, her nostrils flare and her eyebrows scowl. I start to think she may dive at this woman.

'Actually, you nearly got yourselves killed!' Oh, no she just didn't... I see the instant regret on Cora's face, she knows she shouldn't have just said it, it's too late though. Doreen has set off charging towards her, her finger pointed right to Cora, her face beams red with anger, her teeth clenches to a growl. I look on in horror, should I intervene? I know I should, but I've never seen Doreen like this, she looks like a completely different person, not the caring sensible, loving woman I know. Maybe a bit of her humanity has been stolen, also making her way to becoming like and empty heartless vessel.

'You what!' Doreen rages. She almost has Cora pinned to the corner.

'Listen! I'm glad you didn't do as Christos said I doubt I would have not been here now if you had! But you were told to stay at the hotel you chose to go to the boat, that was not us!' Cora raises her hand to try and defend herself from any blows that may land her way, I watch nervously, dreading what may happen next.

The room goes silent for a moment. Doreen eases back away from Cora as we all start to relax, I see the warming face return. Cora breathes a sigh of relief. I start to pace thinking what to do next, being locked in this room is sending us crazy. My head is hurting, my body is aching, and the tiredness is desperately taking over me. I grab my bag from the side and begin to head for the door. Knowing I need to leave this room right now, I can't bear to stay trapped in here any longer. I long for some fresh air to fill my lungs, I need the sun to hit my face, I need take myself out of this mess, just to let myself breath for a moment. I'm only planning a little walk to clear my head and come right back. I'm not totally stupid, I know the dangers, but I'm desperate if I stay for a moment longer, I'm going to go insane.

'I can't just sit here, I need air!' Doreen also grabs her things and follows me to the door.

'You can't leave!' Cora desperately shouts.

'Are you going to stop us!' Doreen demands.

'If I have to, then yes!' Cora tries to block our path but fails miserably. We beat her to the door and fling it open.

'Stop!' Cora pleads.

We look out to the open hallway before we take the first step out. We both do it at the same time, as we turn to face the long corridor that would lead us to the elevators. We both stand frozen as we look down the corridor. It wasn't Cora's pleading that halted us in our tracks. The two us fix our eyes down to where the elevator waits. Cora notices something is up and rushes over to join us. My body feels frozen, as a cool shiver slides down my spine, I know I should be running right now but my eyes are fixed by the elevator doors. This can't be happening!

'What is it?' Cora rushes out to join us in the corridor. She sees it instantly. 'Oh no!' She screams as she sees what we are looking at. Cora starts to fumble for her radio that is fixed on the belt of her jeans. Her hands shaking so much the radio flies out of her grip and flings a few feet away and hits the floor with a bang. 'Fuck!' She scrambles after it now or her knees. Me and Doreen haven't moved, we can't move. Just as she is about to pick it up. A figure appears from round the corner. Dressed in all black with black leather gloves, his face covered in a black ski mask making it impossible to see who it is. They spot us all out in the corridor. I watch the slit for his mouth turn to a smile, he then begins to run right at us. His powerful strides are fast and sharp as he lunges in our direction. Cora looks up to see the masked figure starting in a sprint and quickly grabs the radio and jumps to her feet and begins to run back to us. 'Get back inside!' She screams at us. Her screams throw us back to life, we both jump and bolt for the door. Cora dives on us to push us all through, she slams the door shut, just in time, before he reaches it. The masked figure begins to bang repeatedly on the door. Cora desperately presses her weight up on the door, as though trying not to let it cave in, the lock seems hopeless at this point. Me and Doreen run over and push our bodies up to it, hoping the extra weight helps with the blows. The banging suddenly stops. We all catch our panting breath for a second. We look at one another wondering what is going on, seeing the panic in Cora's tells me we should be scared, of course I'm scared, who is it? Just as things start to calm down and I start to think he has gone. The blows reappear on the door, this time they were harder and faster. Cora quickly takes a glimpse through the peep hole. 'He's going to kick this door in.' She looks at us desperately. Each blow pushes the three of us back. 'We need something to help hold this door!' She screams in panic. I quickly scan the room desperately trying to keep my full weight on the door, but his hard thuds are ricocheting through my body, as each blow makes me scream. I look round at the other women desperately trying to hold the door shut, I know if we don't do something soon, he will break his way in. I spot the side board that's next to the door and know this is the only hope we have to secure ourselves.

'The side board.' I scream. I run over and push the vases and lamp off, they crash over the tiled floor and smashes into pieces, the sound makes everyone stop, even the banging on the door becomes silent. I start to push the side board along the tiled floor thinking it should easily glide across, but it barely seems to budge. This solid oak bit of furnisher would be desired to have at my home, but right now I'm hating it, Doreen sees my struggles and runs over to help, with both of pushing we manage to make the short distance to the door, and finally it begins to slide across the smooth floor. Cora whose got her full body spread across the door dives out the way and helps to place the sideboard as a barrier. The pounding starts to slow down, then suddenly stops the three of us drop to the floor breathless and shaking. Waiting a few moments sure that he would return but nothing happens, instead everything has gone eerily quiet, giving chance for my mind to start wandering, who was it? was it Bill? Surely not he doesn't seem to be the one to get his hands dirty, if it's not Bill then there's more people after us. I try to gulp but my throat is too dry and claggy.

'Who the hell was that?' Doreen struggles to say. Cora fumbles with the radio, trying her hardest to steady her shaking hands. I can't muster to answer her back all I can do is shrug.

'Come in, come in! It's Detective Peters anyone there?' We all wait eagerly for someone to answer. A crackle over the radio appears.

'Detective Hamas here.' His voice is calm, which suggests he's unaware what is happening.

'He's here. We need urgent assistant up to the apartment! There's an officer down by the elevators. Quick! he's going to break down the door!' She says trying to keep calm, but I notice the little quiver in her voice and can see in her wide eyes that she is as terrified as me, of course why wouldn't she be? She's still human and after everything that's already happened, I don't think any of us are in any fit state to take any more, but it's starting to feel relentless, I can only think that things are just getting started.

'On our way, is he still there?' Cora quickly climbs on the sideboard and looks through the peep hole. I watch as she looks through half expecting her to jump back in freight, she doesn't, as see her tilt her head in all directions making sure gets as much view as she can.

'No visual on him.'

'Good we are coming, don't come out of the room, and don't open the door for no one until I'm there!'

'Copy that.' The wait for back up seems to take forever. The only thing we can do is watch each other and keep our bodies pressed as tightly to the sideboard that's blocking the door. Cora keeps checking the time on her watch, as see her getting more and more nervous as each minute ticks by. I realise there's going to be a delay for them getting here, as soon as the slumped dead body by the elevator, it will be the first thing they come to before they get to us.

'He's dead, isn't he?' Cora looks at Doreen, with pain in her eyes. Seeing a work colleague possibly even a friend lay there lifeless without being able to go to him or help him, must be agony for her.

'I think so.' She says with a slight well up in her eyes, she quickly wipes the stray tear and a composes herself back to be professional. However, there is no chance he is still alive, the amount of blood that seeped out from the gaping wound on his neck, his throat had been slit, I doubt many people would be able survive that.

'Oh god!' Doreen pulls her hands to her face and begins to cry into them. 'Why is this happening?' I move closer to wrap my arms around her without answering her, I don't know how to answer her, I'm as confused and in shock as the rest of us.

'You both are going to be fine; help will be here any minute.' She barely finishes her sentence when there's a huge bang on the door. The three of us jump at the same time, is he back? 'Go lock yourselves in the bathroom.' Cora orders us. We do as we are told and run and the lock door as quickly as we can. The sound of my heartbeat pumping away fills the silent bathroom, as I eagerly wait to hear who's there. Another bang on the door appears, this time followed by Detective Hamas's voice.

'It's Detective Hamas open up.' There seems to be a long wait for Cora to reply, which must leave him waiting nervously, as he shouts again. 'It's Christos! Cora, open the door! It's all clear out here.' I now have my ear pressed up to the door, why she not answering? Then we hear the scrap of the sideboard struggling to be pushed out the way, followed by the click of the lock. 'Are you all safe! Where is Lynn and Doreen?' Certain it's him, we slowly open the bathroom door and walk out.

'Has he gone?' I walk over slowly to Cora and Christos, who seem to be a deep conversation, I can hear them planning what needs to be done next, I hear him say, that we need to be moved away from this hotel. They notice me entering and stop their conversation.

'Is he gone?' I ask again still waiting to be answered.

'Yeah, there's no sign of him on this floor, officers are out looking now.'

'The officer by the elevator?' Doreen asks as she ushers up beside me.

Christos looks down at his feet and hesitates before he replies. 'I'm afraid he didn't make it.' I already knew the answer to this. The imagine of the man slumped by the elevator his eyes wide open and totally still, just staring down the corridor. There was so, so much blood. The image keeps flashing in my head. 'We are going to have to move you to a more secure location, grab some things quickly, we need to move now.'

'Where are we going to go? We can't just leave Rita!' I know that we need to, but the thought of leaving Rita makes me feel like we are giving up on her.

'We need to keep you safe, you're a witness and by the looks of it, they will do anything to make sure there isn't any!' A cold shudder runs right through my body. Even with all the police presence, they still tried to come for us. They aren't going to be put off easy, they will keep coming and coming until there is none of us left.

'That wasn't Bill, was it?' Doreen says already knowing the answer. The man was far too slim and short to be him, the slits of his mask revealing his eyes also didn't match. I doubt Bill would be that stupid, he wouldn't risk getting caught, not after all these years avoiding it.

'No! No, it wasn't.' Christos says.

'Who was it then? Is Earnie still in custody?' I listen to Doreen, while I run and grab some things to take with us, knowing I don't have time to pack everything, I just grab some essentials.

'He is. We are not sure just yet; we are looking into it. We have eyes on Bill so it can't have been him trying to attack you, plus that's not his style, he uses people to do that for him.' I thought as much, you can see he would quite happily let other people get their hands dirty and risk getting caught, leaving them to face the consequences while he sits back watching. 'This thing is a lot bigger than you think, they have connections everywhere. We are working quickly to find out who it was, they won't be able to get far, the hotel has been secured.'

'That's good to know!' I say sarcastically, I notice he doesn't appreciate my sarcastic tone with the roll of his eyes. 'Is Rita with him?" He hesitates to answer leaving me thinking there is nothing new to help finding her.

'There's no sign of Rita yet, but we are looking, we need to get you both out of here and into a more secure location first. They know exactly where you are now and they will keep coming.' He stands waiting for me and Doreen to move. 'Please come on we need to go.' We grab our cases and begin to finish gathering some items up.

Within 10 minutes we are ready to leave. Stepping out into the hallway, the body is now covered and the section is cornered off. Apart from a few offices and medics, it's quiet up here. We have too slowly slide passed where the body is laying which makes me feel sick, his lifeless body just metres away. The poor man was just doing his job and someone killed him.

CHAPTER 30

'We have got a car waiting in the parking lot. Detective Peters will be staying with you both along with another officer. I try to listen carefully as I can hoping my brain can absorb every bit of information that Christos is telling us. He gives the us precise orders while we travel down in the elevator. We are told not to leave the officers, told not contact our families, and told not stop in any other location apart from the one we are being sent to. My mind keeps wandering off and I need to shake myself to focus me back on him. My tiredness is burning my eyes, as I fight to keep them open, it won't take me long to fall asleep, it's the first thing I plan to do when we reach the new location, although it's makes me feel like I'm letting my guard down, I maybe am a little, but it's essential I do, I feel like I'm going insane, the stress, panic, worry and lack of sleep is a bad combo for anybody never mind someone who suffers with anxiety, like I do. We are given codes to use if by chance we run into trouble and need help quickly. I watch Christos's lips telling me the word but can't hear it. I need to ask him again what it is. This time I dare not move my eyes, or my focus from him.

'You must remember this! (RED BIRD.) You don't have to say anything else you only need to say that, and we will know, and come right to you.' Christos makes sure I understand what he is saying, I nod and repeat the word to him, he looks at Doreen making sure she knows, she repeats the word back to him. Satisfied that he knows we understand he looks on to see how far we are off in the elevator. I watch the numbers whizz past until it slows then stops on B. "Oh great, the basement level! Could they not have found a creepier place to take us." I think to myself while I silently curse the person who came up with this plan. The skies are now turning dark as it is, so coming to this level and travelling in the dark, I can't help but feel we are going to be easy targets.

The elevator doors ping open as we reach the basement level. The officer who is coming with us is already waiting by the car with the doors already open ready to bundle us in. We pile out and head over to him. The basement or basically the parking lot, which is what it looks to be, is as suspected dark and creepy, the beaming light of the elevator lights up all the way to the waiting officer, without that it would be dark. I look back at Christos. I watch him stay in the elevator as he watches our every move.

'I will be in touch shortly, try not to worry, we will find her.' He shouts as the doors begin to close.

I turn back round to the officer who's eager to get us in the car. There seems to be no one else down here apart from us, the quiet area is interrupted by the sounds of our cases wheeling along the concrete floor, the dim lights are flickering on and off, which makes me move faster to get into the car. The officer takes our cases and places them in the boot. Me and Doreen slide into the back seats while Cora sits in the passenger seat. The officer now climbs into driver seat and is just about to set off. When he looks around and makes sure we are all in, then he glances around the parking lot, with nothing much to see, he carries on and we set off. I hear the doors automatically lock, but I keep my hand on the handle, I'm not quite sure if this is to help prevent someone getting in, or to give me more of chance in case I need to run.

'Where are we going?' Doreen asks politely.

'Not far from here, it's all safe.' He replies with a reassuring smile through his rear-view mirror. I look around the parking lot, it's completely deserted apart from the 4 of us in the car, I wonder if they have locked this area down too, there is other parked cars in fact there's plenty of them, but there's not a single person in sight, well I hope there isn't, I now start visioning someone hiding behind the cars waiting to jump out on us.

The car slowly begins to move, the beam of the car lights, light up the dark parking lot. The Bursting light from the exit sign gets brighter and bigger the closer we get, seeing it get closer relaxes me, we are almost out, I can see the barriers that block our way, soon they will lift and we will be off. As much as a beautiful Hotel this is, though one thing I know for certain is I won't be coming back! I sit myself back into the seat and try to relax.

Something catches me out of the corner of my eye. I bolt back up right and move my face closer to the window, trying to get a better view. There's nothing there, I start to think my exhaustion is making see things. I rub my tired eyes and look again. We are pulling up to the barriers now which makes it easier for me to look. I focus my gaze to the corner of the lot, where I thought I seen something, there's nothing there, just parked cars and the rest is in darkness. I start to turn my head, when I notice it again, this time I'm sure of it, it can't be my eyes playing tricks on me? or can it? I look around everyone in the car to see if they are seeing it, there not, there completely oblivious, Doreen is looking the other way, Cora is on her phone, and the other officer is trying to stick the card into the barriers that will lead us out, I watch as he struggles to fit his huge body through the window, his arm outstretched as far as they can, still he can't reach to slot the card into the machine, I watch as his beefy face frowns in determination, he clamps his tongue between his lips as if this would give him and extra inch to reach, it does not. He's starts to lose patience and aggressively unbuckles his seatbelt, now the podgy officer can lean further and finally slots the card. He smiles to himself as he finally achieves this, only for seconds later, the card spits back out. He takes back his card and tries again, same thing happens every time. He must have tried this at least five times with the same outcome. His frustrated face makes him look as if he's about to jump out and start kicking the machine. Cora finally lifts her head from her phone, wondering what the hold-up is.

'The dam card won't work!' He splutters out and sits himself back in the seat closely inspecting to see what is wrong with it. 'I'm going to have to go to the office and get a new one.' I see Cora debating if this is a wise option, he notices. 'It's only over there.' He points in the direction where I was looking, now it makes sense if I did see something. Of course, someone will be there working the barriers. I shake my head at my over paranoid mind. 'it's the only way we can get out!' Cora gives a nod to him. He heaves his chunky body out of the car, re adjusts his belt, and places his hand on his side arm. He bends down to pop his head through the door. 'Keep the doors locked, you see anything beep the horn and radio in, I won't be a minute.' He closes his door and makes sure it's locked before he heads off to the office. I watch him disappear into the darkness. Cora clutches the radio and cautiously checks every area; I find myself doing the same thing. I now fix my eyes to office. It could easily be missed if you didn't know where it was. It's dimly lit, just like everything else down here, but the cars that have parked in front of it almost blocks the view of the door, the window of the office is dark as if the blinds are closed. I see the officer must have walked in, as I see when the door opens a slight bright beam of light flies out, it quickly goes dark again when the door closes. A couple more minutes then we should be away.

A few minutes pass with still no sign of him on his way back, the doors never re open and there's been no sign of anyone peeping through the blinds. I start to think he's maybe had to request a new card from Christos and maybe that's why it's taking so long. Then I glance over to Cora who is nervously checking her watch, and her phone then the radio, all the while trying to watch for anything outside. She's becoming uneasy, I see her shift in her seat. Then she turns her head around to look at us.

'Have you seen him yet?' She asks with a sharp tone. I can tell that she is nervous. I shake my head. I see a look of dread appear on her face, Doreen props herself up and starts frantically searching around.

'He should have been back by now!' I hear her voice now has a tremble with it. She is putting the radio to her lips ready to call for back up. This isn't part if the plan, he's been far too long, and we are stuck sat in this car like three sitting ducks waiting to be hit like a target.

'There's nothing this side.' Doreen shrieks out. Cora is just about to make the call over her radio. When she suddenly stops, even though the radio is pressed near her lips she does not speak, she doesn't move, her eyes wide as can be glares out the driver side window.

'Cora!' I shout to her. She doesn't answer. I turn to see what she's looking at. The shock slaps me right in the face when I see it. A dark slim figure is hurtling towards us. It moves fast but wobbly. I can't make out what or who it is apart from they are striding at speed towards us.

'Someone is coming.' Doreen shouts out. I look to see the darkened figure getting closer. I feel my heart start to race and frantically start wondering what to do. I keep a grip on the door handle. Is it the officer running back with the new ticket because he has taken too long? The thought is inviting, but it's not his figure, it's too slim and I'm pretty sure he wouldn't move as fast as what this is.

Cora stumbles with the Radio, the dark looking figure is getting closer and closer, the chilling screams are frantic. This isn't someone coming to attack us, this is someone terrified, running for their life. It's a woman. As the woman gets closer, I can see the whites of her eyes, wide and blood shot, terror covers her face. She looks terrible. I look over to her, almost unrecognisable, her dirty bare feet are cut open, leaving a trail of blood behind her, her tiny frame looks even smaller, her usually perfect makeup smeared making her eyes smudge with black, her thin arms are bruised and covered in scratches. She frantically runs right to us.

CHAPTER 31

'Rita!' I scream desperately trying to open the door to get to her, but the dam protective locks won't open. I see the fear in her eyes, her hair is all over the place, she is scared, in fact she's more than scared she's terrified. 'Open the door it's Rita.' Doreen also desperately tries to open her door, we both are pulling at the reluctant handles, but nothing moves. Cora is in shock, she's gone from this moment, her shaking hands won't stop as they jitter uncontrollably on her lap, she doesn't move her gaze from Rita. 'Cora, open the God dam door.' I scream as loud as I could that it burns my already painful throat. A shocked Cora jumps back into the now, she fumbles with panic to find the switch to open the locks. Rita is now at the car and is banging on the windows with her fists, she looks right at me terrified. I keep trying the door, but still, they won't budge. She stops the frantic pounds and looks behind her, she then turns back around to face me again, looking even more scared. She hits harder, each one makes the glass rumble, I see the tears form in her eyes as she loses hope. She then screams. A chilling scream that echoes, it rings in my ears, the scream of sheer desperation. She's petrified and all I can do is watch on hopeless. I claw back at the window, I hit it with every bit of force I have, I will do anything, I can't leave her. I don't realise I'm screaming until I feel the burn rip down my throat.

'Let me in, please let me in, he's coming.' I look behind her to see another dark figure walking. His fast-paced walk storms to us, he narrows his head as if about to charge. He's holding a bloodied knife I watch as the drips fall to the ground. He casually wipes the blood on his sleeve of his free hand, as if getting it ready to use it again. He's not too far away now. I'm on edge, I start pounding the glass, I kick the door, it sends shooting pains through my body, I don't stop. Desperate to get Rita safe, I keep trying.

'The door Cora.' Doreen screeches.

'I'm trying.' Cora finally finds it; she pushes the button. We hear the click of the doors open as the same time as Rita pulls the handle, the door swings open and she dives in, flying her body through my side. She carries on screaming even though she is inside the car, I slam the door shut and hold her shaking cold body as she cries out. Doreen leans over to help calm her. Cora never takes her eyes off the man as he bolts towards us.

The knifed man notices and makes a run to get to us while the door is unlocked. Just as he reaches the handle Cora hits the lock button leaving the masked man looking directly at us, the same man that chased us in the corridor, I'm certain it's him, those piercing eyes, sharp and dark, I'd notice them anywhere. He knows he can't open the door, but he tries anyhow. Realising it's not going to budge; he thrusts his elbow to the window. His heavy thuds are useless against the protective glass, but each one manages to make me jump. Failing to break the glass, he now leans down to look me directly in the eyes, I try not to look at him, I try not show him how scared I am. I'm terrified, he can see my fear as he grins almost licking his lips with enjoyment. Tears are starting to roll down my face, I feel them sliding down my cheeks, each one slowly dropping in my lap. I shut my eyes tight, hoping when I open them again, he is gone. He's not, he taps the tip of his knife on my window to get my attention, I can't help but look, he lifts his knife to the window and points it at me, then slowly pretends to slice it over his neck. I shudder knowing exactly what he is suggesting doing. He will if he gets the chance to, he already has to one person. I slowly turn my face away from him and just look forward I shut my eyes tight and squeeze my lips together to stop my screaming, but more slow tears run down my face. Rita clings on to me and places her head deep into my chest, shaking. He sees us terrified and laughs. He moves to the driver window and bends to look at Cora, he stares deep into her eyes and then taps on the window with the tip off his knife and then points to the lock button. She curls herself up and away from him, making as much space between them as possible. She shakes her head, Refusing his demands. This angers him as he forcefully punches her side of the window. The huge thud makes her jump.

'Fuck you.' She screams at him. He laughs and gives one last thud on the window with his elbow before standing up tall and heading back to the corner office. Finally, we can breathe, we need to move in case he comes back. I know for certain he will. His want for blood is desperate, he wants us dead, they will keep trying and like Christos has said, they won't stop trying until they have killed us all.

'Drive!' Doreen shouts to Cora. Cora jumps into the driver's seat and goes to turn the key. Although the barrier still blocks us we don't care, we will run right into it if we need too. She takes too long, why have we not set off, why aren't we crashing through that barrier at full speed and with spinning wheels. I start shouting at her to drive as my eager eyes check to see if he is on his way back.

'There's no key.' She screams then scrambles around to see if she can find it. 'It's not here.' Rita is in a daze and mumbles things to herself, I can't make out what she is saying, but whatever it is she is repeating it over and over, again. Me and Doreen hold on to her to try and calm her down, she must be in shock, this only makes her want to speak louder.

'He killed him.' She mumbles. We all look at each other, knowing who she means, the officer who went to the office. I had almost forgotten about him with all the rushing panic. 'He killed him, just like that he killed him.' She trembles as if reliving that moment.

'Your safe now.' I try to comfort her, but I don't know how or what to say, my heart aches for another poor officer losing his life to these psychos, while protecting us, I can't help but feel guilty. So much hurt and pain caused by a stupid mistake. I can see the pain in Cora's eyes at yet losing another colleague. She doesn't seem to think about it for too long, she can't, we all can't if we surrender ourselves to the grief, we will be next. Then our families will be the ones left grieving. I can't do that to them, I won't do that to them. I pull myself together ready for the fight.

'We need to move now!'

'The keys aren't here!' Cora is searching furiously through every part of the car, still no keys to be found.

'What do you mean they aren't here?' I dread to think who has them, of course he had taken, he wanted us left locked in here.

'He must have taken them with him.' The colour drains from Cora's face. We all stop what we are doing and stare in the direction of the office, hopeless. A figure starts looming from the shadows, a big smile appears through his cut out black ski mask. As he gets closer, we can see he's holding the car keys. He lifts them up to his head and shakes them, as if to say, "looking for these." He then points the key fob at the car and presses the button to unlock it. Cora dives on the button to lock it again. This seems to become a battle for a few seconds to see who can press the button the fastest. The masked man seems to be enjoying the situation, getting a thrill from his hunt. He teases us every time he presses the button on the fob. Cora is becoming exhausted, physically and mentally we are all slowly dying. He knows he will eventually win!

'Use my radio! Tell them we need back up down here now!' Cora screams at us, we don't move, we are in too much shock. 'Now!' She blares, her shrieks are that loud that it causes my ears to ring, but it makes me move. I jump through to the front grab her radio and remember the code word we were given in an emergency. Unsure what I'm doing I start pressing buttons, until

I hear the crackle sound.

'RED BIRD, RED BIRD!' I scream as loud as I can with my burning throat, I wait a few seconds, but nothing comes back! I try again. 'RED BIRD! He's trying to kill us, help us please!' My shouts become desperate hoping that someone hears me on the other side. Still there is nothing. I begin to cry, are we left on our own? I go to use the radio again, my hands shaking as I watch him get closer and closer to us. Just as I press the button to speak. I hear it. A tiny voice answers us.

'Copy that.'

'Are you fucking kidding me!' I scream out loud. 'Is that all they can say, I've used the code word. Do they not know we are in danger! We are about to be killed!' My furious rant blares round the car and into the radio as I still have my finger laid on the speaker button without realising. I quickly let it go slightly embarrassed.

'We are on our way, try and get somewhere safe, Is Detective Peters there?'

I look over to Cora who's still struggling on trying to keep the doors locked, the mask man is starting to lose his patience and instead steps back and twists his neck to make it crack, he's right by the car now. I can only hope they make it here intime.

'I'm kind of busy right now Christos.' Cora looks at us. 'He's going to get in here, take the radio and run find somewhere to hide, I'm going to try and hold him off.' Cora looks at us with stern look waiting for us to go. 'They will be here any minute now, you need to go.'

'We can't leave you.' I'm shaking so fast that I can barely keep a hold of the radio.

'If you don't, we will all die!' Just then we hear the sharp piercing sound of him hitting the window with the bottom end of his knife. This makes us all jump. He repeats the hit again, only this time he unlocks the door and swings it open, our reactions where to slow, the driver's door is now fully open as he edges his way in to dive for Cora. 'Go now!' Cora screams as he grabs her.

CHAPTER 32

Without another thought I swing open the door where Cora was sat, I jump out of run to the back doors to open it for Rita and Doreen. They both stumble out and fall to the ground, I help them both to their feet and we bolt into the darkness. I look back to see the man now dragging Cora out by her feet. Her feet rapidly kicking back, making him struggle to keep his grip, but with an already injured and tired Cora the man is too powerful and drags her fully out. She smashes to the floor; I hear her yelp out in pain. Something inside me makes me stop running, I turn around to see them scuffing on the floor. I debate running back when I see the defenceless Cora on the ground, the masked man has now pinned her fully, she can barely move under his weight. I can vaguely hear Doreen screaming at me to run, but can't take my eyes off Cora, she needs help, we can't just leave her to be killed. My mind is running riot with thoughts of what I should do.

'What are you doing? We need to go.' This time Doreen shakes me to get my attention. I ignore her and start to move forward to help Cora who's struggling on trying to fight him off! She sees me coming to her, but her eyes aren't filled with relief, they look confused, but I keep edging closer to them.

'Run!' She shouts. Her eyes look back to me in terror, which interrupts her from protecting herself. Then the masked man lifts his knife up above his head and plunges into her side. I gasp and hold my hand up to my mouth, but I carry on running to her. I know the danger what is waiting, but I can't stop myself, her eyes are still fixed on me. She slowly mutters again, I'm just a few feet away from her now. 'Run!' Her eyes are starting to slowly blink until they close. The masked man looks up and sees me close to him, a grin appears through the slit of his mask. I've stopped running now, I know I should be turning and running as fast as I can in the other direction, but my body won't move. The radio is still clutched in my hand, I must be pressing it too hard as now, I feel a burning throb and the pain shoots up into my arm. The man is now clambering to his feet, The lifeless body of Cora just lays there as blood pours from her wound. I start hearing shouting coming from behind me, everything seems to have gone into slow motion, the buzzing in my head is making it hard for me to concentrate. Then I hear the loudest scream from Rita, the echoes bounce round the parking lot. It wakes me!

'Run!'

My body finally moves, I turn around and begin to run as fast as I can, I dare not stop, I dare not look round, I keep going even though every bit of the splintering pain that floods my body cries for me to stop. I follow the footsteps of Doreen and Rita, my lungs are burning, and my body is ready to collapse. I can hear the man's heavy steps trailing behind me knowing they are getting closer with every step he takes. We head to a clump of cars parked over the other end, it's so dark in here, that between the cars it's almost impossible to see, with just the little glimpses of dim light trying to break through stops it from being in total darkness. We crouch behind a big people carrier, hoping to have lost him when running between different cars. We huddle closely together as if trying to blend into the car. The silence is deafening, and the wait is painfully frightening. I feel everyone judder with fear. The imagine of Cora's eyes flickers in my head, and I wonder if her lifeless body is still alive. I feel the pain seer through my hand that's holding the radio, I need to remove it from my grip, I notice the indents printed onto my palm, desperate for the blood to flow. I don't hear the ping of the elevator, nor shouts to suggest they are here to rescue us, there's nothing. Why is it taking so long, have they decided to leave us?

They a lost cause, if they make it, then they make it. Were they ever going to come? Everything runs through my head. It hasn't been that long from the first call to them, it's only been minutes, but when your life is on the line, every second of every minute, surely counts. I place the radio back to my lips, and whisper into it again.

'Please hurry.' My hope dwindles, it's only a matter of time before he finds us, or the police reach us first. Which one that will be, I don't know, but so far, the killer has the upper hand.

I hear his footsteps getting closer in my direction. The three of us just stare at one another knowing he's not that far away now. I close my eyes as if that will help me become invisible and start to pray. He's close now, I can feel it.

'I know your around here! I can practically smell your fear. Come on out I promise I won't hurt you!' His calm laugh sends chills up my spine.

My tightly shut eyes spring open when I hear his cold harsh voice, he's so close I can hear the panting in his breath. I look under the car and can see his feet just a few cars away from us. 'You want to play a little game of hide and seek?' We look to each other wondering if we should move, knowing we are just moments from being caught. I put a finger over my lip to keep us quiet then point in the direction where he is. 'You know I'm going to find you! So why not save me the hassle and just come out.' His voice is getting closer, and I can hear the spring in his step as he jumps round each car hoping to find us. Rita has her head buried in her hands, terrified to be captured by this monster again. Doreen keeps her arms wrapped round her tightly. I look back under the car and see his feet are now at the car next to us, they then turn and head our way. I push Doreen to move to the back end of the car we are hiding behind, she understands what is happening as she slowly gathers Rita and guides her. I follow crouching on all fours, trying my hardest to keep my desperate heavy breathing from bursting out of my lungs, my knees feel every scrape of the ruff floor, the sting of my skin coming away blasts through them, I grit my teeth and carry on moving. We make it to the back end with barely any noise. I look back under the car to see he's now at the other end of the car where we were. His chilling tone disturbs the silence again.

'I can feel your close.' His voices shudders through me, I hold my breathe trying not to make a sound even though every nerve in my body wants me to scream. I can see he's just stood at the other end; his footsteps have now stopped, he must be looking round to see where else to check, I pray he's finished searching round this car. He has. I watch as his feet start heading further away, I breathe a sigh of relief, Doreen watches my every move for any indication to what is happening, she notices my relief and relaxes her tense shoulders. Rita stays curled up in Doreen's arms to scared to even look up or move. Just as I'm about to look for an exit in the opposite direction to where he is heading. Our silence gets broken! The radio screeches filling the silent lot with its roar!

'We are almost here, hang in there!' Christos's voice fills the silence. I quickly press it into my chest hoping to hide the noise, but I know it's too late, he will have heard it. Everything goes silent for a moment. I hope it's scares him off to leave. I look at the other two, their eyes are now wide open in shock. I look back under the car unable to find where he is, my eyes dart everywhere desperately searching but can't see or hear his footsteps. My heart is thudding away, my mind is racing. What should we do now? I know we can't risk staying here any longer.

'We need to run!' I whisper to them. I see a shadow loom from behind me. I freeze. It's too late he's found us!

'Found you!' His husky voice says with excitement. Just as we begin to bolt away, he sweeps his knife and slices it down my arm. I don't stop running, I know I can't or that will be it, even with blood pouring down my arm and the throbbing pain stinging I try to increase my pace to catch up with Rita and Doreen, who are now a bit ahead of me. I keep following their direction, I can feel him behind me getting closer and closer. To the point I can now feel his gasping breathe hitting me on the back of the neck, I know he's going to catch me any minute, his excited laugh rings in my ears, he's that close now, that if he stretches out his arm, he'd probably be able to grab me. I decide to cut through the cars and not to go in the same direction of Rita and Doreen. Hoping it slows him down enough for them to get away I know I'm already going to be caught, but I carry on running, my feet burning, my knees aching and the thudding pain shouting down my arm makes it that limp that I must hold it to stop it flopping. He follows my direction, but I must have gained some pace as I can no longer feel his panting laughs hitting me. I race round a car that's stood alone and turn around to face him.

I see him at the other end of the car waiting to see which way I go. I tease each direction hoping he goes the other way. Instead, he mirrors my every move. His eyes hungry and wild, his teeth clenched into a smile. I can see he's enjoying this. He's like a predator that knows he's caught his prey, enjoying toying with it before the kill, I know that this is going to be my last move, I take a deep breath as I choose my direction. I lunge, but the flexible man is already on top of me as he tries to rip away my protecting arms.

Something catches my eye behind his head, it's coming up quick, so fast that I don't' see what it is. I close my eyes, then there's it is, a huge thud! His head bounces forward and nearly hits me in the face, he doesn't move, I feel his dead weight press on top of me. I open my eyes, wondering what has happened and why I'm not dead. I look into his once smirking face, now bewildered and shocked, his grinning smile has now closed, he slams to the floor, his heavy body almost topples me over with him, his eyes still wide open but no sign of life. Unsure what I've just witnessed I stand and stare at him too shocked to move. I slowly look up to see what has done this, behind him stands Doreen, holding a small fire extinguisher. She's still holding up high above her head ready to hit him again if he moves. Her eyes are wild and focused she doesn't take them off him, not even to look at me. I try talking to her, but she doesn't hear me, it's like her soul has left her body, just leaving a shell behind.

'Doreen. it's okay.' I whisper to her, but she still doesn't notice. I reach my hand to her, she still doesn't move, my shaking hand waits for hers, but she doesn't reach back. Tears are welling up in my eyes, I'm desperate for her to notice at me and to hear me, but she doesn't move an inch. Traumatized and terrified Doreen just stares at his lifeless body.

Within seconds the dimly light parking lot fills with light. Men appearing with guns held out and torches blaring run towards us. I can hear them shouting but their words just roll into blur. I look at Doreen who is still holding the fire extinguisher, her eyes are glazed over. I can hear the police screaming as they get closer, I see their mouths moving, their frantic pointed guns ready to shoot. I shield my eyes from the bright light of their torches, I try to peer through my hands, but the lights are too bright to make anything out, I know it must be the police finally arriving, it's got to be. My distress calls feel so long ago, yet barely any time has gone by. My anxious body is still on alert, it's still in its fight or flight mode, Do I run? I look at Doreen she hasn't notice what's happening behind, she still stands as still as can be. The voices scream loud and clear this time, my urge to run vanishes. It's them finally!

'Put down your weapons, get on your knees and show us your hands!' The police are only a few feet away when they halt, aiming their guns and shinning the torches at us. It has become so bright that I need to close my covering eyes. I do as they wish and drop to my knees holding up my shaking hands. Doreen barely moves, I'm not even sure she has noticed. They scream once again, waiting for Doreen to move. She does nothing. I start to panic; she is going to get herself shot if she doesn't move. I begin to scream at her, even though the pain in my throat is begging for me to stop, I keep screaming and screaming until she notices me.

'Doreen! You need to get down.' She looks at me with a vacant stare. 'Doreen!' I scream again. She suddenly wakes from her state of shock, drops the fire extinguisher and falls to her knees. Her wild eyes are darting everywhere, you can see she is confused, she looks up to me and starts to cry, I just want to run over and grab her, but the pointed guns edging towards us stops me. There close enough now to be pointed in our faces. My body stiffens up as I'm looking down yet again another barrel. I can't understand what they are saying, it's all going too fast. I feel like my body is going to collapse in a heap, my head is swirling, and the parking lot is starting to spin. I noticed my arm is now fully covered in blood, as I watch each drip fall past my face, I hear the drops drip, drip, drip on the floor in front of me, I notice a little pool of blood starting to form at my knees. Just as I'm sure I'm about to fall to the ground in a heap. I hear a voice shouting through the crowd of officers that have now surrounded us.

'Whoa! Hold on there.' I hear a familiar voice appearing from the barricade of armed men, he pushes himself through, I watched as each officer gets pushed to the side. 'Hold down your weapons! These are the victims!' As soon as I see him, I just want to cry, please let this nightmare be over!

Christos makes his way over to us, his eyes frantic and distressed. The armed men step aside for him, which leaves him a path to walk through. When he reaches us, he notices the body on the floor and realises how close things got, again! His eyes look hurt when he sees the state we are in, then I notice the flicker of relief to see us still alive. He grabs us in a hug and tries to help us to our feet. My legs feel too weak to move properly and as he tries to hold us both up, but our weight is too much for him, he struggles to keep a hold, his struggling grunts echo down my ear. Under any other circumstances I'd be rather offended!

'Get over here and help them! We need blankets and medical assistant.' He shouts to his officers. 'Are you hurt?' We shake our heads still too frightened and in shock to move much more. I suddenly feel a cool breeze of air that hits over my body. The whole of my body trembles to the point that the blanket they have wrapped around my shoulders has now slid off and fell to the floor. I watch as I see Christos rush to bend down to pick it up, he wraps it back around my shoulders and fixes it more securely around me. He heads us to the direction of some medics that's close by. The once deserted parking lot is not heaving with people, rushing in all directions, taking pictures, securing areas, treating people. It's amazing what a few minutes can do. I see someone roll out a body bag, the realisation that I was so close to getting packed in one of them, makes me sick.

'Come on your safe now, let's get you checked over and get out of here!' He leads the way, but I stop knowing I need to know more before I leave. Christos and Doreen halt when they noticed I've stopped walking. They watch confused I was walk back.

'Come on we are nearly there; you really need that arm checked before you go anywhere.' Christos tries to usher me towards the medics, but I stand my ground and don't move. This persistent urge won't budge and know I must go back. I need to.

'I need to see who that is.' Before anyone can stop me, I bolt back to the body that's still laying on the floor. I hear Christos's pleads not to, but I carry on and ignore him, I squeeze passed the surrounding officers, they don't try to stop me, which I'm surprised at. Instead, they look on wondering what I'm doing.

'Wait!' Just as Christos gets his words out, I'm already there peeling off his ski mask. Slowly lifting it above his head, firstly it reveals the tense square jaw that's cleanly shaved, I lift it further to reveal the rest of him, stopping just as I get to the eyes, although you can see his eyes through the cut out of his mask, I stop and just look at them for a moment longer. I recognise him, but my mind scrambles to think where from? I reveal the last part of him. His perfect smooth features just there with no emotion. I gasp when I realize that I have seen this man before. He's hotel staff! My mind whizzes back to that day in reception, the overly nosey, strange man! I can't believe my eyes, of course he would have something to do with it, he has the key to the whole hotel. He was figuring us out the moment he knew we were looking for Cora! It's not a surprise he managed to get to Rita and trap her down here.

'It's the hotel manager!' I shout back to Doreen and Christos; they are now making their way back over.

 Just then I think I see his eyes blink, I look a bit more closely to him wondering if he is alive or dead, he certainly looks dead! As I get close enough to him, he bolts up to grab my wrist. I yelp out unexpecting him to move. Before I know it one of the officers is already on top of him then I'm released from his grip instantly. I scramble back and my bum, trying to move away as fast as I can. I watch as a few officers jump onto the frantic man and restrain him, He's screaming and laughing. His laugh creepy and insane, it's clear to see the man is crazy. He catches a glimpse of me through the crowd of officers, his eyes wide and red, sweat pouring out of him while he tries desperately to free himself, he stops struggling for a second and just glares right to me, slaver is dripping out of his mouth from his screams. He purse's his lips and blows me a kiss. He laughs even more when he sees the horror on my face. Before he can do anything else the officers are carrying him out of the way. His screeching giggles echoes through the parking lot. Doreen puts her hand on my shoulder which makes me jump, she bends down to my level.

'Come on we need to get you out of here!' I nod and take Christos's helping hand, I slowly try to ease myself up. A surge of panic runs over me suddenly remembering about Cora and Rita.

'You need to help Cora and where's Rita?' I say flustered.

'They are safe we have got them, come on we need to go!' This time I follow Christos as he leads us away. I do not turn back this time!

CHAPTER 33

The three of us now sitting in a guarded room in the police station, after being taken to the hospital to get checked over, again! luckily none of us have any serious injuries and we should make a full recovery. Cora however is alive, but has been rushed right into surgery, we won't have updates for a few more hours. Although it wasn't an integration room, it still felt cold and hostile. Just plain white walls, with big dark leather couches and a coffee table in the middle separating them. I've never wanted to be at home as much in my life, but we aren't allowed to leave just yet. We have managed to phone our families again but still having to keep it brief. Rita's son, however, was delighted to finally speak to his mum apparently, he was going stir crazy and needed people to come over to watch him, which is understandable. We've been told that our families have patrols checking on them just in case Bill finds a way to them, this is more of a safety precaution rather than any evidence of an attack on them. Everything is being very securely thought out, to hopefully prevent anyone else in being put in danger, we have had too many lucky escapes so far, I can't help but think we may not get another. I look around at us all, the three of us are like shadows of our former selves, broken and traumatized, I know our wounds will soon heal but our minds may never. Considering it's only a few days in of our week-long holiday, we look ready to go home now. So much for coming away to relax the thought flickers in my mind as I casually grin to myself. Our perfectly groomed hair and makeup is splattered everywhere, our bodies aching and covered in bruises and cuts. We barely speak to each other instead we just seem to hold on to our mugs off coffee a bit tighter and huddle around the coffee table. Until we get the news we can fly home. The silence is becoming unbearable between us, as time seems to go so slow. Has this ruined our friendship? Clearly none of us know what to say, we all just process, with what the fuck has just happened! Every now and then one of us will fidget forward looking as though we are about to say something, but then think better of it and sit back into the sofa, knowing that's the easiest option right now.

'I'm so sorry I have put you all through this, I could have got one of us killed!' Rita breaks the silence. The guilt is visible in her voice and face. She begins to cry 'How could this have happened?' I place my mug on the table and wrap my arms around her tiny frame. Somehow without her confidence the once youthful loud adventurous Rita has now turned to a nervous, terrified older woman in just a few days. I know that we are all going to find it difficult to recover but I look at Rita and wonder if she ever will. I've never seen her like this before, even after her husband's affair and the death of her parents. Of course, she mourned and got upset, but she never lost her head strong confident self. This is like a Rita we have never seen. She's barely said a word about what happened to her when she came running out to the car to us, and I've never pressed figuring she will tell us when she's ready, or if she ever wants to, but has happened to her has clearly scarred her.

'It's not your fault, please don't blame yourself.' I stand up to move over to her and offer her some comfort, but her tear-stained face looks the other way when she sees me. She wants nothing to do with us. Doreen also notices Rita's reaction.

'This is not your fault! Now pull yourself together, we are all here safe maybe traumatised, but we are here! Look at the bloody state of us! Now come on, we need to think positive, our kids and grandchildren won't want to see us like this.' Doreen's harsher approach makes me cringe but is soon catches Rita's attention and she now has turned herself round to face us.

'How can you act like that, like everything is okay?'

'Oh I know everything is not okay! But considering we are all sitting here together now, we are going to be able to go home that's good enough from this horrible situation. Anyway, think how bad it's going to be for me going home, my husband is already a dithering mess every time I leave him, imagine what he is going to be like now? I won't be able to go to the corner shop without him having a panic in case something happens. I know he loves me very much but the thought that he might have to cook, clean and wash clothes if something happens to me will traumatize him!' Doreen laughs as tries to make light of the situation which works as we begin to laugh for the first time in what feels like a long time.

Christos then re-enters the room with a raised eyebrow. He wonders why we are laughing after the experience we've all just endured. His face soon changes to a stern look, the barer of bad news. We stop what we are doing and stare back, waiting for him to speak. The room falls into utter silence for a moment. I can see his troubled thoughts appear across his face. He begins to shift awkwardly from foot to foot, then gets the courage to step forward and take a seat on the couch that is facing us. We all just watch and take in every movement he makes, knowing what is bothering him can't be good. One hand presses into his temples, trying to relieve some pressure likely from his ponding head. He begins to open his mouth to speak then suddenly clasps it shut as he hesitates.

'What is up Christos?' I ask although not sure I want to really know. He shuffles uncomfortably in his seat trying to find the courage and the right words to speak.

'The thing is we have the two men in custody facing the charges, that's not a problem, what we don't have is Bill! We barely have enough to connect him to anything, or even being involved in anything that has happened!' He finally says disappointed, I sit in shock not being able to believe what he has said. There's surely got to be something?

'But he is involved!' Rita explodes in a rage.

'We know that, but there isn't enough evidence to connect him to it! If it was him that was holding you in the parking lot, we'd have him! But it wasn't, we had eyes on him the whole time and he never went anywhere near there. Now you say that you left his room of free will, he let you go, it was the hotel manager that led you to the parking lot. Did he by any chance mention Bill wanting you to go down there or did Bill in anyway suggest you go down there?'

Rita leans forward, trying to piece together the memories, she takes a minute in her thoughts before she answers to Christos. 'No! No he didn't, in fact he didn't let up on anything he was kind a polite and there was no threating behaviour from him what so ever towards me.' She looks down at the floor disappointed.

'You don't need to protect him! If he did anything you can say, we are safe now!' Rita cuts me off before I can say anything else.

'I know, but he honestly didn't do anything to me, he was just like a normal man, we went out for coffee we had a little stroll then got a taxi back to the hotel, we were going to get a couple of drinks in the bar, so I said I'm going to head back to my room first to change and he suggested to go to his room first to freshen up as it was closer, then we would go to mine. When we were at his, that's when I got the call from Bill's apartment phone, to say Doreen had taken a fall and had been rushed to hospital, I didn't realise my mobile was missing until then. The hotel manager said he had a taxi coming for me in the parking lot, I didn't think twice about it to be honest I was too concerned about Doreen. So, when I arrived there, he said come and wait in the office until the taxi arrives, I did just that!' Rita holds her head in her hands and looks down at the floor. 'How stupid must I be?' We all seem to shuffle slightly knowing how cunning they've been. Anyone would easily fall for that, I know I would have, I think to myself. 'It wasn't until he locked the office door that I knew something wasn't right, I tried to get out, but he was too strong, the only reason I got away was when that officer came knocking, he seen me and they ended fighting, I seen him stab him, and that's when I ran.' Rita starts shaking as tears are start to flow down her face. Christos butts in to stop her saying anything more, knowing it's too much for her.

'Listen you're not stupid and you did the right thing to run, you might not be sitting here now if you didn't. They are very clever and having been in this game for a long, long time, they know exactly what to do and how to make it look so they are not involved, this is why they have gotten away with it for so long. We only managed to catch Earnie because Lynn and Doreen went snooping where they shouldn't have.' I cringe to myself as he mentions it. 'That saved my detectives life, because she certainly wouldn't have been seen again if it wasn't for them two!' He looks over to me and Doreen and gives us a thankful smile.

'I really need you to remember if he made a phone call that you may heard parts to or if he managed to slip down to see the hotel manager while you were with him, was there anything to suggest they knew each other?' Christos waits eagerly with his pen and notepad.

'No, he didn't. We passed the hotel manager in the reception area, but they never spoke to each other, Bill never even looked at him, but the hotel manager defiantly seen us, I can remember him staring so much at me, which I thought was weird, but with the phone call I just presumed that was why.' Christos nods but I can clearly see his disappointment.

'Thank you for being honest, but we have nothing to connect Bill to this! We won't be able to hold him any longer.'

'There has got to be something?' Doreen insists.

'We have nothing. Earnie and the manager are keeping tight lipped, they've not slipped up with anything. There basically saying that each crime that's happened isn't connected, that they have been random acts, we know they most certainly aren't, but we don't have any evidence to suggest otherwise.'

'This is bullshit!' I stand to my feet in anger. 'We all have nearly been killed in the process and he's going to get away with it! What are we meant to do now? He knows who we are! Are we supposed to look over our shoulders for the rest of our lives because this psychopath gets to walk, he might come back for us!' Christos's face turns red with embarrassment, he stands himself up to join me and places a hand on my folded arms.

'I know this is frustrating, we are going to look over all the data we have and hopefully something will connect him to it. In the meantime, we are going to have a detail signed on to you all to watch over you, until you head back to the UK. We will let the British embassy know, and they will then assign the appropriate regulations for what you will need when you head back home. He's a very dangerous man and he is known over many countries including yours, there is a chance that you all may not be able to go back to your own lives just yet!'

'Your fucking kidding us, right? We all have families back home, we have our homes our friends, you're telling us that we might not be able to go back to that. Rita joins me in standing, her face is furious, the anger of red is rising from her neck right up to her face. Then Doreen stomps herself up. The three of us now beaming out our anger at the poor Detective, who ends up looking lost and helpless in our almighty rage he becomes unsure what else to say to us as he mumbles away.

'This isn't our fault! All our families are going to be made to suffer because you lot can't do your job right!' I'm bouncing, I'm feeling every bit of the anger bubbling inside of me and it's ready to burst out at any minute, I begin to shout and scream in the poor defenceless man's face. 'This is outrageous, I've just lost my fucking husband and you're telling me I'm going to lose my children and my grandchildren, well he's not going to take them from me!' Christos suddenly seems to be backed in a corner by the three of us. He holds his hands up and tries to diffuse the situation.

'Calm down! Look I'm not saying that is going to happen, but it might I'm just being honest and trying to prepare you for what may be. You've got to understand how dangerous they are! You don't want that to your family surely? Look I've got one of my Detectives fighting for their life at the minute, and two officers dead. These fellas don't mess about! I hope it doesn't come to that for you, but it might!' Christos is breathless from trying to explain what could happen so fast that his words and breathing have gotten all mixed up. Me, Rita and Doreen step back away from Christos to give him some room, while we try to process everything. Deep down I know he's right, but the bubbles of anger are still popping away through my body, why has this had to happen to us, out of all the people who could have got their case mixed up, it had to be ours. I take a few deep breaths, my body feels the exhaustion and pain. I begin to make my way back to the sofa with the sudden urge to want to fall asleep, I'm disheartened, every time we start to think this nightmare is over with, something else crops up to rear its ugly head! I'm starting to wonder if we will ever be free of this!

'Can we at least go back to the hotel I think we all need to get some rest?' My drained body asks. Christos weighs it up for a second debating if it's a good idea or not, then allows it to happen.

'I will get you a lift and an officer will be there watching over you.' Christos says while leaving the room, not entirely satisfied with our choice.

CHAPTER 34

After finishing up with all the questioning and safety precautions, which of course the lists where endless, we are able to head back to a new safe apartment, where we will wait with an officer until all the details are sent to the embassy, and the police back in the UK, then they will determine what kind of action will need to be taken. If by chance we need to go into a secure location for a little while, then we won't be allowed to even see our families, breaking the news to them was heartbreaking, they don't understand the full situation, as neither do we, finally getting it through to them that it won't be forever and it will be the safest option for everyone, they all reluctantly agree.

The warm breeze hits me as I stand waiting for the car to arrive, the three us bruised and battered take in deep breaths of fresh air, for it seems like hours of being couped in a stuffy room. The big officer that is going to be watching us is huge, his stern face never changes as he cautiously checks every inch of the police car park, and when any of us stray too far he huddles us back up, like a flock of wandering sheep. Which makes me feel like I'm a tiny little girl again. His face never alters, even when our car arrives, he still keeps that stern focused look. Nothing is going to put this man off his game. He tells us to wait one minute before we jump in so he can do a sweep inside the car, we look on fascinated at how quickly this big bulky man can crouch down on all fours to check underneath without any hesitation. "I can barely bend down and put my socks on without a few grunts and he must be three times the size of me." Already to go with the officer finally satisfied that it's safe, he opens the back door and stands by it and ushers us in. Doreen slides in first and struggles to shuffle her bum across, which holds up the queue and puts the officer more on edge, I see him glance at his watch and roll his eyes, clearly, we are not quick enough for him. Doreen has barely got fully into her seat when the officer has started ushering me in, which now has caused a slight blockage at the door and first seat, which starts to really annoy the man. Although he is becoming impatient and really wants to get us on our way, he still manages to keep his cool and politely asks us to hurry things along as we are behind on our schedule.

Finally, I've scooted myself into position and managed to cock one leg over into Doreen's footwell and the other stays in Rita's, though I feel like I'm straddling the seat a bit too inappropriately, I'm glad I've managed my stiff joints in without any help. I wait for Rita to join us. I look back out to see what's taking her so long and find her angrily staring at something behind our car. I look at the officer whose stern look has for once changed into shock and panic, I try to stick my head out further see what is happening, but then get blocked by the officer sweeping into action, he slams our door shut, which has locked us in as I figure out while trying the handle. Doreen has now got curious and is trying to push herself up to my side to see what is going on, bearing in mind this car isn't very big in the back, she squeezes her big breasts up to me which pushes me further to the door, the next thing I know my face is pressed against the window. Trapped between Doreen's boobs and the glass the only thing I can see is my breath putting a print on the window. Doreen is totally oblivious I have to let out a scream to get her to notice. Finally, she moves and allows me some room.

'Oh, I'm sorry, I'm trying to see what is going on.' She says a little embarrassed as she backs herself up. I just give an eye roll back at her. With both of us now composed in a better manner we peer out desperately trying to see what is going on. The big bulk of the officer has most of the view covered, but I can see he has got his arms wrapped around Rita, holding her back from something. Rita pops out her skinny arm out and begins waving it about, every sweep is getting angrier and more aggressive, the big man looks to be struggling to keep Rita restrained, but he somehow manages to do so. He's lifted her up so he's carrying her now, with what looks to be in some sort of move you would do when your toddler kicks off and refuses to move. He's now bundling her over to our way, his face is puffed red and his grip solid, he opens the back door and gently throws Rita into the back with us, then slams the door shut, he heads over to whatever Rita was going mad at. Me and Doreen look over to her wondering what the hell is going on. Her lips are curled into angry snarl, her heavy breathing is making her grunt, and her body is trembling, rather with anger or freight, she doesn't sit still for a second before she has swung her full body round so she can now look out of the back window. Her rage continues with burst of swearing and sticking her middle finger up.

'FUCK YOU!' She screams.

We don't even ask, instead we swing ourselves round, bumping into each other with not getting our timings right, with a fumble about and a few huffs and puffs, we manage. The three of us peering through the back window. First, I see the officer, he's angry, you can tell he's shouting, because every so often a bit of spit will fly out with his words, his face is beaming red, and his huge hands are pointing into someone's face that's standing outside the other car, it looks like another officer, he looks embarrassed and then heads back into the station. Our officer turns around after a long glare to the people sitting in the car behind and heads back over to us, I debate quickly turning round when he catches us looking but i know I don't have the speed or the agility to do it, so I just stay put and give an awkward smile to him. As he moves away from blocking the view of the car behind, I get a glimpse of two men, but the car has already started to set off. We all turn ourselves the right way and look out of Doreen's window hoping to get a view to who it is. Rita is still mumbling away to herself cursing the whole time. Then I see it.

Their car slows down as its lines with us, staring back at us, with a huge grin on his face is Bill! My shocked look must have made him laugh, he winks and casually waves bye. His car smoothly glides on into the distance. Our officer clearly fuming speaks before any of us do. He asks the driver to wait a couple of minutes before we set off, so they are out of view then he tells him to do a different route before we make the proper one to our new destination. He then turns to us, his eyes are back to being focused on the job.

'Sorry, that shouldn't have happened, he wasn't meant to be leaving until we had gone, someone will be in trouble for that mix up, try not to worry everything is still safe and secure, we are just going to add a few more precautions in, and get another car to follow us.'

I'm too shocked to say anything, Rita is still chuntering and shaking. Doreen however calm as surprisingly can be, says.

'What the fuck, well wasn't that a shambles, thought you were keeping us safe from that nutter, not having us meet up in the car park with him!' Our officer flushes and apologising once more and heads right onto his phone to report the incident.

Finally with all clear and on the move to our new location, everyone in the car is very silent, the driver is focused on the changed route, the officer that's watching over us, is checking everything around him, and continuously checks in on the car that's following us in support, a few cars behind. I sit back and dream of getting home away from the place, wanting to hug my grandchildren and daughters, wanting to get back to my safe secure place, my home. Not knowing what is going to be in store for us before then keeps pinging my anxiety, so I keep shaking the thought out of my head and reassure myself that is going to be last resort for being placed in a safe house. I look over to Doreen and Rita, Doreen is trying to doze but every time the car hits a bump her eyes spring open. Rita looks to be in deep thought, her hands are twitching, and her knee is bouncing nervously. I place my hand to stop the nervous twitches, I ask if she is okay, to which she nods and the continues with thinking. I lay myself back into my seat hoping the journey isn't going to be too much longer, we've been driving for twenty minutes already, and we don't seem to be stopping anytime soon. We've already passed the turning for the hotel that we did stay at, a cold shudder creeps through my spine, I wondered if Bill was there, was he waiting for us, or has he gone on the run with it being a close call already.

Rita springs up straight in her seat. The rapid movement makes us all jump, even the officer turns his head round. We all look at her waiting for her to speak, all her troubling thoughts seem to have cleared, her face has brightened to an almost glow.

'Stop the car!' She shouts. Me and Doreen stare at her in shock. What is she doing?

'Sorry we can't, we need to get you to your new location, no stops have been signed off.' The driver replies while looking through his rear-view mirror at her.

'Stop the fucking car and turn back to the police station! We might just be able to get the bastard!' Her voice is determined and excited. The officer's ears seem to prick up with what she has just said, he swings his full body round so he can look at her properly, he mutters something in his radio, and then just looks at her waiting for her to say more. I'm totally confused what she is talking about, my mind begins to race thinking we have missed something, but my thoughts are blank.

'What are you talking about?' Rita ignores me.

'We need to go back to the station now, if he leaves this country, we won't find him again until he finds us. I can't believe we have had the evidence all along!' Doreen and I sit looking at her confused. The officer just as curious as we are, agrees to turn around, he rings in to tell them we are heading back and instantly gives the nod to the driver who swings the car around in a flash. The speed leaves us all pinned into the seats and once again Doreen clings on to her "Holy fuck handle."

Pulling back up at the station, the drive certainly didn't seem to take as long as leaving, with the driver wasting no time, put his foot down to get us back. Christos is waiting for us at the doorway, I can see the anticipation in his face. He opens the door for Rita, who jumps out eagerly before any greetings.

'Did you find my phone?' She asks Christos.

Christos nods. 'Yes, we found your phone it was shattered, our team has it and is still working on it why? It won't be much use for you now, you will need a new one.'

'Can you retrieve things from it even if its broken?'

'Yeah, sometimes why?' Curiosity is eating away at him, as it is me then like a spark I remember.

'Oh, my goodness the recording!' I shout beginning to remember the night at the bar. Rita smiles back at me and gives me a wink.

'What recording?' Christos looking more confused but is desperate to know more. 'You have a recording of what's happened?' He looks excited.

'Yes, I recorded them at the bar, so we could see what they were talking about and if they knew who had their drugs. I'm not sure what is on it, but it could be useful.'

Christos gives a slight grin then ushers us quickly back in the building. We watch as Christos is frantically making calls and seems to be running up and down the corridor ordering people about. After about 20 minutes he re-joins us. We all sit eagerly trying to figure out his expression, but he's too busy jiggling loose papers in his hands.

'You haven't got it have you?' Rita says bowing her head

expecting disappointment.

Christos pauses in front of us his face showing no signs of anything. I'm sure he keeps us waiting on the edge of our seat on purpose.

'You have only gone and done it! We now have the bastard linked to it!' He shouts in relief as if punches the air. The three of us jump up and bombard him wrapping our arms around him. Doreen begins to kiss him on the cheek smothering the poor man. He tries to peel himself from our grip, as we continue to cling on to him. Finally having some good news come our way.

'That's enough now ladies, please take a seat, we haven't caught him yet, we have a team out searching for him and we have the airport on alert looking for any aliases that we know he uses. So let's celebrate once he's been caught.'

'We have them talking about the cocaine, killing people, also the plans what they were going to do when they found out who had their package. They've both used their names on the recording which is great, and we even have the bar man using Bills second name. We certainly have enough now to link him to it, and with the bar man identifying them and the CCTV matching the time of the recording there's no way for him to get out of it. Unless he's already left the country. All we can do now is wait.' We all nod and take a deep breath, finally we have something to smile about, and the thought of us being able to go home and see our families is brilliant, I can't remember feeling this good for a while.

'Surely he can't have gotten too far away it hasn't been that long since he left here?' I say in hope.

'Well normally I'd say no he couldn't have, but this man has been in this game for over twenty years, and no one has ever been this close to catching him before, so he will no doubt have already had an escape plan in place for when things do go wrong. I imagine when he was brought in for questioning someone will have been alerted to get his getaway prepared. We need to remember he's corrupted a lot of powerful people over the years, including the police in many countries.'

Typical, just as we get some good news, there is always something that brings it down! I think to myself.

'Is he going to get away with this?' Rita cuts in on before Christos can finish his sentence.

'Not if I can help it. Let's not get our hopes up until he's in custody.' Christos gives us a pitiful smile, and suggests we get ourselves comfy. 'This might take a while so how about something to eat and drink while you wait?'

We take a seat and wait for some refreshments and been told that if no news comes in a few hours, we will be taken to the new hotel.

We rest up with a cuppa and try to keep each other grounded and not get carried away just in case things don't do to plan, but the feeling at finally having this nightmare over with keeps fizzing in my head with excitement and relief.

'What a bloody holiday this has been eh?' Doreen tries to laugh it off. We all begin to ease our aching bodies and try and stretch out our niggles.

'Tell you something, I'm feeling really old!' I mutter out as I'm trying to massage my stiff sore calf. The other two look round and laugh while massaging their aching parts.

'It's my back!' Rita cries while placing her hands on her lower back to ease some pressure.

'It's my whole body, I think it's gone into shock it's never had as much activity.' Doreen says laughing. The warmth of laughter fills the cold room, just having the little bit of normality back floods in over us. I look round at us and wonder what I'd ever do without them, the close call on each of our lives makes me appreciate what I have, I now know I won't be hiding myself away again like I was doing before coming on this disaster of a holiday.

Christos re appears in the doorway holding a tray of sandwiches and three mugs. Shocked to see him standing there and his weird expression on his face tells me he hasn't just entered the room. As he stands their ears dropping, a smile creeps across his face. We all bolt upright when we spot him, hoping the young fit man hasn't noticed us trying to ease our old aching joints. Of course, he has though, but he tries to play it down with a little concern.

'Are you sure you don't need to see a medic? I can get someone down to check you over again.' Rita's usual pristine self, springs back into action.

'Don't be so silly we are fine, just stretching that's all.' Christos stares unconvinced at us.

'You sure? You have all had a couple of tough physically days, it wouldn't hurt to get someone to come take a look. Il phone them now.'

'Christos! We are just getting fuckin old, put the phone down.' Doreen jumps in.

A shocked Christos does just that and takes a step back from the table where he's just placed the tray. 'Okay then, I shall leave you for a little while, if you need anything I'm just down the corridor.'

'Thanks.' I smile to him as he scurries back out the room hopefully avoiding any more drama from us.

'Shall we?' I lay my hands out and grab a mug. We all do the same and lay back into the big comfy sofa.

A hour soon passes by without realising. We get ourselves lost in conversation as we all try and take our minds off the situation, but everyone now and then I wonder if they have caught him, and how long it will be before we are allowed to fly back to the UK, desperate to be with my family, who are worried sick, having countless calls and messages wanting to know what is happening, wishing that I could tell them more news, but I can't I've decided to tell them I'm going to try for a sleep to hopefully stop the persistent calls and messages. Although my mind is far too active at the minute to rest, but there's only so many times I can keep repeating myself and reassuring them that I'm fine, so hopefully they will get the hint and a wait for me to call them with some news. I feel a pang of guilt when I hit send knowing I'm telling a little white lie, they are of course just worried about me.

Christos once again shocks us by lurking in the door way. This time his face is stern, and his hands become twitchy, he's unsure to rub his chin or place his hands in his pockets. The three of us just stare waiting for him to say something. The dread is reappearing through my spine, by the look of his face, tells me this isn't good news. I hear Rita take a gulp and she grabs my hand. Doreen clearly can't take the anticipation any longer and stands up.

'Just spit it out Christos, what is going on?'

He fumbles for a little longer, he looks down at the floor and places a hand on his head. Me and Rita glimpse at each other, while the fear reappears its ugly head.

Christos suddenly lifts his head in snap, and a big cheeky smile appears on his face. 'We've only gone and caught the bastard!' He springs his arms out in joy. 'Your free ladies, we've got him!' Still sitting down in disbelief, trying to let his words sink in for moment. The realization hits me I jump and scream, then the next thing I know it we all are jumping for joy. 'We caught him trying to board a flight, we just and so made it. He almost thought he got away, his smirk soon changed when he seen us though, weirdly he didn't try to run, but being surrounded he likely thought there was no chance.' Christos says as happy as what we are.' 'You all are going to be able to see your families in the morning.' The pressure has instantly been lifted from the three of us as we dance, scream and hug one another. What a perfect way to end this nightmare.

We finish up statements and get word from the UK side that they are happy for us to come home and to finish whatever needs to be done on home soil. We say our goodbyes and finally get on our way to the new hotel, where we will spend a night and fly back home in the morning.

That night is the best sleep I've had in a long time, and waking up refreshed without the worries we have had all holiday is defiantly appreciated.

The sun shine bright and the skies are clear blue as we wait to board our flight home, our families are already making the trip to collect us from the airport. Although still bruised and sore and traumatized, we don't actually look too bad considering what we have been through, although I need to thank the more heavily applied makeup for that. We relax while we wait, knowing in only a few hours' time we will be back home. The thought makes me smile as a sip on a large glass of wine.

CHAPTER 35

A few months after the holiday life is becoming much more normal, our bruises heal but our minds are scarred, which leaves me waking with nightmares, but slowly it is getting better. The counselling has been brilliant it also taught me how to deal with my grief from losing my beloved husband. After almost losing my life and my two best friends I no longer shut myself away instead, I've let myself live again. My family still check on me daily, but they are slowly realising I don't need to be watched 24 hours a day. Rita is still going to therapy, which is understandable considering the amount of trauma she endured from being held hostage, however her elegance is still intact you'd never know looking at her what she's been through, she puts up a good shield to the outside world. Doreen has kept up her new found strong confident self and has made us join a self-defence class, which is pretty good but secretly I hope we don't need to use it. Our bond has grown stronger and stronger. We keep in touch with Christos and Cora also. Cora is recovering well and is heading back to her police duties any time soon, the pair are heading out to come visit us this weekend to celebrate the sentencing of Bill and Earnie, hopefully they will be behind bars for a long time, they still however, say they have no involvement in each other's crimes, luckily the recording is valuable to this. The hotel manager has already been sentenced with already a list of crimes already on record and footage of him leading Rita to the parking lot, we have been assured he won't be seeing any outside world for a long time. Apparently, he isn't in Bill and Earnie's gang, they are thinking he's been paid by them to do that job, but he also still says it was all his doing and Rita was just randomly chosen by him! Which obliviously sounds pathetic, of course it wasn't random. We have also been approached by reporters trying to get us to sell our stories, however we all don't want all of it dragged up again and our families still don't know the full extent what we went through, and we want to keep it that way. Our secret, our troubles, we've locked it away in an imaginary box, never to be spoken about unless absolutely necessary. We don't know who leaked what had happened to us or how they got our contact numbers, but they soon stopped the pestering when they knew that none of us were going to talk.

I smile as I write down in journal. My therapist suggested I do this as may help letting my feelings out, and surprisingly it has helped, I just got to make sure that they aren't left around when my family call.

A sharp bang on the door jolts me out of my writing. I wonder who could be banging on my door this early in the morning. Still dressed in my pyjamas and dressing gown I head to the front door, I peer through the glass, something I always do now since the holiday, I see what looks to be a delivery man. I keep the chain lock on the door when I open it. A young man stands there with small box. Seeing that it is a delivery man I unlock the chain and open the door fully. I take the box from him and re lock my door. I look down at it as I head back to the kitchen wondering what I've ordered. My mind comes up blank. I place it on the counter and double check that it is for me and hasn't been delivered to the wrong address. The sticker has all my details correct. So, I shrug to myself and begin to open the perfectly packed brown cardboard box.

I peer into the open box and lying there was crisp white letter and a red rose laying on top of it. I lift out the rose and admire its perfection, but my mind races wondering who could have sent this, I've certainly not been on any kind of dates, and I defiantly don't have any admirers that I know of. I place the single rose on the counter and reach in for the white envelope, I look at my name written perfectly in bold letters. I look confused trying to figure out whose writing it could be, I don't recognise it at all. My heart flutters with curiosity as I begin to peel open the letter, inside was a perfectly written note.

I jump and knock over my mug of coffee when I start processing the words that I'm reading, I gasp and throw the letter on the counter, only seconds later to pick it back up and read again. I need to make sure that I have just read what I have and that I'm not going crazy. My hands begin to tremble, my heart starts to pound, and I can feel the panic attack preparing itself to erupt. I read out the note loudly to myself this time, taking in everything perfectly written word.

SEE YOU AGAIN SOON.

LOVE B.

I Grab the letter and the rose and fling them into the bin, I pace around trying to understand it, but I can't. I turn back to the bin and grab the letter and rose back out and place it back in the box knowing that this will need to be checked. Thoughts begin racing through my mind. Is it Bill? Has he got out? Or is it someone else trying to scare us? I can't stay calm long enough to think clearly. I grab my phone and begin to dial with my shaking hands. It doesn't take long before someone answers.

'Did you get one?' I can't get my words out fast enough, but hearing Rita's muffled sobs on the other end tells me her answer before she says.

'Yes, and so has Doreen we are coming over now.' We don't even say a goodbye as my phone goes silent. I get a chilling shiver up my spine as the room suddenly goes ice cold. I jump up and race round checking all my doors and windows are locked. My phone begins to ring so loud through my silent house that it makes me jump, I look at the caller to see its Christos. I answer and place it to my ear. His words hit me like a tonne of bricks falling. I fall to my knees and begin to cry.

'How can this happen!'

Printed in Dunstable, United Kingdom